I0659034

SAGEBRUSH ALLEY

Sagebrush Alley

by
Patricia Jones

Sastrugi Press

Copyright © 2018 by Patricia Jones

Sastrugi Press / Published by arrangement with the author

Sagebrush Alley by Patricia Jones

All rights reserved. No part of this publication may be distributed, reproduced, or transmitted in any form or by any means, including recording, photocopying, or other electronic or mechanical methods, without the prior written permission of the publisher, except in the case of brief quotations embodied in critical reviews and certain other noncommercial uses permitted by copyright law. For permission requests, write to the publisher, addressed "Attention: Permissions Coordinator," at the address below.

Sastrugi Press
PO Box 1297, Jackson, WY 83001, United States
www.sastrugipress.com

Library of Congress Catalog-in-Publication Data
Library of Congress Control Number: 2018963253
Jones, Patricia
Sagebrush Alley / Patricia Jones—1st United States edition
p. cm.
1. Fiction 2. Woman Authors 3. Western States
A young woman working on an advanced degree finds herself in a fight for her life when she crosses paths with a man who kills a game warden without hesitation.

813 Jon –dc22

ISBN-13: 978-1-944986-54-4 (hardback), 978-1-944986-55-1 (paperback)

Printed in the United States of America
10 9 8 7 6 5 4 3 2

Sastrugi Press
00135

In memory of my brother Stan Wilson.

Acknowledgments

The author wishes to thank the people who helped to make this book a reality. Dianna, Russ, and Gable Gillett for walking the trail to the falls with me as a memorable occasion; for the early readers Beth Kelsey and Keith Jones, for Clay and Gayla Rowley for geologic and technical information; Bud Stewart of Wyoming Game & Fish Department; Sgt. Danny Keller of Sheridan Police Department, Nancy D. Wall, Elizabeth Harrington, David Hugh Pickering, and Angie Knox for editing; Aaron Linsdau of Sastrugi Press; and, last but not least to my husband Keith for his encouragement, care and support over a very challenging year.

Prologue

A third of the way up the trail, Dana Cameron paused to catch her breath. The day had turned from sunny to overcast, reflecting her disheartened mood as she climbed steadily up the pathway over embedded rocks, roots, washed-out sections, and logs strategically placed to hold back spring run-off.

As a graduate student in botany at the University of Wyoming, Dana was in the Sinks Canyon of central Wyoming, doing field research for her thesis. Resources she trusted had brought her to the area two weeks previously in search of the elusive plant she based her thesis on.

With each step Dana took, her black binoculars swung back and forth from a strap around her neck. She lifted them to her eyes, adjusted the focus, and earnestly searched the hillside that rolled gradually upward off to her right. The ground was covered in grasses, sagebrush, early-blooming wild flowers, and boulders upon boulders.

The air felt heavy with humidity, making her trek arduous. She moved on a short distance, pausing on the crest of a small rise as her eyes swept the surrounding landscape.

Dana's gaze moved along the brow of the incline onto the canyon wall that loomed up into sheer cliffs of granite, jutting hundreds of feet skyward. After working in the area for over a week, she remained amazed by the vastness of the canyon wall, which stretched on and on up into the valley. From where she stood the walls evolved from black to gray and back to black as shadows passed over various parts of the cliff face.

Reluctantly, she returned her attention to the hillside and the task at hand. Perhaps she was mistaken about where to look, or it was too early in the year, or weather conditions had not been conducive to growth.

Dana was ready to move farther up the trail when a brief flash of color a good distance up the incline caught her eye. Quickly she moved the binoculars back to her left. A smile slowly crept across her face.

She lowered the glasses and stepped off the path, carefully avoiding a clump of prickly pear cactus with swollen yellow buds just on the verge of opening. Then she struck off up the hill in the direction of what she had seen.

In several places small streamlets of scree flowed down off the footings of the canyon wall. Dana slipped and nearly lost her balance on the loose gravel as she kept her eyes focused on a sheer-faced boulder that she was using as a reference point. The rock had seemed like a large, dark, refrigerator box back on the path but the closer she approached and the higher she climbed the larger it grew.

A slight mound loomed ahead of her and Dana momentarily lost sight of her objective. She stopped for a moment to catch her breath before resuming her climb, pulling herself up the last few steps by a handhold on a clump of arrowhead balsam root blossoms growing rampant on the hillside. She fell to her knees, exhausted, and peered over the rise. Her rock that was her reference point stood about ten yards away and, on the ground to its right, she hoped to find the object of her search.

Just as she got to her feet, the air was splintered with a scream that echoed out over the valley. Her attention was jerked upward to the top of the big rock, where a large animal lay crouched down, its tawny body ready to spring. It was a cougar.

The animal's long rope-like tail swung back and forth and it pawed the air in front of it with one of its huge paws, amber eyes fixed on Dana, while the muscles in its hind quarters rippled under the warm morning sun. Its mouth opened wide as it released a second challenge.

"Eeee-ooow!"

Dana pulled her body upright and scrambled to her feet. She tried to think of what she had read about big cats. Could she scare it off by yelling, or would that only hasten an attack? She knew there were reports of them carrying off small children; that couldn't apply to her, but if it attacked it could do her a world of hurt. She looked around for anything she might use to repel the large cat.

But, with a snarl in Dana's direction, the cougar apparently decided she was not a threat. It gradually slunk back off the edge of the rock, stood, and with a parting grumble turned and jumped off the back of it. Dana gulped in huge breaths of air as she attempted to calm her racing heart and watched as the cougar scampered farther up the hillside.

When it had disappeared from sight over another mound, Dana

swallowed the constricting lump in her throat and tried to compose her shaking body. Would the cougar circle back around to where she stood? She knew they were stealthy animals and good at keeping out of sight. She tentatively moved up to the rock and touched it with her trembling hands, trying to regain a sense of stability.

After slipping the straps of her backpack off her shoulders and arms and dropping it to the ground, Dana examined what she had seen from the trail.

"Sugar to hell!" she exclaimed as disappointment overtook her. Falling to her knees, she bent down to find what had deceived her from below. It was only a large piece of mica that had managed to reflect a ray of the morning sun so that through her binoculars it had appeared to be a clump of her plants.

She slouched back on her haunches, laughing without humor at the fact that the mica had tricked her into thinking she had at long last found a specimen. On top of that, she was still shaking from her close encounter with the big cat.

Her sour amusement soon turned to frustration over being unsuccessful once more in her search. It was already 13 June. Perhaps it was still too early in the year for the plant to be visible, let alone in bloom, or the information about the plant reappearing was in error. In any event she had been foiled in her search yet again.

Though tall and slender, she was nearing thirty years of age and she felt each one of them at that moment. She stood up slowly and looked around before reluctantly lifting her backpack and starting down the slope.

She was nearly back on the main trail when she heard a loud boom from farther up the canyon, followed by a second report. *What now?* It sounded almost like a gunshot. She froze where she stood, not knowing if someone would emerge from behind another rock or take a shot at her. It wasn't the hunting season. Who would come all the way out here just to do some target-shooting?

Dana advanced farther, stopping periodically to scan the adjacent hillside to see if she could spot where the blast had come from. Nothing. Slowly, she moved forward.

She felt almost in a daze, slowly turning in all directions. After several minutes without seeing anything or anyone, she decided that someone must have been target-shooting after all. As her nerves calmed, she returned to her original mission.

According to one of her sources at the university, the plants she sought should be in bloom during late spring and into summer. However, she suspected that with the late spring the area had experienced this year, plus the frequent rains, it might simply be too early for them to have broken dormancy. Perhaps the better plan would be to get off the main trail and search the nooks and crannies of the hillside for the plant, relying on a description of the foliage she carried.

Related to several of the small wild varieties of *dicentra,* the one she sought was thought to have died out in mountainous areas during the recent droughts that had dogged much of Wyoming. *Dicentra,* or longhorn steer's head, was known to have a fleshy stem system, with single-stalked, deeply divided, round leaflets upon which developed pink blossoms. Some of the blossoms, she knew, could have variations with streaks of dark purple or brown.

Dana had become captivated by the plants. The shape of the flower itself closely resembled the much larger domestic plant called *love hearts* or *bleeding hearts,* which had grown in her grandmother's garden many years ago. When she had come across the wild version in her search for a subject for her graduate project, she had been immediately reminded of those happy days as a child spent on her grandparents' farm. The deciding factor had been their cyclical appearance and the disappearance of this specific variety.

More than once during the past few days, however, she had wondered about the wisdom of her choice.

CHAPTER 1

Without warning, Dana felt the cave floor begin to angle downward. Her hands slipped forward on the slick granite surface as her body began to slide. Her flashlight flew out of her grasp and she could see its beam flashing end over end away from her. Her senses were shrieking in fear. Was she sliding into a deep abyss? Was this how it would end?

Clawing frantically at anything that would stop her slide, she found only open space and smooth granite. She could feel her fingernails being shredded into jagged pieces.

But, instead of the deep chasm she feared, Dana slid headfirst down a short incline and came to rest against a protrusion in the floor. Her flashlight lay three feet ahead of her, its beam directed straight forward. Reaching out her right arm, she stretched to retrieve the Maglite then slowly pulled herself into a sitting position.

Flashing the light around in all directions, Dana discovered she was in an actual cave. The space was quite large and the ceiling was definitely high enough to allow standing. The crevice she had just crawled through was visible behind her, and actually only a couple feet higher than the cave floor. Two feet. When she had begun to slither out of the fissure, she had feared it would be dozens of feet, or more.

The floor was by no means level. Small mounds Dana took to be rock formations rose up in various places, some small, others tall and slightly cone-shaped.

Locating her stick, Dana slowly stood up, letting her left foot bear her weight. A wave of dizziness brought on by the pain from her injured right foot nearly brought her to her knees again. She stood still for a few moments, waiting for the lightheadedness to pass.

Gradually, surveying her surroundings, she realized she was in a big, amorphous room that extended ahead of her as far as her light would reach. A musky, damp smell, similar to what she had noticed in places in the forest where deer bedded down, wafted around her. Once more, she directed her Maglite around the perimeter of the cave.

Off to her right, Dana could see a mound of rubbish. Could that be where the smell was coming from? Feeling steadier, she hobbled warily over to study the debris and found it consisted of dried leaves and grasses, small branches, and even the skin of some dead creature, nestled between rocks and the wall.

Dana began to wonder if she had stumbled upon the den of some animal, perhaps the cougar she had faced days earlier. She remembered the game warden did say he thought the animal had a den in the area. A strong, fusty odor emanated from the material and she now saw there were tufts of animal fur and what appeared to be small bones scattered throughout the lair. And there was another odor she could not immediately identify.

It had to be the home of a larger animal, Dana surmised, given the size of the bed and the bones of small animals. Was the animal whose den she had just found out for the day hunting and would it soon return? Did the creature gain access through the same entrance she had used, or was there another approach close by? Either way, she needed to be vigilant.

Dana briefly considered returning to the opening, but then remembered the danger outside and changed her mind. The complete lack of sound was eerie. She had not heard any clamor from her pursuer for some time now. Because of the twists and turns she had made in getting this far inside the cave, it was hardly surprising she could not hear him any longer. Perhaps, when he had been unsuccessful in getting to her, he had given up and gone away. The thought gave Dana little comfort, however. She knew he would not give up that easily.

It was likely only her imagination, but as Dana played the light around the cave it seemed as if the walls and the floor were shiny in some places. She wondered if it could be water. That would certainly account for the musty smell. Because of the uneven base beneath her feet, she stepped gingerly as she went deeper into the chamber.

Dana turned suddenly toward the fissure when she heard a dull *whump* in the direction from which she had come. It was followed moments later by a second *whump*. She became conscious of a cloud of dust enveloping her as she flashed her light around. She quickly looked around for a place to conceal herself. It was possible the animal whose den she had found was returning to its lair. But there were no hiding places. For several minutes she stood where she was, frozen, listening, her senses on high alert.

Gradually, the stale material in the cave settled down and the extreme quiet returned. No animal appeared, and eventually Dana shuffled forward again.

Before she had gone twenty feet she felt exhausted and found a place against the wall where she could sit with her right foot elevated on one of the flatter rocks protruding from the floor. Even knowing how perilous a situation she was in, what with her injured foot and the maniac waiting for her outside the cave entrance, it felt good to have a respite and a chance to ponder her situation. She was determined that once she was rested, she would find a way out of her predicament.

As Dana leaned back against the cave wall, the events of the past few days crowded into her thoughts...

***

At lunchtime on the day she had thought she had found a specimen of her plant and had come upon the cougar draped over its rock, Dana stopped by a large, gnarled limber pine a few feet off the trail. The main trunk of the tree had been hammered by winter winds until it was bent over and deformed, approximately three feet off the ground. A small grove of aspen just leafing out grew adjacent to the shaded spot where she settled with her back against the mutated trunk.

From her backpack, Dana pulled a bottle of water, a sandwich, and an apple she had packed that morning. As she consumed her lunch, she was lulled by the sound of the unseen river below her. The river itself was obscured by the thick foliage of shrubs and tightly-packed but spindly pine trees as it rushed down from higher elevations.

On the opposite bank of the river, the forest rose to meet the canyon wall. She watched a kestrel soar along the trees and the low-lying brush, ever watchful for its next meal.

Still mulling over her discouraging morning, Dana spotted a figure coming up the path in her direction. The man was dressed in a red canvas shirt, jeans, heavy walking boots, and a cap with some kind of insignia on it. As he came closer, Dana identified him as a game warden. His shirt appeared to have the logo of the Wyoming Game and Fish Department above the left pocket flap.

When he spied Dana sitting in the shade, the man slowed his progress, removed his cap, and wiped his forehead. He was a man in his late forties or so, she guessed, of average height, a bit on the stout side, with a sunburned, wrinkled face.

"Good place for a rest," he said as he approached.

Dana took a gulp of water to wash down the last bit of her sandwich. As she wiped a drop from her chin, she pointed to the emblem on his red shirt.

"Looks like you're the law around here."

"Name's Henderson," said the game warden as he removed his water bottle from a carrier. "Game and fish department."

Dana squinted up at him. "I'm a plant biology student from the university, doing research here in the canyon this summer on a sub-species of the *dicentra* plant."

"Having any luck?"

"I thought I'd found a small clump this morning back down the trail a-ways. Turned out it was some mica glistening in the sun. I'm thinking I need to get off the trail and into some of the less-traveled areas. I've been here nearly two weeks now and have yet to find a thing."

"Is this a plant that needs sun?"

"Essentially they're shade-loving plants, so I've been looking on the north side of big boulders and sheltered areas."

"That shouldn't be a problem in this region then. Still snow in some of the protected areas like that farther up the trail."

"In the time I've been here, I've concentrated my search along the lower trail. I'm gradually working my way up higher."

The game warden bent down in a crouch. "I walked the Popo Agie this morning. There were quite a few fishermen along the river, so I didn't pay particular attention to the plant life."

"Is it rough going down along the river?"

"Yeah, brushy in some places, especially across the river where it doesn't get as much sun as this side of the canyon. Fishing's still iffy this early in the year, though. Water's pretty rough and still a-ways from settling down; I'd say we're right at the peak of the run-off."

"You just called the river the *po-Po-zhia*. That sounds almost like a

French word."

"It's an old Crow Indian word meaning 'gurgling river'. You're right, though, a lot of visitors say it the way it's spelled. The locals have a lot of fun with it and call dudes the Po-po-aggies."

"I've heard it pronounced like that," she said, grinning. "How far up this way do you patrol?"

"All the southwest section of Fremont County. My partner takes the northern section over to the reservation. The lower canyon is a state park; this upper half is part of the Shoshone National Forest. Are you familiar with this area?"

"I'm getting there. I've read as much as I can get my hands on. My advisor at the university helped convince me to look here in the canyon for samples of the species I'm studying. Plus, he has connections with a geologist in Lander who, I hope, will be able to shed some light on the role some rocks play in where my plants grow."

"Sounds like you've got a plan then."

"Just so I find some plants to study," Dana said wistfully. "They were thought to have gone extinct, but with additional rainfall over the last few years they've apparently been seen round here."

"You know about the Sinks, and where the water rises?"

"I've read about them but haven't had a chance to see them yet."

"You drive past them every day on your way up here. You really should stop one day and have a look-see. The Popo Agie River disappears underground then surfaces a quarter mile down the road in a pool before continuing its course down out of the foothills."

"Sounds interesting. I've just been so focused on getting started on this research, I haven't taken the time. I'll have to check it out."

"Yeah. We've lost several of the trout from the pond where the water rises this spring," Warden Henderson said, taking a long swig from his water bottle.

"You mean they're dying off?"

"Naw, some 'sportsman'," he replied, raising both of his page fingers in open quotes, "seems to think that's the reasonable thing to do and has removed, near as we can tell, 'bout ten to fifteen of the bigger fish."

"How big are you talking?"

"Some of 'em weigh quite a bit. Mostly rainbows, some browns.

You see, the trout migrate upstream when they spawn. Fish can't get through the underground barrier back to the main stream above the Sinks, so they stay in this pool where they are protected and have an ample food supply."

"That's awful that someone's taking the fish illegally," said Dana, as she stood and brushed pine needles and dirt from her shorts. "Have you caught whoever is responsible?"

"Not yet. Still under investigation. That's why I'm being extra vigilant along the Popo Agie, keeping an eye out for any suspicious behavior, watching for illegal campsites."

"You ever come across a cougar in this area?"

"Oh yeah, there's an old guy that hangs out here about. Why do you ask?"

"I had an encounter with him this morning. Thought he was going to jump on me." And she went on to explain how she and the cat had come face to face.

"Think he's probably got a den farther up. Never come across it, though. There weren't any cubs around were there?"

"No. Just the big cat. And the strange thing is, shortly after he disappeared, I heard what sounded like gunshots, quite a-ways away."

Henderson stood and placed the cap back on his head with a quizzical look on his face, as if he had just remembered something he had to do. "Well, best keep movin'. I wish you luck in your research." As an afterthought, he added, "Guess you know it's illegal to remove any plants from the wilderness."

"I do know that, but I will be examining my plants in depth by measuring the size of blossoms, checking leaf shape, and photographing them."

"Probably see you around again then."

The warden tipped the bill of his cap as he moved on down the trail.

Dana gathered the remains of her lunch, placed them in the empty sandwich bag, and stuffed it into one of the side pockets of her backpack, making sure she had not left anything but crumbs behind. She certainly didn't want to get cross-wise with the game warden.

She stepped back onto the trail. The noonday sun was warming and the clouds that had looked like forerunners of rain showers had mostly dispersed. She pulled on her sunglasses and set off up the path.

Five hundred feet farther along she took a side trail, much less traveled. It was rather steep and wound around rocks, the ever-present sagebrush, and cactus before switchbacking up the side of the hill.

Dana searched carefully around any boulders that offered a shaded mini-climate. Eventually, where trees no longer grew and the sagebrush became less abundant, the path split into three less visible trails. She could plainly see where the scree flows had originated at the foot of the cliffs. She wiped the sweat off her brow.

Still nothing.

Chapter 2

After tramping the main trail and several side paths in fruitless searching until just after three in the afternoon, Dana was discouraged by her exploratory skills and returned to her vehicle at the trailhead. Soon she was making the thirty-minute drive back to her apartment in Lander.

Coming up with a proper plan for her exploration had to become a priority. Any field scientist worth her salt knew that was an essential step in the work she had under way. Intellectually, she had learned that making a diagram of the area to be searched should be a huge part of her planned work. However, enthusiasm for her work once she had arrived at the canyon had taken precedence over what she knew to be the right approach. She had been anxious to get out on the trail to explore, even without a plan in mind.

As she drove, she thought back to the previous March when, during spring break, she had spent a couple days in Lander, searching for a place to live during the time she was in Sinks Canyon doing her research. She hadn't been eager to leave the close-knit, supportive, friendly environment of the university community, but it was a necessary step in the process to obtain her degree.

Lander, nestled in a long narrow valley on the eastern slope of the Wind River Mountains was just a short drive away from Dana's research site. She had been intrigued by the story she had been told by a clerk in the newspaper office who had been sharing some of Lander's storied history.

It seemed the town had originally been named after one of a series of military forts at the early town site. However, as skirmishes between early homesteaders and Indians settled down, a man by the name of Frederick Lander had made the growing town his headquarters while he surveyed the Oregon Trail through nearby historic South Pass, back in the late 1800s. Mr. Lander was a rather flamboyant young man who courted and married the daughter of one of the more prominent families. The townspeople were so impressed by him that they renamed their growing town after him. But soon after the marriage he took his new bride back to Pennsylvania whence he had come. Many in Lander, upset over this turn of events, wanted to change the name again. They were soon disabused of that idea when the town fathers said 'no', that would be considered 'capricious'.

Dana had discovered her apartment quite by accident. She had been chatting with a waitress at The Bronze Spoon after she refilled her coffee cup. She was relaxing for a bit between chasing leads for a place to call home while she did her research up in the canyon.

The waitress, chirpy and middle-aged, wore a name tag that said Marissa. She glanced down at the newspaper Dana had open to the classified ads section. "You lookin' for a job, button?"

"No. Actually, I'm looking for an apartment to rent this summer."

"Summer's a hard time to find a rental here," said Marissa. "We get lots of seasonal people looking for the same thing."

"What do the seasonal people do?"

"Recreation mostly, construction jobs, and the guest ranches bring in a lot of people to work during the summer."

"The places I've looked at so far are either way too big for me or in pretty bad shape."

"I hear you." Marissa moved on down the line of tables and stopped to converse with another customer.

Dana returned to poring over the small selection of rental possibilities.

Marissa was shortly back at her table. "Say, I just remembered. Aberdeen Calhoun, a nice Irish lady over on Canby Street, owns a large Victorian place and she's recently had the front portion of her carriage house made into an apartment. By all accounts it's pretty classy. From what I've heard about Aberdeen, I think she'd be pretty particular about whom she rents to, but I'm thinkin' you'd qualify."

"Do you know if it's still available?"

"Wouldn't hurt to check it out."

After paying for her coffee and leaving the restaurant, Dana wondered how the waitress had determined she would be qualified to rent the apartment. By her appearance? Late twenties, shoulder-length auburn hair, pert nose, hazel-eyes... Her demeanor? Well-mannered, pleasant, engaging, she hoped... The way she was dressed? Brown wool tights with a beige turtleneck, and warm winter boots reaching nearly to her knees. Nothing especially distinctive there.

She had been a bit intimidated by the waitress's comment that Aberdeen Calhoun would likely be finicky about who she rented her apartment to. Well, she would soon find out. She pulled out her smartphone, entered Aberdeen Calhoun's name and found her address.

As Dana returned to her car a brisk March wind was blowing some errant snowflakes around as if the weather could not decide if it was still winter or if spring was trying to move forward. Dana left her parking slot and drove toward the area of town to which Marissa had directed her.

She found Canby Street easily and slowly cruised along the avenue of stately older homes until she came to the correct house number. It was a huge three-story Victorian home with a dark red-brick foundation and painted gray siding, with maroon trim on the doors, windows and dormers, and a wrap-around porch on two sides. Pine boughs from winter decorations still adorned the windowsills and an artificial fir in a maroon pot stood to one side of the front entrance.

Dana parked on the street in front of the house, took a deep breath, and walked up the curved walk toward the porch. Off to her right she could, indeed, see the carriage house. It was a significantly smaller version of the main building, even to the extent of the downsized bay window on the front painted in the same two colors.

As she was about to step up onto the first step, Dana's eyes were drawn to the flowerbeds on each side of the south-facing front facade. Spring blooming bulbs were beginning to push their way through the soil and mulch and would soon be making visitors welcome.

As she rang the doorbell Dana wondered anxiously if she stood any chance at all of finding a place to live in such a desirable neighborhood. The door was opened by a tall, fairly elderly woman with sharp, angular features. Her black hair was parted down the middle and secured in a large chignon low on the back of her head. She was wearing a simple grey wool dress and was in her stocking feet.

Dana's first thought was that she might be the maid. In a hesitant voice, she asked, "Mrs. Calhoun?"

"Aye," the woman replied.

"I was told downtown that you might have an apartment available in your carriage house."

Mrs. Calhoun looked Dana slowly up and down. "Why don't you come inside?"

As she stepped into the entry, Dana glimpsed an elegant formal living room to the left and a much more casual gathering room to the right. Mrs. Calhoun led her into the gathering room where an attractive brick fireplace, painted white, emitted a warm welcoming glow.

The old lady directed Dana to a high-backed chair to one side of the fireplace, while she took its mate a few feet away. There was an open book lying on her chair, so she picked it up, inserted a marker, and laid it aside on a convenient table.

"'Tis true, I do have an apartment, newly done I might add, but it'll be rented soon. To a nice young woman who'll be teaching music at the high school, come late summer."

Dana listened intently as Mrs. Calhoun spoke in a brogue she found a little difficult to understand immediately. To her ear, it sounded more Scottish than Irish. She explained why she needed the apartment.

"I will have my research completed by late July. Is there any way you might agree to let me rent the apartment for June and July?"

Mrs. Calhoun pondered her question for a moment. "That could be a possibility. Perhaps we should go look at it."

"I would like that very much."

Mrs. Calhoun slipped into a pair of low-healed grey pumps lying on the floor to one side of her chair. Dana got glimpses of more nineteenth-century furniture as they walked through the house. She noted colorful upholstered chairs and sofas, heavy drapes, lush oriental rugs and, as they passed the dining room, a handsome maple buffet table with a large round table and chairs to match.

Finally they went through a modern kitchen and out to a mud room at the side. Mrs. Calhoun slipped into a short tweed coat, took a key from a short bureau beside the door, and led the way out to her porte cochere. They then followed the driveway around to the back of the carriage house.

"My garage is in the back of the apartment," said Mrs. Calhoun, gesturing with a wave of her hand toward the back of the smaller building.

They walked across the dried, crunchy lawn to the carriage house, stepping around patches of late-winter snow. Mrs. Calhoun unlocked the door of the apartment and they stepped into a small entrance that opened into a pleasant living area. Along the far wall was a small dining table with a tall casement window near it, and a counter separating that space from a compact kitchen. To the right of the kitchen was a door leading into the medium-sized bedroom and bathroom and, tucked into a niche beyond the bedroom door, a small utility room with a stackable washer-dryer combination and a closet. The apartment was fully fitted out with furniture which, though previously used, looked in good shape and complemented the style of the rest of the apartment. The back wall had no windows and Dana realized the garage Mrs. Calhoun had spoken of must be on the opposite side of it.

"This is exactly what I've been looking for," said Dana.

"We just finished the painting last week and got the furniture moved in. If you think this would work for you, I would be happy to rent it to you for June and July."

A big smile spread across Dana's face. She asked a couple of questions about the appliances, then Mrs. Calhoun told her what she wanted for rent and they agreed on the terms.

Mrs. Calhoun gave a sigh of satisfaction now business was concluded. "Now, why don't we go back to the house and I'll brew us a cup of tea."

Thrilled that she had found an apartment, and already looking forward to returning to Lander to pursue her research in June, Dana felt a big step had been taken toward moving forward with her life.

Back in Aberdeen Calhoun's home, they sat across from each other at a table in her sunroom just off the kitchen, sipping tea.

"Your home is beautiful," said Dana.

"It's bonny enough, though sometimes I think to move to a smaller abode now it's just me ambling around the place."

"Your husband?"

"Poor Ned died these eight years gone."

"Oh, I'm sorry."

"Neddie and me moved here from Scotland near sixty years ago to raise the sheep. We built a grand flock, too, me and Neddie."

"Do you still have sheep?"

"My son and his family have taken over the business now."

"So you have family around then?"

"Oh yes, and the wee bairns are the joy of my life."

Dana wrote out a check for her rent and handed it over. Now everything was set for her to come back to Lander in early June.

***

As Dana pulled up outside her rented apartment she was anxious to hit the shower and wash off the dust and grime that had accumulated on her, in her hair, and on her clothes. She might even get in a short run around the neighborhood before dark. She planned on relaxing later and reviewing the notes she had made during her spring semester field botany class. She was particularly interested in re-reading the information on the plant she was studying to see if she had missed anything important.

Dana had just placed her backpack and cap on pegs inside the entrance of her apartment when her cell phone chirped. A tortoiseshell cat that had adopted her within a day of her move to Lander, and that she had named Flag, intertwined herself between her bare legs as she dug the phone out of her pocket. Flag had acquired her name because of her long, thin tail, which was tipped with beige fur and which she carried straight up in the air as she promenaded around the apartment.

Dana reached down with her right hand to pet the young cat as she answered the call. "Hello?"

"Dana, it's Arnie, just checking to see how you're doing."

Arnold Watt, Dana's mentor, academic advisor, and sponsor of her thesis at the university, kept a tight rein on his graduate students. This was the second call she had had from him in the time she had been in Lander.

"Dr. Watt. I just got back into town. I've been up on the trail in the canyon all day. The weather hasn't cooperated much until today, but they tell me it will soon dry out."

"Have you had a chance to meet Jed Ahrens yet? Think he could give you some ideas on where to look for your plants."

Dana knew Dr. Jedadiah Ahrens was a former colleague of Arnie

Watt's in the geology department. He had retired from teaching but was still active in research.

"I have his phone number right here on the counter and will try him this evening."

"Good, good. I was thinking you might want to include a chapter on some of the specific geology in the area. I think that would justify your hypothesis better."

"I'm finding some very divergent igneous formations and, based on material I'm reading, I'm thinking there must be some mineral the *dicentra* extracts from certain rocks."

"That's what I'm talking about. You want to be able to prove with empirical data why your plants grow where you find them."

"True. But I've yet to find a specimen, so it's frustrating so far."

"You need to stay focused on your research, and be sure to talk to Jed. I know he'll be able to help you."

"Thanks. I will."

"Okay, then. How's everything else going?"

"I'm pleased with my apartment. Oh, and I've made a new friend."

Dr. Watt's voice perked up. "Young and handsome, I hope."

Dana looked down at Flag. "Not exactly. Actually, she's pretty sexy..."

CHAPTER 3

After they had completed the call, Dana moved to her kitchenette. As she lifted a small bowl from the drying rack, filled it with water and placed it on the floor for Flag, she mused about Arnold Watt's comment regarding meeting someone young and handsome.

Nearly two years before she had been overwhelmed after her relationship with fellow student Jeremy Vanderhoff had fallen apart. In addition to being her advisor, Arnie had taken her under his wing after her break-up from her fiancé.

After high school Dana had taken a couple years off. Well, four to be accurate, doing secretarial work, short stints as an auctioneer's gofer and as a landscaper's assistant, while she decided what she wanted to do with her life. It was while she was working for the landscaper and becoming familiar with plants— which ones required sunshine, which liked shade, and which weren't particular— that she realized she had an affinity with the study of botany.

Following her broken engagement to Jeremy, Dana had found it hard to pick up any portion of her life that might lead to an emotional connection. She had truly loved Jeremy and, like so many others before her and many yet to come, had thought she had known her lover well. However, overcoming the trouncing of her confidence in their relationship had been painful. She likened their separation to Jeremy dying.

Arnold Watt, in counseling her, had attempted to make her see it was far better that she had learned Jeremy's true nature before they were married and before there were children involved. Taking Dr. Watt's thoughts to heart, she had become more cautious, unwilling to expose her heart to any more harm. Now she tended to limit her friendships to women, couples, or fatherly types.

And, thinking of fatherly types, she decided she should try calling Jed Ahrens. She found the snippet of paper with his number under a small gneiss rock paperweight in the shape of a nearly perfect dome and entered it into her cell phone. She had come across the rock on the first day she had been up in the canyon and as an inveterate rock hunter had brought home the gray and white striated specimen. Reflecting on her conversation with the game warden, she wondered if she had committed a blunder in removing the rock.

After the phone rang several times, an abrupt, gravely, male voice came on the line directing any callers to leave a short message and, if it merited his attention, he would return the call. Dana left her name and number and explained her relationship with Arnold Watt, the project she was working on, and requested that he call her back.

***

The long-anticipated shower refreshed Dana and she emerged from the bathroom rubbing a towel over her head. Flag jumped off the back of the sofa and greeted her with her usual chattiness.

"Are you as hungry as I am, little girl?" Dana asked as she opened a cupboard door and reached for the bag of cat food she kept there.

Having satisfied Flag, she pulled the remains of a tuna mixture from the refrigerator. She made a sandwich and added a glass of iced tea and a small salad, which she then carried to the sofa. Flipping through the TV channels, she got caught up on the latest rerun of *Friends* and settled down to relax with her meal. Flag stretched out on the floor by her feet.

During the night, she heard rain gently falling outside her bedroom window. Perhaps, she thought dreamily, the moisture would encourage her plants to push through the ground cover and flourish.

***

Tuesday morning, Dana had an early breakfast of cereal, toast, and coffee, and was in her Honda ATV on the road back to the canyon. The rain clouds of the previous night had dispersed and the sky was a perfect, cloud-free shade of azure. Traffic on the road was light, seemingly only an occasional rancher from the valley she was passing through on their way to town for morning coffee with other like-minded folk at one of the local gathering places.

The green alfalfa fields along the road caught Dana's eye. In a couple of places, baled hay from the previous summer had been stacked or rolled into one corner of the fields for storage. Or the rancher had opted to leave the bales in the field, making it easier to feed the cattle that wintered on the homelands.

She kept a close eye on the shoulders of the road, wary of the mule deer that fed during the early morning. Remnants of last summer's tall grasses grew thick in the barrow ditches and the deer were prone to jump out of cover for greener grass across the road.

Dana slowed and then stopped near Lance's Curve. A doe stepped out onto the two-lane ahead of her, looked in her direction, across the road, then back at the grassy roadside she had emerged from. She stamped her right front hoof a couple of times and speckled twin fawns only days old tentatively moved out from the tall grass behind her. Dana smiled as she watched the doe and her offspring continue across the road, down the embankment, and through the grass to the river below them.

At Bruce's Trailhead, she parked in her usual space on the second row at the end of the parking lot, parallel to a buck fence that enclosed the area. The only other vehicle on the lot was a worse-for-wear dark blue Dodge truck with an equally well-used over-the-cab camper on the back. She had noticed it at the trailhead on more than one occasion. She knew people occasionally parked and camped at the trailhead, although she recalled Warden Henderson telling her it was discouraged. Perhaps the possessor of the vehicle was an early riser who had not stayed at the trailhead overnight and was already on his way up the trail.

Dana was leaning into the back end of her SUV, rearranging a couple of items in her backpack, when another vehicle pulled into the lot beside her. The green pickup had a Shoshone National Forest decal on its side. Three young men emerged—college-aged, local, seasonal workers, she surmised. They were completing a conversation they had obviously started while driving about some girl they had met at a local bar the night before.

Dana raised her head to acknowledge them.

"How ya doing?" asked the tallest of the trio, as he opened the tailgate of the pickup, then pulled out a gas can, followed by a chain saw.

"Good morning," she replied.

The other two were stretching, arms extended over their heads, leaning from side to side and, Dana suspected, finding it hard to wake up.

"Looks like you're going to be doing some serious work," she said, motioning toward the equipment.

"Yeah, we're the clean-up crew. Have to make sure the picnic grounds are clear of debris, the outhouses cleaned, and cut up any fallen trees along the trail," he responded as he gestured in the direction Dana would soon take.

"I'm Dana," she said, offering the youth her hand.

"Good to meet ya," he replied, "I'm Joe. This here is Edeen, and that clown is Adam."

Edeen was a Native American, big-boned and with a mop of shiny back hair, while Adam was a bit on the chunky side with carrot-red hair. Dana looked twice, hoping the hair was natural rather than the result of the current fad of Jell-O dye jobs. They both acknowledged Dana's greeting.

"What brings you up here this mornin'?" Joe asked.

Dana explained her project and the amount of time she had spent searching areas off the trail. "How far off the trail do you cut down trees?" she asked as she zipped shut one of the pockets of her pack.

"Only if something is hampering passage on the trail. The forest service likes to keep the area as natural as possible. We do pick up a lot of litter people leave behind, like pop cans and plastic bottles, but most people are pretty good about cleaning up after themselves. How do you go about this research?"

"Mostly by trial and error until I worked out a grid to walk. My biggest problem is learning to be careful with all the gravelly rock up away from the main trail."

"It can be dangerous," Joe replied, "We've seen a couple people take nasty falls up on the incline." He looked down at Dana's shoes. "Looks like you've got good hiking boots on, which is wise."

While they had been speaking, Joe's two companions had been jostling each other in the shoulder and cavorting around like colts.

"I think they're awake," said Dana.

"Yeah, it's time I put these two comedians to work. You have a good day, Dana," said Joe.

Adjusting her backpack comfortably on her back, Dana bent to retie the lace on her left hiking boot. Then she pulled on a brown and gold ball cap with the logo of a bucking bronco to shade her head and tugged her ponytail through the adjustment tab in the back. After closing the door of her Honda, she wished the young men a good day and walked across the lot toward the trail.

She saw no sign of activity around the pickup camper.

The previous evening Dana had taken her topographical map of the upper canyon and, using a red pencil, had divided it into sections. She was determined that the most methodical way to go about her search, and not miss a specimen, was to break her exploration into doable segments instead of just exploring willy-nilly as she had been wont to do before.

Following the scheme she had laid out, she left the trail at the information kiosk and began crisscrossing her way back and forth over the first designated area above the trail, then moved up and down the lower foothills. As the morning progressed, the climbing became more arduous as the canyon wall loomed above her.

By mid-morning the sun was hot overhead. She stopped for water and a short rest.

As always when standing still, Dana carried on gazing around at the nooks and crannies where her plants might be growing. But now she became aware of a mewling sound. Unsure if it was just her imagination or the breeze playing in a grove of aspen below her, she lifted her head to listen. She heard the unusual sound again. With her right hand, she shaded her eyes from the sun and looked along the hillside.

A slight movement on an outcropping surrounded by several large limestone rocks farther up the incline caught her eye. An animal, reddish-brown in color, emerged from among the rocks, turned around, and disappeared back among the rocks. The mewling sound that had aroused Dana's interest was coming from the same area. The animal reappeared and moved a few feet away. Dana got a better view of it now and was able to identify it by its bushy tail as a red fox. The mewling now made sense to her as she guessed it was a female who had been inside her den with her kits.

With a sigh, Dana returned her water bottle to its pocket in her pack. She needed to continue walking the next slice of her search area. She turned her head to get one more glimpse of the fox den. In doing so she inadvertently stepped onto some of the loose gravel she had complained about to Joe earlier that morning.

Her feet went out from under her, her backpack became dislodged, and she landed hard on her behind before sliding several feet down the incline. As she got her breath back from the jolt she had just taken, not only to her body but to her pride, she muttered at her carelessness and scolded herself "lesson to self, pay better attention where you place your feet". She reached out to the dumpster-size rock she had nearly slammed into, and braced herself against it for stability so she could regain her feet.

While at the kneeling stage, her eyes were drawn to the base of the rock where a small mound of green was growing. She did a double-take and then bent forward to scrutinize the plant more closely. Her mind racing, she wondered if it could be what she was seeking.

She looked up to get her bearings. The plant *was* growing on the northeast-protected side of the rock. It wasn't in bloom, but she could see tiny buds dangling like dainty earrings from the thin stems. And, it wasn't just one plant. As she brushed leaves away, she discovered more of the same plants struggling to reach the warmth of the sun.

From the pocket in her vest, Dana drew out and unfolded a sheet of paper that contained a detailed description of *dicentra minutea*. Had she at last found the long-sought-after plant? The plant some still believed to be extinct? Though related to a common larger variety, more than one article she was aware of had stated categorically that her plants had disappeared from the ecosystem several decades earlier. Her plan was to prove that the plants went dormant, sometimes for years, sometimes for even longer, dependent upon prevailing weather conditions, before reappearing.

She spread the paper out and looked from the plant before her back to the paper, checking the leaf shape and description, stem length, bud size and configuration. The plant she had just found answered its description perfectly—a thickset stem system, with single-stalked, deeply divided, frond-like leaflets upon which the blossoms would develop.

After positively identifying and photographing the plant, Dana couldn't help the exhilaration she felt. A smile stole across her flushed face with the realization that she had finally found a sample of her elusive plant. She took extensive notes in her field book, including the plant's size, height, physical condition, the dimensions of the flower buds, the surrounding soil, and its placement as to sun and shade. Then she scraped a small portion of the surrounding soil into a plastic bag, identified the location, and placed it in her backpack.

CHAPTER 4

The following morning, Dana parked in her usual spot at the trail-head and walked about a quarter mile up the trail to an aspen tree where she had stuck a piece of duct tape. The tape was to mark where she should leave the main trail and to guide her back to what she was now thinking of as the mother lode of *dicentra* she had discovered the previous day.

She was drawn back to the site to identify the type of rock her plants were growing near. It was one more item to check off her list. She thought about the thousand other items on her endless list and consoled herself that she would eventually succeed.

After examining the shed-sized granite rock that protected her plants, Dana was startled by a sharp clinking noise. She looked down toward the trail, but it was hidden by foliage. Many people who walked the area used walking sticks, and when the metal tips hit rocky surfaces they made a sound not unlike what she had just heard. She turned back to her plants.

There it was again. This time the noise sounded more like steel against steel. She was concentrating on returning articles to her backpack and attributed the sound to hikers or small animals capering around the rocks. The sound came again, closer, more distinctive, and she looked around, trying to see where the strange sound was coming from.

Always aware that bigger, wild animals might be in the vicinity, she had no desire to encounter one of them, especially a bear. Dana knew that she was no match for anything bigger than a medium-sized dog.

"Ahoy, below!"

The sound of another voice on the hillside seemed incongruous. Dana looked around her and back down to the trail in confusion.

"Above you," the voice called out.

She raised her head to the steep canyon walls, looking to the right and to the left, before looking directly over her head. There, dangling from a rope more than three quarters of the way down the face of the cliff, was a man, swinging slightly.

"You surprised me," Dana called. "I didn't realize anyone was nearby, let alone hanging from the canyon wall." She didn't know why it hadn't occurred to her earlier. The game warden had said the canyon was a favorite of rock climbers.

"Yeah, well, I'm just about to start my ascent. Thought I'd say hello." The stranger was clad in a gray tee shirt, blue shorts, and a black cap, and had a two-day shadow of beard. His long legs, swinging in the saddle of his harness, were butternut brown. "I've seen you a couple times along this trail before, but I was too far away to say hello."

"I'm scouting these hillsides for some research on a specific plant, for my graduate thesis."

"Having any luck?"

"As a matter of fact, I am. Took me a few days to organize how I should go about the process. These plants are pretty elusive, though."

"You have good information that they grow here?"

"I do. Just yesterday I found a good-sized grouping," she said, motioning to the nearby boulder that sheltered her discovery. "They're shade-loving, so a little later in breaking dormancy."

"Must take a lot of patience."

Dana nodded her head in agreement. "Are you climbing alone?"

"Mostly I do. My free time is pretty sporadic, so I just take off when work permits. It isn't very easy to schedule time with others."

"You must be able to see for miles from up there," said Dana as she raised a hand to shield her eyes from the sun.

"Pretty much. 'Course, I have to pay attention to what I'm doing while rappelling, too."

"This the only area you climb?"

"I climb all along these canyon walls. Something different to experience every time."

As Dana stood talking with him, a slight wind began wafting through the nearby aspen and she noticed thick, dark clouds amassing to the south. A loud clap of thunder boomed a short distance away and resounded through the wide canyon. Both of them knew that they didn't want to be caught outside in a lightning storm.

"I'd better get away from this rock, if that squall's moving in," said the climber, and he quickly tightened his rappelling gear and pulled his leather gloves back on, preparing to ascend the canyon wall. "Good luck in your research."

"Thanks," Dana called, as she waved to him and then watched him make his way up the wall.

CHAPTER 5

The same blue pickup-camper, now with a two-horse trailer attached, was parked in the lot of the trailhead again when Dana arrived on Wednesday morning.

As she walked past the trailer, she could see two horses through the metal grille and hear them shifting around inside. One of the horses nickered and she glanced inside, hoping they had sufficient water, particularly if they were going to be left in the trailer for any length of time. The horse next to the side lattice turned its head toward her and rolled a large glassy eye in greeting.

Back on the trail, the rain showers of the previous day had moved on. Just enough had fallen to settle the dust on the track, which was now drying out and in good condition. As she moved up the trail, she sidestepped more than one batch of horse dung.

The recent rains had refreshed the wild flowers that grew on the hillside and along the trail, and the purple mountain lupine, yellow daisies, blue columbine, and tall stalks of light purple gay feather grew abundantly in and around the sagebrush. The tall grasses were lush and bore developing seed heads that swayed in the slight morning breeze.

Dana's path opened into a treeless area that was exposed to the early morning sun. In more than one place she came across more dried dung that had been trampled by the feet of both animals and humans until all that was left was bleached strands of hay.

After leaving the main trail Dana began climbing a zigzag upward track that wound around rocks and sagebrush. Prickly pear cactus was starting to bloom and their bright yellow blossoms made it easier to avoid the vicious spikes on their pads. She paused for a moment to orient herself. She was just beyond the site of her discovery of the *dicentra* the previous day and she was anxious to explore up closer to the cliff wall to see if they might be growing there as well.

Rounding the edge of an SUV-sized boulder, Dana was distracted by movement farther up the hillside. She stopped for a moment with one arm braced against the enormous rock. Whatever she was seeing, it was quite large. Once again she wondered if it was possible she had come upon a bear scrounging for food.

As she stood pondering whether it would be prudent to retrace her steps to the main trail, the object stood upright and she realized it was a human form. Then the figure bent over again and picked up a good-sized rock, which it then tossed down the hill. The rock came to rest against the base of a sturdy alder. Now the individual was down on hands and knees as if pawing through the dirt.

Checking her location, Dana realized the site where the figure was at work was where she had seen the vixen two days earlier and had heard her kits mewling. Dana pushed off the boulder and started on up the hill, shouting and waving her arms. As she neared the person on the ground, she was able to tell it was a male. As her yelling reached his ears he turned slightly and looked over his shoulder.

"What do you think you're doing?" Dana demanded as she came up behind the man, barely containing her anger. She noticed that on the ground to the man's right lay a heavy burlap bag and some twine. She could only assume the worst.

The man, bulky in build and wearing an Aussie Outback hat, slowly stood up, holding a digging trowel against his right leg. He had a leather cord around his neck from which hung dark glasses. The sleeves of his green canvas shirt were rolled to his elbows, revealing heavily tattooed skin, and his hands were encased in heavy leather gloves. He wore a khaki vest with numerous pockets, some of which appeared to be stuffed. He peered at Dana with piercing blue eyes, as if he wanted to swat her away like a pesky fly.

"Whadda ya mean, little lady?" he growled, giving her a head-to-toe inspection. He wiped his gloved hand across his mouth, dragging a line of brown saliva across his cheek before wiping it on his shirt, and then whipped off his hat, revealing a shaved dome.

Dana could faintly hear a soft mewling sound.

"This is a red fox den and there are kits down there."

"You don't say?" he said, as a sneer developed around his mouth.

"I wonder what the game warden would have to say about you trying to dig them out?"

"I just heard 'em cryin' for their mama," he countered. "Thought maybe she abandoned 'em."

"Right," she responded, "suppose that's why you brought along the bag." The horrible image of her grandmother butchering chickens for Sunday dinner flitted into Dana's mind. She could only imagine what had been in store for the kits.

"I always carry that along. Never know when I'll find an artifact of interest."

"Artifact? These are live animals."

"You're prob'bly right," he said, kicking the dirt around the opening he had created at the base of the speckled gray limestone pile.

As angry as Dana was, the thought suddenly occurred to her that perhaps she had been a bit hasty in confronting the man on her own, especially with no other human anywhere near. She had no way to protect herself if he decided to take a swing at her with the pointed metal trowel he still held in his hand.

As if to bear out her thought, he scoffed, "Guess you feel obliged to police the area, huh? Jest like that interfer'ng game warden."

"You don't have to get snippy. I just feel it's the right thing to do to make sure no harm comes to the wild animals."

He grinned at her in a condescending manner, showing stained and yellowed teeth. "I'd best git on up the trail," he said as she stubbornly stood her ground with her arms crossed over her chest. He turned, replaced the hat on his head, and snagged the burlap bag with his left hand. She could hear the clink of metal rattling together in the bag and wondered what other paraphernalia he just happened to be carrying.

Well, that went well, she thought cynically as he made off.

Dana had no way of knowing if the man's intent had been to dig the kits out of the den or if her imagination had simply got the better of her, but what other reason would he have to move the rocks and soil away from the opening to the burrow? Furthermore, what fate had awaited the young foxes? Was he after their pelts, or did he plan on raising them himself? Maybe he planned to sell them to a zoo.

She watched him saunter down the incline in a crisscross fashion. As he walked he returned the trowel to the bag, then rolled everything into a tight bundle and carried it under one arm, using his free hand to swat at insects that buzzed around his face. He turned to look back at her once. There was an angry scowl on his face.

Mad as she had been when she confronted him, Dana's ire slowly dissipated. Who did he think he was to be so blatant about what so obviously was against the law? As the game warden had cautioned her recently, the wildlife and plants in the forest were protected from being dislodged by the public.

She waited till the man had regained the main path before going slowly back to the large boulder where she had been resting before the encounter. Her expectation was that the mother fox had been biding her time out of sight of the scavenger and that she would return shortly to check on her litter. She peered around the boulder again just in time to see the mother fox slip down into her burrow.

Having wondered many times in recent years where she had developed such righteous indignation over anything she deemed wrong, Dana had come to credit her maternal grandparents for instilling that quality in her. They had lived on a farm in the eastern part of the state. They grew a few acres of alfalfa and a like amount of great northern beans, ran a few cattle, and planted a huge truck-farm that generated produce that was sold to the public in the late summer.

As a young girl, she had spent many happy hours following her grandfather around as he fed the animals, telling her in his quiet voice about each. She had learned that the pigsty was off limits, as the swine could be testy at times; how to milk a cow and feed the barn cats with an occasional squirt of milk directly from the cow's teat; and how to reach lightly under the hens in their nests and gently withdraw the eggs.

Dana smiled ruefully as she recalled an occasion when her younger brother and a visiting cousin had challenged each other to see who could rope one of her grandfather's sows. However, once they had got the rope around the pig's neck it had become so tight the sow was soon down on the ground, choking. The two boys fled to the farmhouse and told her grandmother what had happened. She grabbed a kitchen knife and returned to the pigpen with them, where she managed to saw the rope off the sow. She also gave those boys a stern warning not to leave the yard again and, to Dana's knowledge, they had stayed clear of the sty thereafter.

During those times when her grandfather was in the fields, Dana had helped her grandmother in her vast gardens. In the springtime, she assisted with the planting and the weeding. When it came time for harvesting, she helped pick, wash, and prepare vegetables for storage. While her grandfather was quiet-spoken, her grandmother was more colorful in her speech. Grandmother traced her lineage back five generations, to an emigrant German family, and on occasion when she was frustrated or angry, such as during the pig-tying episode, she spewed out a string of cusswords in German—*die scheisse, verdammt, mein gott.*

Her grandmother raised a brood of chickens each year and began harvesting them as fryers by late July. Those family members who still lived in the vicinity had gathered around her grandparents' large oak dining room table on many a Sunday for fried chicken, mashed potatoes and gravy, fresh greens and vegetables from the garden, topped off by homemade ice cream to follow.

As much as everyone enjoyed such a meal, Dana recalled watching many times on Sunday mornings as Grandmother selected a couple of plump fryers from her flock, stretched their necks on a chopping block and lopped off the heads with a small axe, before flinging them aside to let them flop around and rid themselves of as much of their blood as possible before she dressed them for cooking.

When the sweetcorn, squash, potatoes, and cucumbers were mature, Dana had helped sell the items from a roadside stand. Later, during her teenage years when she wasn't in school, she had handled the sales with the assistance of one of her younger siblings. She smiled wistfully as she remembered how, on one occasion, a young man a year or two older than she was appeared at the stand with his mother. Embarrassed that she had mentioned to her sister that she had a schoolgirl crush on him, Dana had jumped when her sister gave her a jab in the side, with the result that she dropped one of the squashes they had picked out as she was sacking it.

***

It was still rather early and many of the casual hikers on the trail

33

didn't show up until around noon. A series of waterfalls up near the head of the canyon was the destination of many of those who traversed the trail. Consequently, there were few people along the passage at this time of the day and Dana was feeling a bit uneasy after her encounter with the forager.

She wondered if the camper and horse trailer at the trailhead belonged to him. Though she had no wish to cross his path again, she wasn't going to be intimidated in her research by his odious behavior. Perhaps the wiser plan would be to work back along the hillside up to the base of the cliff wall as she had contemplated earlier. The plan she had laid out and was trying to follow ended where the boulder field thinned out, about sixty feet shy of the rock face.

Hoping to see the game warden, Trig Henderson, she kept an eye pealed along the trail. He had told her he had quite a large territory to cover, so it was extremely unlikely he would be back on the Popo Agie Trail again today.

The going was slow as she picked her way gingerly through the rock field, unhurriedly checking around likely places where she had determined her plants thrived. By noon, she had found a couple of new clumps and had made additional notes about their habitat. Blossoms on one cluster of plants were just opening, while a second was just starting to set on its fragile stems.

Perched on the edge of a flat granite outcropping, Dana had a wide view of the main trail below her as she logged some of the data she had just gathered. True to her expectations, day-hikers, in groups of three or four, came trudging up the trail, some with walking sticks to assist them over the rough spots, invariably with backpacks, all of them chattering. Voices seemed to carry noticeably hereabouts, likely because of the canyon walls which, though a great distance apart, still reverberated with any sound that was made.

She watched as two horseback riders headed up the trail to the upper country. Would those be the horses in the trailer she had passed that morning at the trailhead, she wondered? She had been told ranchers used the trail to check on cow herds and that during the hunting season it was utilized to reach established camps.

Throughout the morning, she had watched for the man she had confronted at the fox den in case he returned. The chances were that he was probably well up to the falls and beyond, maybe with other quarry in mind. She decided she was spending far too much time worrying about meeting up with him again and that her time would be much better spent on the study of her plants.

Wind moved through the canyon, gradually building in intensity as Dana sat absorbing the panorama below her. Overhead the clear skies had been invaded by heavy, gray, low-lying nimbostratus clouds, while behind Dana, over the northern cliff face, darker and more threatening clouds filled with rain were moving forward.

She closed the field book she had been working in and gathered up her equipment. During the time she had been working in the area, she had learned that such winds and clouds were the forerunners of early afternoon summer showers. Thinking of the hikers she had seen just minutes earlier on the trail, she hoped they carried rain gear with them.

Dana made her way down to the trail as the rain began spattering around her. From there she hurried back toward the trailhead. The sage-sweet smell of rain-drenched sagebrush permeated the air around her and she inhaled it deeply. She had a rain jacket in her backpack but didn't stop to put it on. Besides, she had an ulterior motive for cutting her day short.

Back at the parking lot, there was another late-model pickup with a first-class horse trailer attached. It was empty and likely accounted for the riders she had seen from a distance on the trail. There were also several other vehicles that hadn't been there earlier.

The blue camper and the horse trailer that had been parked down the row from where Dana had parked that morning remained. And the two horses were still inside. How someone could go off and leave the animals standing in the trailer all this time she couldn't understand. At least with the rain shower they should be getting a respite from the heat. She tried to see inside the metal trailer to see if water was available but the angle of the grillwork hid the floor. The horses inside the trailer shifted as she walked around the unit. The pickup-camper had an Idaho license plate on it. However, as she moved on around to the back of the trailer, it had a ten-county Wyoming license plate on it, so she knew it was local and must be leased or borrowed from someone in the area.

A rumble of thunder and the first drops of rain sent her scurrying to unlock her vehicle, stow her equipment, and scramble inside.

CHAPTER 6

Back in Lander Dana stopped at a supermarket, donned her rain jacket, and dashed inside to replenish her supply of her favorite twelve-grain bread, milk, and cereal. By the time she finished her shopping and returned to her car, the rain was coming down in sheets.

At her apartment, Dana gathered the bag from the market and hastened to the protection of the covered entryway of her digs. Inside, she placed the food items on the counter separating her small kitchen from the living area and brushed the rain from the shoulders and front of her jacket.

That done, she pulled her cell phone from the pocket of her shorts to check it for any messages then pushed the button to see who had called. There was only one communication waiting for her attention. Shedding her jacket, she hung it on the back of one of the oak dinette chairs before turning to the phone.

"This is Jedadiah Ahrens. Believe you called about getting information on geology. I'll be inside during the noon hour." Click.

Well, that was short and sweet. Dana had understood from Dr. Watt that his geologist friend was quite old, so that likely accounted for the abruptness of the message. She pondered what being inside during the noon hour meant then checked her wristwatch. It was 11:45 a.m. She would give him time to, presumably, have his lunch then return the call.

It was fortunate she had cut her day short. Had she remained up in the canyon any longer, as had been her practice, she would have missed the opportunity to connect with the geologist today. She checked the time of his call and realized he had called merely minutes before she arrived home. He had probably known that with the rain coming down so hard, she would likely not be out in the field.

She made a quick trip out to her car for her backpack then changed into navy cotton slacks, a long-sleeved green pullover, and warm socks with her loafers. Returning to the living room, she opened her notebook to review her observations as she nibbled on an apple. Raising her head occasionally, she peered outside as the rain pelted the tall rectangular bay windows of the room.

At 12:30 she returned the call to Jed Ahrens. The phone rang three times before he answered.

"Jedadiah Ahrens."

"Dr. Ahrens, this is Dana Cameron. I called you to see if we might meet. Arnold Watt is my academic advisor at the university." She explained about being in the area doing research in Sinks Canyon on the elusive *dicentra*. "Arnold suggested that with your knowledge of geology in this area, you might assist me by answering some questions I have about the habitation of the plant I'm studying."

"Don't know how much help I can give you, young lady, but I'll be in my shop this afternoon."

"Would it inconvenience you if I were to come by?"

"No, suppose not. You know where I live?"

She didn't. He gave her directions to his home on the north edge of Lander.

***

With no let-up in the rain in sight, Dana sunk her arms into her anorak, pulled the hood up over her shoulder-length hair, and returned to her Honda.

She was completely unfamiliar with the area of town to which Dr. Ahrens had directed her. When she came to the end of Tweed Lane, the pavement ran out and she drove forward on a rain-splashed gravel road with small pockets of standing water. The road, surrounded by aspen and small pines, took a turn to the left, then back right, before she found a mailbox on the right with "AHRENS" in prominent black lettering. She turned onto a narrow lane that meandered through further trees and low-growing shrubbery, which opened up to reveal a large, immaculately landscaped yard, with a two-story cedar home in the middle of it.

A curved driveway arced around the entrance to the house. Dana parked to the right side and surveyed the area before leaving her car. As she was heading toward the main entrance, she spotted a small wooden sign posted at the edge of the lawn. It had "Shop" scribed on it and an arrow pointing to a smooth rock path that led around one end of the house. The walk led along a flower-edged path to a small building made of river rock that differed greatly in appearance from the main house.

The shop was situated behind a detached three-car garage of the same cedar material as the main building. Jed Ahrens's shop was squat and appeared to be quite old, with a crumbling foundation and few windows.

At the entrance was a screen door, an obvious modern addition. Dana peered inside and gently opened the door.

"Dr. Ahrens?"

An old man looked up from the table in the middle of the room where he was working. He had a thin, grizzled face, with a scraggly gray beard, sharp gray eyes, and thick white hair. He had been bent over a microscope, with a pen in his right hand, apparently making notes on a pad to one side.

"Well, damn, girl, don't just stand there," he said, motioning Dana into the room.

Dana came forward, extending her hand. "Thanks," she stammered, feeling as if she were intruding on significant work. "I'm Dana."

"Thought you might be," he said, ignoring her hand.

There was only one room in the shop. It was lined with shelving, most of it filled with different types of rocks, field notebooks, and small tools. Picks, axes, and shovels hung from a small space on the back wall. On the north wall was a fireplace built of the same gray river rock.

The fireplace reminded Dana of one she had seen in an old mountain cabin she and her family had stayed in many years before. The fireplace was obviously still used, as a large, well-worn, leather-covered recliner chair and small table were placed in front of it. On the table lay several trade magazines in various states of disarray.

"So, you're one of Arnie's grad students. I thought he was taking a sabbatical this year."

"I believe he postponed that until after next spring."

As she moved closer to where he was sitting, Dana realized Dr. Ahrens was in a wheelchair. He pushed himself away from the table and motioned her to a chair around the corner from where he was positioned.

"What's this about finding *dicentra minutea* up in the canyon?"

"Are you familiar with *dicentra*?"

"I'm more familiar with *dicentra uniflora*. Don't know much about the smaller species." Seeing the look of surprise on her face, he continued, "Yeah, after your phone call I took a look in one of my old botany books and saw mention of it. Think I read an article recently that talked about it being pretty much extinct."

"That's what's exciting about it," Dana said. "I believe I have found a few pockets of it along the west side of the canyon, above the campgrounds."

"Seems unlikely," he said, "what's your proof?"

Dana pulled her field book out of her backpack and opened it to the pages where she had made notes of her first and subsequent discoveries: the drawings, the measurements, blossom size, and leaf and stem descriptions.

The old man began reading through her notes, peering closely at some of the notations and drawings she had made.

"Uumph." The sound came from deep in his throat. "You take good field notes."

"The first specimen I found was not in bloom yet. It was budded, so I had to make explicit drawings to compare with my material at home. That evening I made a copy from my plant biology book to carry with me."

"I see," he said as he came to the textbook page she had inserted in her notes. "And why do you think this plant has reappeared in this area?"

She had known that question would be coming. "It's been found in the foothills of the Snowy Range near Laramie. One of my professors has seen sparse patches of it and an acquaintance of his claims to have seen it along the trail here last summer. He got me enthused, plus, the domestic form of *dicentra* has always been a favorite of mine."

"Can't always let our sentiments make decisions for us," he groused.

Dana took a double breath. "I'm aware of that. However, I believed, and still do, that the evidence is strong enough to warrant my research in this area due to the presence of some of the same rock types that seem to suit them. Plus, the spring rainfall here has increased over the past few years."

"Uumph. Seems you've done your homework."

They were both leaning over her observations when an inconspicuous back door Dana hadn't noticed before banged opened.

"I picked up your saw blades in town, Unc."

Dana raised her head and saw a tall man coming into the room, wearing a ball cap and laden with two large paper-wrapped packages. The older man raised his head and pointed with his right arm.

"They can go on the table, by the lapidary saw, Jax. Thanks."

"Didn't mean to interrupt you," said Jax. He turned to deposit the saws on one of the tables near a complicated piece of equipment after seeing his uncle engrossed in conversation.

"Jackson, this is one of Arnie Watt's graduate students, working on a project up in the canyon this summer," said Dr. Ahrens as he turned back to her notes.

The man walked toward them. Dana stood and held out her right hand to greet Jax. She did a double-take, looked at him closer, and realized he was the rock climber she had exchanged greetings with a couple of days before. Today, though, he was clean-shaven and dressed in more business-like chinos and a long-sleeved blue shirt.

"Well, hello there," he said, recognizing her instantly, "if it isn't the seeker of plants."

"You're the rock jock."

They both laughed at their descriptions of each other.

Jax removed his cap, which was adorned with a bright insignia too small for Dana to read and swished it through the air, spreading a swirl of raindrops around him. His brown hair, with its tendency to be curly, framed his high forehead, wide cheekbones, and firm chin.

"To what do we owe the pleasure?" he asked. "Given up on your project?"

"Not at all. But it's hard to get much work done on days like this."

"What's this about geologic relationship?" demanded Dr. Ahrens, cutting his nephew off. He had lifted his head from what he was reading, with a finger holding his place in Dana's notes.

Dana turned from Jax and looked over the geologist's shoulder. "A couple of articles I've read, plus other data in one of my textbooks, seem to indicate that minerals in some rocks act as nutrients for my *dicentra* plants. Do you have any knowledge of that? I would like to show a correlation between the plants and the rocks."

Jax looked at the notebook over his uncle's other shoulder. He seemed to have taken the interruption by his uncle in his stride as if it was an expected feature of their usual interactions.

"Uumph. You have the articles you're talking about?" Dr. Ahrens inquired as he pushed back away from his worktable again and Dana and the nephew made room for him and his wheelchair.

"I have that information at my place," she said.

"Like to see them," he muttered, implying he had reservations about the authenticity of her articles. Then he turned to Jax. "What are you doing out here today? Too wet to make any progress?"

Jax looked at Dana over his uncle's head and smiled knowingly at her, then crossed his arms over his chest. "The concrete crew poured a small amount this morning but they called it off at noon. Couldn't keep up with the rain."

Jed gave a short grunt.

Dana looked quizzically at Jax. "Are you involved in a building project?"

"I'm the architect on the hospital's new extension."

"You must have a hands-on approach if you were out with them in the rain this morning."

"Have to. Not a day goes by but some change in the plans comes up, and I'm responsible to see that any change is okayed by the hospital's Board of Trustees. Nine times out of ten, it's going to cost them more money. And, if that's the case, it slows us down while we wait for the board to take action. It's a lot like herding chickens."

"So on those rare occasions when you're not needed on the construction site, you escape to the mountains and climb rocks?"

"You got it," he said, an engaging smile creasing the corners of his brown eyes.

"Be a wonder if he doesn't break his fool neck," interjected Dr. Ahrens. "I've seen some of the places he climbs."

"Unc, you know I use every safety precaution."

He gave another short grunt.

"Well, I should leave you to what you're working on," said Dana, motioning toward the microscope. "Sounds like the rain may be letting up. I'll drop those articles off for you to read, if you'd like. I would really appreciate your input into what I'm doing and any suggestions you have."

"We'll see what your material has to say."

"I can't help but notice your shop here," said Dana, looking around. "Did all this rock come from this area?"

"You bet. All the rock in the construction of this building was collected from the creek, cut, mortared and set in place right here by my great-uncle when he moved his family out here from Ohio to start a new life in the early 1900s."

"So this property has been in your family for many years, then."

"The family built a ranch house eventually and used this here building as a barn. A fire mostly destroyed the ranch house about thirty years ago. That's when I built the present house."

"Your house and grounds are lovely."

"I appreciate that."

Dana gathered up her notebook and moved toward the door.

"Hang on, I'll walk out with you," said Jax. He turned to his uncle and patted him on the shoulder. "We still on for dinner tomorrow night?"

Dr. Ahrens glowered, then nodded. "Uumph."

CHAPTER 7

Outside, Dana found that not only had the rain let up but blue sky was breaking through the remaining clouds, with the sun barely hidden behind one large mass.

"Your uncle's quite the character," said Dana as Jax joined her where she stood admiring a big clump of pink irises.

"Pretty set in his ways," he said as he set his ball cap loosely back on his head. "Have to admit though, his bark is much worse than his bite."

"I noticed some engraved stones around his shop. Does he do those?"

"If people find a specimen they want etched and bring it to him, he does it for them. Not as many as he used to, though."

"You mean he carves, like, names?"

"Etches. He uses a special tool to actually chisel about a quarter inch into the stone. So yeah, plus street addresses for their yards, businesses, just about anything."

Dana nodded, understanding. "These flowers are beautiful," she said, raising her arm and sweeping over the wide area of perennials that were in bloom or budded. "Who's responsible for all this?"

"My aunt planted and cared for them. Since she died a few years ago my uncle is alone here most of the time and not as sharp as he used to be. That's why I worry about him sometimes. He does have a housekeeper who comes in daily. She prepares meals for him. And a gardening service comes once a week to mow and weed."

"It's very impressive," Dana said, leaning over to touch a petal. "I'm a flower lover myself."

"I kind of gathered that after hearing about your project, and seeing Unc's reaction to the work you've done."

"He obviously knows his geology."

"One of the best in the area. He used to spend a great deal of time out in the field. Lately, he's been studying a lot of fossils that have been found on the west side of the Windys."

"Windys?"

"Sorry, the Wind River Mountains. We're on the east range here."

"Oh, right, haven't heard them called that before. But back to your uncle, can he still get out and about?"

"Not so much now, but he gathered numerous samples before his accident and people bring him specimens, which he continues to study and classify. He still writes an occasional article for newsletters and magazines."

"What happened? I mean, how did he get injured?"

"He was out in the field, and fell."

Dana had a sense that wasn't the whole story. "What kind of fossils is he studying?"

"Mostly fish, crustaceans, leaves, plants, even small mammals."

"He must have been working in the Fossil Butte area, then."

"I believe so. If you're interested in fossils I know he would be glad to talk about them."

"Think I'd better stick to my own knitting right now."

They had reached their vehicles.

"Maybe I'll see you up in the canyon again," said Jax, opening the door of his silver pickup truck.

"I'll remember to look over my head," Dana replied, sliding into her own car.

***

The rain had disappeared and it had become a warm, pleasant afternoon. After leaving Dr. Ahrens, Dana drove to the Fremont County Library and looked through historical documents on local botany, hoping to find information on related species of the plant she was tracking.

As with many research items, one article led to another and, before she knew it, it was after 4:00 p.m. Dana had found numerous articles on *dicentra,* but only one small notation about her species, saying it had disappeared from the area in the late 1960s. She returned the articles to their folders and left the library, speculating about temperature changes or some other causal principle that had caused them to go extinct.

She made a snap decision to drive through McDonald's pickup window to get a hamburger and a yogurt parfait before heading home.

***

That evening, Dana was just finishing feeding Flag when she heard a small thump outside her front door. She had got used to reading the small local newspaper when she was seeking an apartment back in the spring and still preferred it to the Internet version.

She picked up the paper and opened it. The headline across the top of the paper read, LOCAL GAME WARDEN FOUND DEAD. She quickly perused the article as she settled in numbed surprise at the counter with a glass of sun tea and her meal. The person the article was about was none other than Trig Henderson, whom she had so recently chatted with on the trail. How could it be? He had seemed like such a robust person.

In the second paragraph of the article, it stated that the well-liked warden had been found by workmen in a brushy area south of the trail along the Popo Agie River, halfway up the track to the falls. Officials were uncertain if the death was from natural causes. The body had apparently fallen from a sharp outcropping of boulders and had numerous cuts and bruises. The story went on to talk about activities the game warden had been involved in locally, his surviving family members, and concluded that the case was still under investigation.

Dana took a bite of her burger and slowly absorbed what she had just read. She felt a sense of shock at the news that someone she had so recently spoken with had died. Then her cell phone rang.

The caller on the line was Arnold Watt. Dana swallowed her mouthful of food and answered.

"Hi, Arnie."

"What's going on?" he asked. "Heard you lost a game warden up that way."

"I was just this minute reading about it," she replied. "I hadn't heard about it before."

"You really have been in the sticks. It was on the news this morning."

"I chatted with him quite a bit just a few days ago. He gave me some not commonly known information about the area."

"From what I heard on the radio, they don't seem to know what happened to him."

"It's been an adventurous day here. I was out in the field this morning and had an encounter with a guy who was trying to dig a red fox and her kits out of their den, then I got rained out and came home. Then, this afternoon, I went over and met Dr. Ahrens."

"Oh, yeah? How did that go? How is the old guy?"

"Well, he's in a wheelchair."

"Yeah, I knew that. How's he doing?"

"He's a little crotchety, but he looked at my notes and thought I had done a good job on them. He wants to see the articles I have on the role rocks play in supporting plant life. What happened to him? His nephew was there and mentioned an accident, but he didn't offer any details."

"He got hurt after he retired from teaching. Was still doing some serious free-style rock climbing without a safety rope and fell, smashing up a hip and pretty much ruining a leg. I understand he had his eye on a rock extrusion about fifty feet up the side of a nearly vertical face, and slipped."

"Oh." *So, that's why he's so sensitive about his nephew's climbing,* Dana was thinking. However, the day she had seen Jax in the canyon, he had been using ropes and a harness. From the little she knew about rock climbing, she felt he focused on safety.

"Well, good, good… glad you connected with him," Dr. Watt continued. "Was Jed able to help you any in building a case for a relationship between the make-up of rocks and plant life?"

"He wants to see the two articles, then we'll talk some more. I think he has some doubts about my material."

"Sounds about what I would expect. I wanted to mention, too, Dana, that you'll need to find several clumps of your plant and, if possible, in diverse locations."

This last statement took Dana aback. Did he really think she would base her entire project on one specimen, or even two, or three? Trying to keep the defensiveness out of her voice she kept her tongue firmly in her cheek as she responded. "I'll keep that in mind, Arnie."

"Now, tell me more about this fellow who was after the foxes."

"I think he was intent on either taking the kits and selling them or destroying them for their skins."

"Did you report him?"

"Interestingly enough, I had met this game warden earlier in the week on the trail and was hoping I would run into him again today but, of course, that didn't happen."

"Maybe you should report the poacher to the…" he paused momentarily, "…oh, I don't know, maybe, the sheriff's office?"

"I could do that, but I'd hate to cause a problem over something if I don't have any proof of it." She switched the phone to her other hand and deftly changed the subject.

CHAPTER 8

Dana left her apartment a few minutes earlier than usual on Thursday morning. She had made copies of the two articles on dependency relationships between plants and rocks, one quite short and the other more extensive, placed them in an envelope with his name on them, and drove out to Jed Ahrens's place.

When she arrived, the door to the shop was closed. Dana turned the knob, but it was locked. She squeezed the envelope between the door handle and the frame, guessing he probably wasn't as early a riser as she was. Hoping to talk to him in person about the articles, she told herself she would follow up with him later.

Dana retraced her route back into town and out the opposite direction, heading for the canyon.

The morning was bright and sunny. Luminescent clouds along the eastern horizon were fading from pinkish-orange to light lavender as the sun made its way higher into the sky. Dana hummed along with the country music station on the radio as the singer wailed about *leaving the right one behind once again.*

She parked in her usual spot at the trailhead, noting that the blue pickup-camper she had seen before was parked farther down the line. The rear door of the horse trailer was open, the ramp was lowered, and there were horse droppings leading to the trail's entrance. So the pickup-camper occupant was clearly already on his way up the path. It seemed strange that he had left the trailer door open, but maybe that made it easier to reload his horse once he returned.

The trail was tricky from the previous day's rain. Small puddles of water still lay in places on the uneven path and where the soil partially covered rocks it was slick. Dana found herself watching carefully where she stepped. A sprained or broken ankle was not a pleasant thought.

She was determined to prove her theory about *dicentra* favoring a sheltered location, one protected from the elements, correct. The plants she had found thus far had been on the shady side of larger boulders and, interestingly enough, well above the main trail. Unfortunately, that also meant there was considerable scree the higher she climbed, and the danger of slipping in the loose quarter-sized pebbles made the going extremely slow.

Dana's plan for the day was to trek up the trail to the waterfalls, which she had yet to see, and then do her field work on the way back. A couple of hikers she had met on one of her previous excursions had told her the falls were spectacular, particularly this early in the season. She knew the water in the Popo Agie was fairly high, with the run-off from the mountain snow filling it to its banks, so she was anxious to see the falls while they were at their best.

As Dana progressed up the trail, she occasionally had to sidestep more fresh horse droppings. She was thinking if the rider was the man she had encountered yesterday, he must have a partner, as there were clear signs of the tracks of two horses.

As the sun rose higher in the sky and warmed the earth, she stopped to remove her fleece jacket and folded it into her backpack. The rain had encouraged yet another wave of multicolored wild flowers along the hillside and next to the trail. She scanned them as she strode along in hopes of spying a clump of the evasive *dicentra* among them, but they apparently chose to grow separately.

A murder of crows was perched on the blackened, dead branches of several trees in one area. A spot forest fire had obviously laid waste to a span of the hillside. Their raucous calls back and forth to each other broke the stillness of the morning, scattering the colorful finches and robins as they rummaged for seeds and worms on the ground.

Hearing the sound of a power engine ahead, Dana paused for a moment. Who could be making such a racket in this pristine area? She continued forward and, over the next rise, her question was answered. Her first clue was the carrot-red hair of one of the two people she saw off to her right. It was the clean-up crew, minus one.

When they saw Dana approaching, the chain saw was shut down.

"Hey, Day-na," said Edeen. He sported a yellow handkerchief, folded in a roll and wrapped around his forehead to absorb perspiration.

"Hi, guys, did you leave Joe at home today?"

"Naw, he's down in the brush somewhere, taking a whizz," said Adam, puffing from his labor after wielding the power saw.

"Sorry I asked," Dana mumbled, half to herself as she unloaded her backpack from her shoulders. "That must have been a nasty wind last night."

"Yeah, we've got a couple trees to take care of today." Adam gestured to a tree they were cutting into small pieces, part of which lay across the trail. "Have to trim the branches, then cut it up and get the pieces to the picnic and camping sites for firewood."

"Do you work just along this trail?" she asked.

"Naw," said Edeen. "Tomorrow we go up the switchbacks to other camp sites. Keeps us busy, going from place to place."

Dana knew that beyond the trailhead the road led up a series of sharp switchbacks on its way up the side of the mountain into the eastern Wind River Mountains and a vast recreational area.

"How far up the trail you going today?" asked Adam. He and Edeen exchanged a fleeting look.

"I haven't seen the falls yet. Thought I'd check them out today."

"Last night, we heard about a sow grizzly and her cubs in the area," said Edeen. "Be a good idea to be on the alert for them."

"Thanks for the warning," said Dana. "Isn't that a little unusual, for a grizzly to be in this area?"

"Been told the game and fish released a pair of grizzlies way back in the toolies several years ago and they're starting to show up here in the lower elevations," offered Adam, then added with a grin, "since you're going to the falls, you might pick out a good place to ride them, once the water slows down."

"Aw, man," said Edeen.

"Yeah, it's a hoot, like riding a roller-coaster," said Adam. "Me and my buddies used to do that a lot, back in my high school days. Sometimes we'd use those old, round plastic sleds. Course we took some nasty bumps, too."

"You must be talking the upper slides, huh?" asked Edeen.

"No way I'd go over the big falls."

"You two have definitely piqued my interest in seeing them," said Dana.

"You know that plant you're out beating the bushes for?" asked Edeen, changing direction, "the bleeding hearts?"

Dana's ears perked up. "Yes. *Dicentra* is the botanical name."

"Was talking with my grandmother last night, and told her about your work. She says my people use the roots from that plant for toothaches. Guess the crushed leaves also make a tea that soothes nerves and helps sprains and other cuts and scrapes."

"I didn't know that," said Dana. "Have you ever used it?"

"Never seen it made up," said Edeen, "but I remember once, after falling during a pick-up basketball game and scraping my knees, grandmother rubbed some kind of concoction on me."

"She should have rubbed it on your head," said Adam, giving his co-worker a friendly punch on the shoulder.

By that time, Dana had her notebook out and was scrambling to write down the information Edeen had shared. She would look into the healing aspects of her plants later when she had access to her computer.

"Whatever it was, it took the sting out of my scrapes."

"I've heard of other potions Natives have handed down over the years," said Dana, "but hadn't heard of this one. I'll do some follow-up exploration on my plants. Really glad I ran into you guys today." She turned and was getting ready to pick up her backpack when she turned back. "Have you, by chance, seen the blue pickup-camper that's parked at the trailhead most days?"

"Yeah, I've seen it," Adam said. "Think it has a horse trailer hooked on it today."

"Have you seen who drives it?" asked Dana.

"Some dude who thinks he's a mountain man," said Adam.

"Know what he does out here? I mean, you ever see him carrying anything?"

"Just on his horses. He was packing up when we left the trailhead this morning," said Edeen.

"He takes both horses?"

"Yeah," said Edeen, "always trails one of them."

"Why you asking?" asked Adam.

"I kind of had a run-in with him, and was just wondering. It's probably nothing."

Adam and Edeen shared a mystified look. They both acted as if they wanted to respond, but didn't.

"Do you know where he goes with his horses?"

"It appears he goes all the way up the trail to the top," said Edeen.

"Might be taking supplies up to one of the camps," suggested Adam.

"You're probably right. Well, I need to keep moving and let you get back to work," said Dana.

"Be sure and keep an eye out for the bears," said Adam, as he bent over the chain saw, preparing to re-start it.

"I appreciate the information," said Dana, picking up her backpack and fitting it over her shoulders. "You guys have a good day."

"You, too, Day-na," said Edeen.

CHAPTER 9

As she climbed higher, Dana became aware of a dull roaring sound that increased the farther she trekked. She must be nearing the falls. The trail opened into a series of steep switchbacks, winding around a thick field of sagebrush before leveling out into a wholly dissimilar vista, leaving the occasional trees and shrubs behind.

Suddenly she came to a large, flat rock outcrop and the sound of rushing water was deafening. Creeping forward, she found herself on the ledge that was the viewing site of the lower falls, from which the roaring sound was emanating.

The falls cascaded over a curved crest not more than a hundred yards from where she stood. It reminded her of Niagara Falls, on a smaller scale, with foamy spray churning out near the base. Streaming rivulets of water not contained by the overflowing riverbed were spilling over side channels of the Popo Agie's main course.

Dana slipped off her backpack and pulled her water bottle out, tossing down a couple of long swigs, then sipping from the bottle periodically. She scanned the spectacle of the roiling water as it poured over the rock formations that dictated its course down the river. The sun's reflection gave water particles flying through the air the appearance of precious stones in all colors of the rainbow, as if someone had flung them from the top of the falls. The cascading water drowned out any other sound.

She was content to spend time watching and listening to the mesmerizing water gushing over the summit as if being released from captivity. Melting snow from the mountain ranges much, much higher up had made its way into the run-off that created the display she was observing. Dana had always been intrigued by the phenomenon of water originating in the mountain ranges, forming creeks that merged with rivers, making bigger and yet bigger rivers, before reaching the Gulf of Mexico. She knew that on the opposite side of the continental divide of the Wind River Mountains the run-off went through the same process, some of the water likely ending up in the mighty Colorado River before providing irrigation for the southwestern states and California.

Eventually, she shook herself out of her musing, fascinating though it was to contemplate the water, and slowly picked up her backpack.

The goal for today was to see the smaller falls farther along, so Dana moved on up the trail. It led her over a narrow wooden bridge that spanned a small rill with ferns, chokecherry, and red-twig dogwood bushes growing thick on its banks. She was re-entering a forested area with tall pine trees beginning to close in around her as she gained elevation with each step.

After a while she came to another set of falls, smaller in width, but dropping a longer distance into a large pool at the bottom. The water surging over the falls poured down in a cloud of sprinkles, some of which settled on Dana like a refreshing shower.

A wooden bench had been placed nearby for visitors to sit on to enjoy the sight and rest from the arduous climb, but Dana chose to stand as close to the shimmering water as possible. The sound of the torrent flowing over the brink gradually became secondary to the wonderment of the vista. All was peaceful and she was deeply absorbed in the pleasure of the scene laid out before her.

Small butterflies, some blue, some yellow, hovered at the edge of the pond, occasionally dipping into the cold, mountain water for a sip. How had they discovered this idyllic spot? Dana stood, fascinated by the beauty of the pool, until her gaze drifted to the summit of the falls. Off to one side, a small rainbow arced off the falls, refracted by the sun and droplets of water into a spectrum of light.

At last she grudgingly moved farther up the trail to where it split into two paths. She took the one to the left. It followed the waterway until she came to another beautiful pool, complete with more colorful prisms of light. Above the pool was a tiered series of short falls like a wide staircase. Dana guessed these were the falls Adam had spoken about, which he and his buddies had sledded down. They looked on the wild and treacherous side but she could see how young guys would be tempted to challenge each other to slide down them. Maybe, but only once the water calmed down.

As before, the streambed could not handle the amount of cascading water. It overflowed into smaller rivulets off each side of the falls and eventually into the pool. The ground beneath Dana's feet was somewhat spongy from the abundance of water and she discovered thick masses of moss growing not only on the ground but also on the sides of several of the trees. In places protected from the sun, small patches of snow remained. To go farther up this path, she would have to crawl over fallen trees and shrubs and deal with very boggy soil.

Instead, Dana retraced her steps, walking back to the split in the trail. Going in the opposite direction, the trail took a sharp angle deeper into the forest. She chose instead to return to the serenity of the long falls, where she took advantage of the bench and sat for a time, riveted by the tranquil setting.

Few places she had visited had given her such a sense of complete peace, contentment, and a feeling that all was right with the world. This place, though, engendered all those feelings. The rushing water plunging into the glistening pool, the surrounding pine forest, and the sweet-smelling blooms of the shrubbery surrounding her all contributed to the feeling of harmony she was absorbing into her soul.

Dana was jerked from her contemplation by a reflection on the surface of the outermost edge of the pool. It wasn't a product of the colorful prisms caused by water, but looked more as if a metal or glass object had caught a spark of sunshine. She stood and walked as close as possible to where she had seen the unusual glinting in the water. There was no piece of glass, no metal.

Dana realized belatedly that the reflection could have been occurring for some time before she noticed it. The crows that had been so palpable earlier had disappeared. Or perhaps they just couldn't be heard over the roar of the water. She had seen no other hikers on the trail or here at the falls and quite suddenly she felt isolated and vulnerable.

She moved a few steps farther along the edge of the pond and the gem-like colors that had captivated her changed yet again. Then, for a second time, she saw the odd flash on the water, and felt an eerie feeling creep up the back of her neck. At the same time, it felt almost as if someone was watching her from the cover of the forest.

She whirled around, thinking that other hikers were approaching on the path. No one.

Was it only her imagination or did she hear movement in the forest, a snapped twig, maybe the rustle of something moving through the underbrush? She listened intently, unsure if her senses were playing tricks on her over the sound of the falls. *Must have been a deer or an elk stirring*, she reasoned. On the other hand, she didn't want to encounter a more troublesome wild animal, such as the grizzly bear Edeen and Adam had mentioned. She turned her head, concentrating.

There it was again. Now she heard a slight jingle, then an abrading sound, as if something was being rubbed together or against the trunk of a tree. She stood listening for several moments, took a deep breath, and ran her eyes over the thick swathe of pine trees before her. Again, she was sure she heard some sound that didn't seem quite right in this setting.

She thought of Jax and wondered if he or some other climber was dangling from ropes and working his way up or down the face of the canyon. He had been using climbing cams, straps, and carabiners when she had seen him climbing on Tuesday, but the canyon wall was some distance away. There was also no way she could see the sheer face of the rock wall through the surrounding foliage.

Feeling annoyed at herself and her uneasiness, she gathered up her backpack and was settling it over her shoulders when she paused momentarily. Was that the snicker of a horse or, letting her imagination get the better of her, a grizzly about to charge? She turned for one last look at the falls and the pond, then quickly returned to the main trail, anxious to leave the uncanny feeling she had experienced behind.

A strap on her backpack, which was barely hanging on one of her shoulders, caught on a tree limb. She jerked the strap and it ripped away from its underpinning as she hastened away.

Dana quickly retraced her steps back over the wooden bridge and past river birches growing in the slough along the spongy creek bank. She cast more than one glance back over her shoulder at the shadow-filled forest before reaching the flat openness and the boulder lookout at the main falls. Gathered at the edge of the precipice was a group of five hikers, and Dana gave a sigh of relief to find others in the area. She exchanged greetings with them and moved on.

Once back at the switchbacks, she left the main path and began picking her way cautiously around sagebrush, bitter brush, and the ever-present prickly pear cactus, climbing steadily up the incline toward the cliff wall as she had planned. Being back out in the open, with the sunshine spilling over her, warmed her soul and eased her anxiety.

The south-facing canyon wall loomed before her. Looking in both directions along the vertical rock face, she saw no climber anywhere. Well, that eliminated one possibility.

The sagebrush and other plants gradually gave way to the scree field. She paused for a moment to observe any larger boulders that looked promising cover for her plants. As her eyes roved farther up the canyon, a faint movement caught her attention. She raised her binoculars, and above the forest line, at the very summit, she spotted a horseman, trailing a packhorse over the incline.

CHAPTER 10

Back in Lander later that afternoon, Dana stopped by the Leather and Soles repair shop on South Third Street and dropped off her backpack to have the torn strap repaired. As she stepped back out the front entrance of the ageing, grey-brick establishment, down one step to the sidewalk, she met Jax Ahrens, who was waiting to enter.

"So, we meet again," he said, grinning at Dana as he held the door open. "I have a climbing shoe that needs to be reinforced."

She laughed softly. "Yeah, my backpack got snared on a tree today, so I just dropped it off."

"How goes the research?"

"Better, actually."

"Hey, let me drop this shoe off, I'll be right back," he said as he disappeared inside the shop. He returned almost immediately.

"They must have been expecting you," she said.

"I'm a regular customer. I wear holes in the toes of my climbing shoes, so they see me every so often." He looked farther up the street. "I was just going to get a bite to eat. You interested in joining me?"

Feeling slightly camp-soiled, Dana looked down at her sweat-stained tee shirt and dusty hiking boots. She was about to decline, when she realized he was in a similar state himself, having obviously just come from his work site.

"I'm pretty grungy," she said hesitantly. "I haven't been home yet to get cleaned up."

"Nah, I usually go to this little mom and pop place up the block," Jax said, motioning farther along the sidewalk. "They won't mind."

***

They found a booth halfway back on the right side of The Bronze Spoon restaurant and settled in. Tall glasses of frosted iced tea were soon sitting in front of them as they considered the menu. They both ordered sandwiches and onion rings before picking up their earlier conversation.

"So, how'd you get caught up with your backpack today?" Jax asked.

Dana smiled faintly, took a sip of tea, and pondered whether she should even mention the silly episode she'd had that morning near the falls.

"You didn't happen to be climbing this morning, did you?" she asked, avoiding his eyes.

"Wish I could have. It was a perfect day. But I've been tied up on a hitch with the electrical contractor most of the day. Why do you ask?"

"I had a bizarre thing happen." And she went on to tell him about the surly man she had stopped from destroying the fox den the previous day, that she suspected the truck and empty horse trailer parked at the trailhead lot that morning belonged to the same person, and then the curious reflections and eerie feeling she had experienced at the pond below the upper falls.

"Sure it wasn't just an animal moving around in the forest?" Jax suggested.

"I thought of that, especially since I ran into the guys on the clean-up crew earlier. One of them said they had heard reports of a grizzly and her cubs in the area. When I got back out in the open away from the forest, quite a-ways up on the hillside, I saw a rider with a couple horses way up above the tree line."

"Sooo, you're saying... what exactly?"

"I don't know what I'm saying." She paused for a moment. "You're probably right. My imagination just got carried away."

Jax seemed to sense there was more to the story. "So you think the guy you confronted yesterday over the foxes is the same guy with the horses?"

"Seems rather coincidental that the two things happened in such a short time."

"I understand your concern if this guy was digging out the fox kits. But you have to admit it's a big leap to connect that and the uneasiness you felt at the falls this morning."

An angry feeling stole up Dana's neck as she recalled the wrath she had felt. She had to bite her tongue to keep from spewing out all her fury over the incident with the foxes, coupled with her experience that morning when her senses had been on such high alert. But Jax was probably right. She was making a connection that likely just wasn't there. Instead, she told herself, she should be focusing on why she was even in the canyon. Taking a deep breath, she decided it was time to move to a safer subject.

"I dropped a couple articles by your uncle's house this morning. I haven't been home yet this afternoon to see if he called."

"Yeah, I had a late breakfast with him today and he mentioned he had been reading them. He likes nothing better than a challenge that gets him going in a different direction. I know he will want to discuss them with you." He raised his hands from the table as the waitress brought their food.

"I'm looking forward to hearing what he has to say. You check on him quite often?"

"Well, I do. He gets engrossed out in his shop and doesn't always stop to eat. Besides, I like to be with him."

"I take it you're from Lander? That you live here?"

"No, I don't live here. I'm from northern Colorado. As a matter of fact, right now I live in a small house trailer out at the construction site. That way I can be close by when problems pop up. My office is there, too, so it makes it handy for the contractors to stop by."

"I'm surprised you don't stay with your uncle."

"He wanted me to, but it just works out better this way."

"So, you must go home periodically."

"Yeah, gotta check on the three, or is it four now, mouths to feed."

Dana's eyes opened wide.

"Juuust kidding," Jax responded, grinning. "Nothing to go home to except an empty apartment."

"Guess I thought you were married. You seem like a family-type guy."

"Nope, just me. How about you?"

The question caught Dana by surprise, and she felt a familiar tug at her heart. She looked down at her plate, moved her sandwich around to a different position, and then lifted her head slowly with a faint smile on her face.

"This is just so awkward to talk about." She fell silent for an uncomfortable few moments with her head bowed, before slowly looking up. "I was engaged once, a couple years ago, but it didn't work out."

"That's too bad. You dump him or he dump you?" Jax asked, watching her with dark, hooded eyes.

"That sounds so belittling," she protested as she picked up an onion ring and took a bite. "But, actually, I guess you would say I asked him to leave."

"His loss," Jax said lightly, as if trying to cover his thoughtless comment.

Dana swallowed slowly. "Mine, too. I really cared for him, but it... it was bad, felt like a stab in my heart." She took a deep breath. "This is difficult to discuss. I found out he was dealing street drugs to students at the university."

Jax sat back in the booth, a grimace on his face. "Oh crap, I'm really sorry."

Dana told him how she and Jeremy had become engaged in her final semester of her undergraduate college work. He had moved into her small apartment with her. Before long, she had put together several suspicious phone calls, unexplained trips to Denver, and meetings with dodgy students. Then she had found a stash of several small packets of white powder in his closet and confronted him.

At first he had denied her accusations, but he relented when she demanded either he explain his actions or she would report him to the police. The next day he was gone and she hadn't heard from him since, although as he was leaving he had vowed to "get even with her."

Heartbroken, she had moped around much of that summer before enrolling in a master's degree program in botany in the fall. Arnold Watt, the botany department chair, had been aware of what had happened and took her on as his advisee, supporting her emotionally through the early course work. Once she had become stabilized again, he had been instrumental in encouraging her as she made the selection of her thesis project.

"You think this Jeremy was serious about getting even?" Jax quizzed her.

"I have no idea," she replied. "I just hope he is far away."

"I know it sounds a little rough, seeing how you felt about him, but it may be best if he's been caught and is in jail. That was a contemptible thing he was doing."

"I know. Part of my problem with the whole situation is that I didn't go to the police. I keep thinking about all the kids he sold to and how it has probably affected their lives."

"Those are hard decisions to make, especially when the heart is involved," Jax said wistfully. "So… what did you think of the falls?"

"All I can say is they give new meaning to beauty."

"How far up did you go?"

"To the tiered falls. The ground got a little spongy at that point. I guess the soil can't absorb all the water."

Jax nodded in agreement.

"Did you happen to know the game warden who worked in this area?" Dana asked.

"You mean the fellow they found up in the canyon?"

"Yes."

"Met him a time or two when I was climbing. Can't say I really knew him."

"Too bad about him falling the way he did. It's hard to imagine how that happened."

Jax took a long drink of his tea and set the glass down. "The word at the work site is that his accident is somewhat suspicious. Guess they're doing an autopsy to find out."

"What makes the authorities think it was something other than an accident?"

"Apparently he had some unusual injuries, especially to his head. Accidents can happen, but he was an experienced rough-terrain guy, so if he fell off a rock that's a little hard to swallow."

"Sounds like you don't buy the accidental fall."

"Not sure. Time will tell when the medical reports come back."

"Speaking of accidents, I'm curious. When you climb in the canyon, do you always go down from the top or do you sometimes climb up from the bottom?"

Jax laughed before answering. "You're just full of questions today, aren't you?"

She let his comment pass and tilted her head to the right and back, as if agreeing.

"I've done both," Jax explained, "but mostly I drive up to the top of the wall. There's a somewhat rough road that goes up and I can access the rim from up there. As I said the other day, it's a beautiful view of the whole canyon, plus all the mountains beyond that can't be seen from down in the canyon."

"So, do you always use full equipment when you climb?"

"I always wear a harness and belays when I'm descending. That's after establishing my anchor, then I use carabiners to hold me in place as I rappel."

"And rappelling is when you descend?"

"Yep."

"And the other day when I was on the rock? And the storm came up?" She smiled at the image of finding him suspended from the cliff above her.

"I had to bail that day."

"And bail means you hightail it out of there, huh?"

"Retreat back up the wall, before the lightning got too close."

"I guess lightning can be dangerous for a climber."

"Oh yeah, that granite pulls it in like a magnet. I was with a group of climbers down in Colorado a couple years back. An electrical storm blew up without much notice. Lightning hit the formation about fifty yards from us and zinged a wide swathe up to the summit. Burned several trees and shrubs growing in the rock. They sizzled and popped just like wood burning in a fireplace."

"Yikes. Did anyone get injured?"

"No, but I can tell you it scared the hell out of us! You never saw such a mass exodus off a cliff!"

"Correct me if I'm wrong, but I sense your uncle is concerned that you climb."

"That's because he thinks I crack-climb on occasion, even though I've explained to him, over and over, that I take every safety precaution."

Seeing the puzzled look on Dana's face and knowing another question was coming Jax smiled and hastened to explain. "Cracking is when a climber begins at the bottom of a wall of rock, usually without any safety devices, and goes up. Sometimes in this granite there aren't any toe or finger holes so, in a nutshell, I put in a crampon and, by sliding my rope through, I pull myself up."

"And wear out the toes of your shoes."

"Yeah, that happens, but sometimes, on other rock formations, I get lucky and find a bollard, which is a knob or small rock outcropping to get my rope around, so I don't have to use crampons. Sure saves on the shoes."

CHAPTER 11

Lying in bed that night Dana was unable to sleep. Her mind roamed over the happenings of the last few days. She was still curious about the man she had confronted at the fox den. His attitude and his demeanor troubled her. He had seemed almost brutish, and as if he had every right to be digging the kits from their burrow, or maybe it was that he thought she had no right to be questioning his intent. Okay, she knew some people took such things personally and she could accept that, but still his conduct was uncalled for.

Then today, the eerie sensation she had had up at the falls. She was sure either a metal object or piece of glass had caused the strange reflection on the water.

She shivered as she recalled the chill that had crept up her spine. And then, of course, a few minutes later, when she had been out in the open on the south-facing incline of the canyon, seeing a horseback rider leading another horse along the horizon... she wondered if it could have been the same man. When she stood at the falls, could he have been watching her from the cover of the forest?

She knew it would be wise to take Jax's advice and not try to connect the two incidents. The feelings she had experienced at the falls may have been caused more by the seclusion of the place, the clean-up crew's mention of bears being in the area, and her imagination simply working overtime.

Night thoughts had been her bane for two years now. She couldn't escape a night like this without recalling the awfulness of discovering Jeremy's ugly side, the confrontation, the break-up, and his threat to get even. Even though she had been able to put most of that experience into perspective in the intervening period, she tossed and turned for over an hour before sleep overtook her.

She also had some help from Flag in finally dozing off. Feeling a slight jolt at the foot of her bed, she sat up in alarm. She was aware of small tentative steps moving around on the covers, then she felt the young cat making a nest and settling down on one of her feet, bringing with her a calming awareness that she was not alone.

***

The following morning, Dana drove out to Jed Ahrens's home. He had left a message on her phone the previous afternoon saying he would like to talk about the material she had left for him.

After parking her car and stepping out, she heard the sharp ring of rock being chipped and realized he was already at work in his shop. She walked slowly along the path between the house and his shop, enjoying the beauty of his perennial beds, with new varieties already blooming since her previous visit.

She tapped lightly, then opened the screen door to the shop and entered.

The old man looked up from his workbench as she walked toward him.

"I got your message."

"Come on in, girl," he said, motioning her forward. "Just finishing smoothing these pieces of obsidian. One of my customers makes knife handles out of them."

Dana approached his work table and bent over, looking at the pieces of glossy black rock he had shaped into lengths of six to eight inches, two inches wide and an inch thick.

"What pretty pieces. Obsidian isn't found in this area, is it?"

"Not that I'm aware of. Usually this rock is only found in small pieces, too. Extraordinary to find a piece as big as this one started out. Hawaii is the best place to find a specimen this big. Comes from all that volcanic action." He laid out his handiwork side by side, wiped his hands on a cloth, and pushed back in his chair.

"I read the articles you left for me. Seems they're based on good research. I think you wanted to incorporate some of that material into your thesis?"

"That's right," she said. "My hope is that you would be able to verify the material and that we might discuss your knowledge of the relationship between plants and rocks."

He rolled his wheelchair near one of the easy chairs before the fireplace. Picking up a brier pipe from the table, he knocked the ash from the bowl into an ashtray and refilled and tamped the tobacco before striking a match and drawing on the pipe. A pleasant scent of cherry wood began drifting throughout the room.

Dana slipped into the chair across from him.

"As you already know from the material you gave me, the soil derived from rocks influences the plant life that grows in the soil. Some of what I'm telling you may have been presented in your class work, so bear with me. Anyhow, there are three rock classifications: igneous, meta-morphic, and sedimentary," he said, naming them off on the first three fingers of his right hand. "Igneous rock is rock or minerals that have solidified from molten or partly molten material that was generated at depth within the earth."

Dana had her notepad out, ready to jot down any new, relevant information he might share.

"Now, having said that, this area contains rocks of both types of igneous rock—intrusive and extrusive. Intrusive rock is formed at considerable depth by crystallization of hot molten magma derived from the earth's core. Intrusive rock, by definition, does not reach the surface, but we do see it when it has cooled, solidified, and been exposed by erosion. It is generally granite-like in character. On the other hand, extrusive rock is hot molten magma that has erupted onto the earth's surface and has usually solidified in the form of lava flows or consolidated volcanic ash."

"Would that also include, say, basalt and rhyolite?"

"Basalt and rhyolite are among the minerals associated with extrusive rock. Pumice, another example of extrusive rock, is a light-colored, lightweight rock that usually has the chemical composition of rhyolite. Igneous rocks are generally rich in acidic minerals." Jed adjusted his position in his chair then, using the stem of his pipe as a means of emphasizing his subject matter, continued. "Sandstone is among the sedimentary rocks that were formed as a result of the consolidation of loose sediment formed when fragments of older rock were transported by water and laid down in layers. Limestone is also a sedimentary rock, but it has been formed from the remains of plants or animals, usually at the bottom of the sea."

"I'm finding trees and shrubs growing out of cracks in large outcrops of rock."

"There you go, that is an indication that the rock is of intrusive origin and it contains a substantial amount of quartz in its composition. The abundance of quartz in the soil you're finding in the cracks, along with the concentration of rainwater flowing into the cracks, provides an environment suitable for growth of evergreens and shrubs."

"I can't get over the size of some of the boulders where I'm looking. They must weigh tons."

"That they do. They're called perched boulders and they were distributed over the area by glacial movement. Glaciers in the Wind River Mountains were localized small glaciers, compared to the massive continental glaciers that moved out of the northern part of our continent. Even so, ice from the smaller glaciers has tremendous power, capable of breaking up and moving large chunks of rock as the ice moves down the slope, rolling some of them until they are round."

"And the canyon walls?"

"The walls you see were cut through the thick beds of the Madison Formation, which developed nearly 300 million years ago. The Madison is made up of limestone, sandstone, and some shale. These layers formed at the bottom of the sea over millions of years. When the sedimentary layers were slowly forced upward far above the seas—such as during the time when the Rocky Mountains were formed—streams formed by rainwater began flowing over the beds and forming channels that cut the canyons like we see here."

"I find it incomprehensible to think of the power those glaciers had in breaking up rock formations and leaving such huge boulders behind."

"Very powerful, very powerful."

"So, kind of related to that, are you aware of any volcanoes anywhere in Wyoming, other than up in Yellowstone?"

Jed Ahrens scratched his head, "There's a place called Rattlesnake Hills east of here that is of volcanic origin. Then, some of my geologist friends think Devil's Tower, over in the northeast part of the state, may have been formed by a volcano. I'm not so sure. That would have required the soil around the tower being worn away by the elements over the centuries, leaving just that cone-like structure as it stands today. Which could be a volcanic plug. There are definitely hot spots in several locations around the state where mineral formations develop into hot springs, fumaroles, and terraces. Of course, you know all these mountains we have are the result of pressure on tectonic plates of rock that caused the sediments to break and slide over one another, or rise vertically to become mountains."

Dana slowly digested all that Jed had just explained, feeling as if she had just sat through three sessions of physical geology. She flipped through several pages of her notebook and found a reminder she had made for herself. "Getting back to my plants, are you aware of any medicinal qualities of the *dicentra* plant?"

"No, but that should be more in your area. Why do you ask?"

"I've run into a seasonal work crew a couple times up on the trail, and one of them, a Native American, was telling me his grandmother makes some kind of brew from *dicentra* that is good for toothache and for taking the sting out of abrasions."

"Wouldn't be surprised. Been told a lot of wild plants have curative qualities, especially the herbs."

"Absolutely, and I plan to find out more about that feature of my plant."

"Say, you might also want to check in the lower part of the canyon for your flora. There would be some change in altitude, but I don't know if it's enough to make a difference in their growing conditions."

Dana could tell Jed was getting restless after sitting basically in one position for so long while they talked and realized it was already nearly lunchtime. She gathered up her notes and offered to see him over to his home, but he explained that his housekeeper would soon be coming to collect him.

CHAPTER 12

After leaving Jed Ahrens's shop, Dana drove downtown and stopped by the leather repair shop to pick up her backpack.

As she came out the door of the shop, she glanced up the street on South Third where her Honda was parallel-parked. A man was bent over and appeared to be looking at something near her vehicle. She probably wouldn't have noticed him except he was the only person on the sidewalk and so close to her car. Then, as she advanced along the street, the man stood upright and turned slightly so that she was able to see his profile.

Dana halted, stunned. The man glanced in her direction then abruptly turned away and hastened along the sidewalk to the far end of the block. In a moment he had turned the corner and was out of her sight.

Dana had been half a block away from the man, but the way he walked, the profile, the stature, the way he swung his shoulders, scared her. Surely it was her imagination. But he sure looked like Jeremy. *What would Jeremy be doing in Lander?*

Dana quickly walked to the corner but there was no one on the street. The man must have disappeared into one of the shops. Why had he been looking at the rear of her car? She walked a few feet down the side street before realizing how foolish it was to follow him. She had no desire to confront Jeremy even if she did catch up with him. But she was curious as to why he had been examining her vehicle.

The more concerning issue was why he was in Lander. Because she was here, alone, presumably, away from the protection of her friends and the support of people at the university. Was he bent on making trouble for her?

Dana returned to her car and sat in it for a few minutes, trying to reason out what she had just experienced.

Stop it! she told herself. *You don't even know if it was Jeremy!*

***

The sun was at its zenith, high in the sky, by the time Dana parked at the trailhead. It was early afternoon and, as she stepped out of her car, the heat enveloped her like a dry blanket. The familiar dull drone of insects in the grass and nearby trees only contributed to the intensity of the hot arid day.

Enthused by the conversation she'd had with Jed Ahrens, she could now be more selective in her search for specific rock formations. She was also eager to check out some other sites he had recommended, and yet the episode downtown and the possibility that she had seen Jeremy made her apprehensive.

That afternoon, instead of searching the upper hillsides, she was going to look below the trail. She wanted to check along the bank of the river to see if that more shaded environment might harbor any of her plants.

The landscape below the trail was filled with numerous smaller tracks diverging from the main trail like capillaries, obviously made by fishermen going down to the river. The area was also thick with shrubbery, rocks, and saplings. In some places it was exceedingly steep.

Dana struggled down several of the paths but most of them ended in well-trodden trails along the river. These places were muddy, filled with small rocks and twigs, or ended in a boulder that overlooked a popular fishing hole. She searched several different paths, a process that quickly became as frustrating as attempting to find a way out of a labyrinth cut in a cornfield.

After nearly poking out one of her eyes with a branch from a dead alder, and having found none of her *dicentra,* she called it quits. She couldn't imagine why Jed Ahrens had thought this particular area might be a likely place to search. It simply wasn't conducive to the environment her plants needed.

Perhaps she had misunderstood his directions. On top of everything else, the upper river was penetrating deeper into the canyon and as she looked at the terrain around her, she realized she had a seriously steep climb ahead of her to regain the main trail. The one positive aspect of the situation was that at least there was no rocky scree to navigate.

The farther up-river she had gone, the more difficult her trek had become due to the dense growth surrounding her. As she retraced her steps through the thick foliage along the riverbank as far as possible before climbing out, her meandering mind wondered if she had been anywhere near the place the game warden's body had been found. It could be very close by.

It was an unsettling thought.

***

It was nearly 4:00 p.m. by the time Dana returned to her Honda. She was tired, dusty, sunburned, and covered with scratches from the thick undergrowth she had trekked through close to the Popo Agie. She had seen numerous hikers on the trail, both coming and going, and had chatted with a couple when she regained the trail.

They were a middle-aged man, dressed in tan shorts and a purple polo shirt, with a canvas backpack, and his female companion in similar attire. They had stopped on the path and were drinking from water bottles.

"Have you been up to the top of this trail?" the man asked.

"I've been up to the falls," Dana replied. "Are you headed up there?"

"Is it worthwhile?" the female asked breathlessly. "I don't know how much farther I can go."

"The falls are definitely beautiful. Just take it easy walking up. I should also mention I've been told a grizzly and her cubs have been seen in the area."

"What do you think, honey?" the man asked. "You want to go on?"

"You do have that bear spray, don't you?" she asked.

Dana stood looking from one to the other as they discussed what would be best for them. The female rummaged in the backpack and came up with a canister of bear spray.

"I'm up for it," she pronounced.

"Good luck," said Dana.

In the parking lot, Dana lifted the back door of her SUV and placed her gear inside, then looked around. The place was nearly full of vehicles of all sizes and shapes.

An empty water bottle she had been drinking from slipped out of her hand and rolled away toward the passenger side of her car. Tired and stiff, she bent to pick it up, then emitted a sound of dismay. Along the whole side of her vehicle was an ugly scratch.

"Ohhh, how?"

She stood up, then leaned over and ran her hand over the scored dark green paint. She stood for a moment, stunned at what she had found. Though her car was not new by any means, it was in great condition and she had taken care to see it remained that way. She was looking at one continuous scratch, and she didn't see how another vehicle parked close to hers could possibly have caused it.

When had she last checked all around her car? Had this been done previously, without her noticing? No, when she parallel-parked downtown this morning near the leather repair shop, she had walked around the back of her car and she surely would have noticed.

Was this what the man she had thought was Jeremy had been doing when he was looking at the rear bumper of her car? She didn't remember taking a look at the car at the time and might not have noticed this damage.

What if it *was* Jeremy? Why had he been examining her car? For what reason? She shivered at the idea of him tracking her down, then knelt down and looked under the back bumper of the SUV. She could see nothing untoward. Maybe he had followed her from Lander and waited until she was out on the trail, then "got even" with her by damaging her Honda.

She stood and looked around the lot again. There was no one in sight. Sickened at the damage to her vehicle, she closed the rear door and got behind the wheel. She sat for a moment, trying to think where she had been recently. Only out to Jed Ahrens's place, downtown, and here at the trailhead, apart from parking at her apartment. As she sat stewing over her discovery, she remembered she had also stopped off at the library recently. Certainly, she would have discovered this damage had it been done before.

She inserted her key into the ignition, pounded on the steering wheel in exasperation, then started the SUV and drove out of the lot. At the end of the upper row of cars, Dana noticed the faded blue pickup-camper.

CHAPTER 13

Back in town, Dana went to the police department where she was asked to fill out an account of the damage to her vehicle. Then she went to her apartment and notified her insurance carrier of the scratch on her CRV. The day was getting on but she clicked on her cell phone and scrolled through it, finding listings for several car repair shops.

She also checked for messages on her cell phone. There were two. The first was from Jed Ahrens, asking her to stop by to discuss some of the questions she had posed. *Hmmm,* she wondered, *what was that about?* She had just talked with him that morning. Oh well, he always had information she found useful.

The second message was apparently a wrong number, consisting of a moment or two of heavy breathing, then a cut-off. She looked at her caller identification but did not recognize the number.

She jotted down the names and addresses of three auto body repair shops and returned to her vehicle.

The foreman at the first shop, which was a dealership, looked at the damage and said it would be nearly three weeks before he could get to it. She thanked him and moved on. She sensed he wasn't very interested in the job.

The next shop, located in an alley in the industrial part of town, was what appeared to be a small one-man operation called Yogi's Cars. She entered the dimly lit shop through an open single-garage door. Sliding her sunglasses up to the top of her head, her eyes slowly adjusted after the bright sunshine outside.

There were three vehicles in the shop, in various stages of repair. Someone was working at the rear of a black van, sanding the passenger side rear fender. Dana stood for a few moments taking in the contents of the shop. Yogi appeared to operate his shop out of the garage at the back of his own residence. A few basic supplies were hung on one wall, with a couple of pieces of equipment she couldn't begin to identify arranged on a workbench. Rubber piping, gaskets, and washers were also on display. Dana moved farther inside as the man at work on the van became aware of her presence.

After shutting off his machine, the man removed a plastic mask from his nose and mouth and let it dangle around his neck. "Sorry, didn't see ya come in."

"Are you Yogi?"

"That would be me."

Yogi was short in stature, with thin brown hair that stood out in tufts as a result of the mask he had been wearing. He was dressed in brown coveralls, with dried smudges of red, green, and orange paint. He stood up and squinted at Dana.

"I hate to interrupt you but my car has been damaged and I need an estimate to have it repaired," she told him.

"You betcha. Whad'ya have, a fender-bender?"

"Actually, no," she replied and explained as they walked out to her car. She told him where it had been parked, that she had been away from it a good share of the day, and that when she returned to the trailhead, this was what she had found.

"Looks like ya been keyed," Yogi said as he bent to inspect the line running along the passenger side of her CRV.

"I thought perhaps someone had parked too close to me and scraped it while opening a door, or... gosh, I don't know," she said, shrugging her shoulders.

"Nope, it's been keyed," he said adamantly. "I seen this same pattern more times than I can tell ya."

She stood in contemplation for a moment. "You mean someone did this intentionally?"

"That would be my 'pinion. You and the boyfriend just have a partin' of the ways?"

Was that what had happened? Was it possible that Jeremy had found out where she was this summer? She *had* thought she had seen him downtown earlier in the day. But when confronted with that actual possibility and the idea that he was "getting even" she rejected the idea as preposterous.

"Ah, no. What do you think?" She suddenly wanted to get an estimate and leave such thoughts behind. "I mean, can it be repaired and repainted to match the original color?"

"I can do that. Might take a coupla days ta get the paint in. These newer vehicles are easy to match. Your VIN number gives me all that information."

"So, you've seen this kind of damage before?"

"Yep." Yogi took a ring of keys out of his coverall pocket, selected one, and demonstrated how the damage was likely done by running the tip of the key along the side of Dana's vehicle, just above the surface. "Quick and easy way ta make this kind of a scratch."

A slight shiver ran up Dana's arms as she absorbed what Yogi was saying. What kind of anger or combativeness would cause a person to damage another person's property in such a way?

"I have to get one other estimate before I give the go-ahead, but I would appreciate your giving me a figure for the insurance company."

"You bet."

Yogi scratched his head, took some measurements, and got the other information he needed from the door panel. In no time, Dana had a sheet of paper with her second estimate for repairs and labor on the seat beside her.

She drove to the third business she had identified, realizing they might already have closed for the day. It was a shop that specialized in striping and colorful designs, flames, and logos on cars, trucks, and vans. But she was in luck. A sign on the door indicated they were open until 6:00 p.m. or by appointment.

The clerk she spoke with was very focused on the nuts and bolts of his business. He gave her an estimate, which happened to be $200 higher than Yogi's, and she had her final bid. Another person who didn't want her business, she guessed.

She quickly made a decision as to which shop she wanted to do the work. Driving back to Yogi's, she asked him to go ahead and order the needed supplies. He mentioned he would need her car for two days to make the repairs once the paint arrived.

CHAPTER 14

Dana checked the time and decided to run back to Jed's while she was out. His message on her cell phone had sounded excited, so perhaps he had additional subject matter to share with her on her plant.

The road into his place had completely dried out and she rolled down her car window as she drove through the trees and shrubs lining his shadowed drive. Parking in her usual place near the shop, she approached his work area and peeked through the glass of the door.

There were no lights on inside and she could hear no sounds coming from the shop. It was nearly 5:30 p.m. so he had probably finished for the day and gone inside.

Dana turned to go back to her car, then on a whim decided to follow the walk around to the back of the sprawling house.

Running along the rear of the cedar dwelling was a large stone patio. Pieces of rock had been thin-cut in various shapes and perfectly fitted to create an attractive, natural-flowing outdoor living space. Low-growing shrubbery and shade-loving hostas grew around the edge.

As she stood admiring the attractive setting Dana became aware of a scrabbling noise coming from beyond a heavy, concrete dining table several feet away. Colorful metal chairs surrounded the table, but on its far side was an open space where the sound was coming from.

She hurried over to the table. Jed Ahrens's wheelchair was lying on its side and he was struggling to pull himself out and away from it.

"Dr. Ahrens!" Dana called fearfully as she knelt beside him.

A trickle of blood was running down the left side of his face. He looked flushed from his efforts to regain an upright position.

"Damn chair," he grated, "always catches on that one paver. I gotta get Jax to grind it down for me. He's been so dang busy lately, haven't had a chance to get him over here."

She helped him into a sitting position and then, on her haunches, pulled his chair backward and set it upright. "Are you alright?"

He was rubbing his right knee and she knelt by his side again, touching his forearm. "Do I need to call an ambulance, your doctor, maybe Jax?"

"Naw, not the first time this has happened, nor likely the last. Pull my chair around here, if you would," he said motioning to his right.

Dana found a tissue in the pocket of her shorts and dabbed at the blood on his upper cheek. "Are you sure we don't need to have you checked? Is your knee hurting?"

"Hit my damn good knee on the table support when I went over."

"How long have you been lying here?"

"Not long. Um, maybe ten minutes," he admitted. "Couldn't call anybody. My phone's on the charger inside."

As they spoke and she ministered to him, his facial features gradually returned to their normal color. Dana moved around to his right side as he directed her on how to lock his wheelchair into place so it would not roll. Between them, they were able to get him onto his knees, then up on his feet. With a sigh he sank back into his chair.

"That's more like it," he said, wiping perspiration from his forehead. "What're you doing here, Dana?"

"You left me a message this afternoon to stop by."

"Oh, yeah, guess I did call."

Dana supposed it was possible he was lonely and simply craved someone to talk to.

"Can I get you anything? Would you like a cup of tea?" she asked.

"Uumph. I'd like something stronger," he said slyly, "but guess I'd better stick to tea."

Dana walked over to the entrance and slid the screened patio door aside before going in to his ultra-modern kitchen, complete with two wall ovens, refrigerator with wooden doors matching the dark grey cabinets, and granite counters all around.

"Tea's in a canister by the cook top," he hollered after her.

***

Jed Ahrens and Dana sat at the outdoor table, sipping the tea she had just made.

"You look a little peaked yourself, Dana. You okay?"

Dana hadn't realized the damage to her car had affected how she was looking. "Somebody keyed my car in the last day or two. I just discovered it this afternoon at the trailhead. I don't think it was done before today, but I may be wrong."

"You report it?"

"Just to the police and my insurance agent. I've got an estimate for repairs that will probably get done next week. I need to drop my car off at Yogi's when he gets the supplies in."

"Yogi's a good man," he said.

"That's reassuring to hear."

"Let's keep this little incident with my chair tipping over between you and me, girl," said Dr. Ahrens, as he tapped the side of his head where she had applied a Band-Aid.

Dana looked at him skeptically for a moment. "Is that such a good idea? You know, you're likely to get a colorful bruise from that knock."

"I'm always bumping my head into something in my shop. Jax or Hildy won't give it a second thought."

"Who's Hildy?"

"Housekeeper. She had to leave early today, some kind of appointment in town. Always leaves me a light supper in the fridge."

Dana sat with the index finger of her left hand resting above her upper lip and allowed a devious grin to spread across her face.

"It's against my better judgment, but okay."

"Naw, this old noggin has had several hard knocks."

"Suppose you did some of that when you used to climb?"

He lifted his head and looked at her over the top of his eyeglasses. "You know about that, huh?"

"Arnie told me you used to do a lot of climbing when you lived in Laramie."

"That I did. But the blows I took to my head were when I was working on field trips and expeditions."

"Expeditions? As on trips outside the United States?"

"Oh yeah, mostly South America. Peru, Chile, one trip to Central America."

"What were you doing down there?" she asked. "Some of the pyramidal structures in Central America and especially in Peru, like Machu Picchu, have always intrigued me."

"Aw, some colleagues and I have studied the ancient cultures there and what became of them. Little out of my area, but I worked on identifying the stonework in some of the edifices and where it came from."

"That's what I'm talking about."

"Yeah, the Incans had quite an empire in Peru for about a hundred years. Still quite the mystery as to why their culture disappeared."

"I've read there are likely several sites throughout that whole area that haven't even been discovered yet."

"Oh yeah, the dang jungle covers everything. You should get down there some time."

"I hope to, eventually. Don't know if I mentioned I want to concentrate on paleobotany when my degree is complete. I anticipate there is much work to be done here in the U.S., but the southern Americas are surely of interest."

"What's your goal for a job in your field?"

"I'm open to several possibilities, but right now my interest is in working for a natural history museum, in identifying plant fossils, of course. I truly enjoy the field work."

As she listened to Jed Ahrens, thinking they had many similar interests, Dana smiled inwardly. She realized what a multi-faceted, fascinating man he was. He had even begun to loosen up with her after initially exhibiting a brusque attitude.

As Dr. Ahrens talked about the trips he had made, Dana felt like he was speaking to her as a professional colleague. It was only after she was home that evening that she realized they hadn't even got around to further discussion about the relationship of her plants to various rocks.

That would likely be a conversation for another day.

CHAPTER 15

Saturday evening found Dana relaxing on the sofa in her living area. Flag was curled up on the back of the sofa, with one paw resting on Dana's shoulder. She had her laptop open on her lap and was entering some of the technical data she and Jed Ahrens had discussed.

Earlier in the day, she had gone by to check on Jed to make sure he had no ill-effects as a result of his fall the previous day. He was back to his usual irascible self and told her she shouldn't be concerned about him. The scraped area around his upper cheek was like an angry red rash and she wasn't sure how he was going to explain that to Jax and Hildy.

On the way home, she had dropped her car off at Yogi's and he had said he would try to have it ready for her by the early part of the following week.

Dana's cell phone began playing the William Tell overture, which was her ring-setting. It was Jax.

"Unc tells me you're without a vehicle," he said.

"I am. Did he tell you what happened?"

"Yeah, you have any idea who did it?"

"As I told your uncle, I discovered it a couple days ago up at the trailhead in the canyon."

She told him about the circumstances, how she had found Yogi's repair shop, and that she should have her car back within a few days.

"You sure this Jeremy guy isn't in the area?"

Jax's comment caused Dana to pause for a few moments before answering. "Uh, I thought about that, too. As a matter of fact, when I was downtown a couple of days ago, I actually thought I had seen him."

"And you're just now getting around to mentioning that? Was it him or not?"

"Yes, well, I've been busy. The person I saw got away before I could get close enough to tell. But how would Jeremy know where my car would be parked or, for that matter, what kind of a car I drive now."

"Lander's a small town. Wouldn't be too hard to track you down if he is, in fact, here."

A chill again swept over Dana at the notion that Jeremy might actually be in the area. Just when she had thought she was getting a healthy grasp on her life again, the idea that he may be living up to his threat was distressing.

"Well, anyhow, I'm probably wrong," Jax resumed. "I thought, since you have no wheels, you might be interested in going for a ride tomorrow. I can show you the area Unc said he suggested you look at in your research. Besides, I haven't been fishing for a while."

"He did say you would know the area he was talking about. He told me a couple days ago about an area where he thought I should look, but since talking to him again I don't think I was in the right place."

"Yeah, this could work out for both of us."

"Sure. I can always use the help."

There was a brief pause at the other end of the line. "Say, you don't happen to know why Unc is avoiding me, do you?"

"What makes you think he's avoiding you?"

"We were supposed to have dinner last night, but he called mid-afternoon, said he was going to have to cancel. Something about a job he needed to get finished."

"Well, he probably did." *Oh boy, Jed Ahrens likely didn't want Jax to see his raspberry-colored face...*

"Then, today, I suggested lunch and he said he was still busy and that he would see me in a day or two."

"What do you think? He and Hildy have something going?"

Jax snorted before replying, "Have you seen Hildy?"

She hadn't.

They agreed on a time that would work for both of them on Sunday.

***

On their way to Sinks Canyon early on Sunday afternoon, Jax drove his pickup truck at a moderate speed in consideration for the large number of vehicles coming to and from the popular site.

They picked up lunch at a fast-food drive-through, and ate as they drove. Jax had told Dana as they started out that he would show her the Sinks and the Rise, where the Popo Agie River disappears underground and reappears a quarter of a mile downstream.

"You know a lot about this area," Dana observed. "Were you raised in Lander?"

"Nope, but I visited my uncle and aunt. I spent lots of time with Unc up here in the canyon in the summers. You can imagine what it was like as a kid, following him around. He taught me how to fish and to identify the different rock formations and the flora. Once, we were out hiking just above the river when he stopped all of a sudden, cautioned me to be quiet, then pointed out a fawn hidden in some tall grass and river birch about five feet away. He wouldn't let me go one step closer, said if we messed with the fawn, the doe might abandon it. We backtracked a few feet and walked a wide arc around it. Farther up, across the highway, we spotted the doe, who was biding her time till we passed."

When Jax spoke of his uncle, Dana was reminded of the dilemma she found herself in as to whether or not she should mention the fall Dr. Ahrens had taken. Since he hadn't raised the issue that afternoon of his uncle canceling on a couple of meals, she decided to ignore it. Jed had more or less told her he didn't want to worry Jax, but she was concerned he might fall again, with no one around, and that such an event could have dire results.

"I'm not surprised," she said in reply to Jax's story. "In the short amount of time I've known your uncle, he's talked a lot about how he cares about the wildlife and wants others to do the same. And that goes double for the geological and botanical side of nature."

"Sounds like you two have had some serious discussions about your respective areas of expertise."

"You could say that," Dana said, smiling.

Jax nodded his head in her direction as he slowed down to make a left turn.

They parked in a gravel lot, walked around several other vehicles, and climbed a set of wooden stairs up to the Popo Agie visitors' center. Inside was a display of plants and animals widespread in the area, displayed in their natural habitat, which drew Dana like a moth to a flame. One of the animals on display was a life-sized bighorn sheep. They spent several minutes inside before walking along the path that led down toward the cave-like opening known as the Sinks.

The path led down over a series of steep rocks and more than once Jax latched onto Dana's hand to help her over a particularly precarious place. It was late June and the spring run-off was at its high point, with the Popo Agie swollen with swift, foaming water, over-running its banks and flowing into several side channels.

They walked down the path as far as they could before water halted their progress. Jax explained that when the water receded by late July, there was a sandbar one could walk along and actually see the river water being swallowed by the thick, cave-like mantle of limestone.

"This probably wasn't the best day to come here," said Jax as they joggled among the many other visitors to get as close as they could to the rushing water where it poured underground. "When the water slows down, it's actually possible to walk a-ways down into the opening."

"Is the river as wide underground as it is here?" Dana asked.

"Good question. Nobody knows for sure, but apparently the passages narrow down to just small fissures."

"So you couldn't go into that cave and follow the riverbed down to the Rise?"

"No way. Naturalists have put dye into the water here as it disappears underground to determine if the two places are connected. The dye reappears at the Rise, sometimes hours later. Like I say, because of the time it takes for dye to pass through the quarter-mile passages, it has been surmised that there are a series of interwoven underground channels the water moves through."

"Might be interesting if they could put one of those miniature cameras in to see where the water goes."

"That's a good idea, but I don't know if the passages are even big enough to make that possible."

They retraced their steps back up to the visitors' center, where they spent a couple of minutes in the shade of the building before strolling to Jax's truck. They then drove a short distance back down the highway and turned left into another parking lot.

A short trail took them to a wooden deck overlooking the Rise. Again, people were thick along the rails of the viewing site. Dana and Jax waited patiently as people looked their fill then moved on.

A lagoon of deep blue spread out below them, at least, Dana guessed, seventy-five feet down. At the point where the water emerged from underground, the pool roiled.

"This is what I wanted you to see," said Jax.

"Oh, my gosh. Look at the size of those fish!" Dana exclaimed. In the pool below them a number of good-sized trout were thrashing about, competing for the bread people on the deck were throwing down to them.

"Those are rainbow trout, maybe a few browns. They get to be ten to twelve pounds in size."

"Why are there so many of them right here?"

"Trout swim upstream to spawn and, since they can't get through the underground waterways, they stay here. They're protected, so there's no fishing in this area."

"This is what the game warden was talking about," said Dana, remembering the conversation she had had with Trig Henderson. "He said somebody had been poaching some of these fish."

"Seems to happen every so often. Some young Turk comes along, thinks he can beat the system."

"Looks to me like it would be hard to get down to the edge of the pool with all the brush surrounding it," Dana observed.

"That, or they might try to drop a line from up here. I'm not sure just how they go about it."

They eventually returned to Jax's truck and turned onto the road up into the canyon. Shortly afterward, he slowed again and drove off the highway at a pullout on the right side of the road.

He pointed up to a scrub-covered incline that zig-zagged up the side of a gorge that split the side of the hill. "This is where a good-sized flock of bighorn sheep used to hang out."

"That's incredible! This close to the road?"

"I think this was a good place for them to get down from the high country through that cut in the hill," he said, pointing upward. "It's hard to make out but there's a good animal trail through the under-growth."

"Have you been up there?"

"I have. But the flock has mostly died out. They think pneumonia killed them off."

Jax chuckled as he removed his ball cap and ran his fingers through his short, brown hair. "One of the last was a ram named Bam Bam. He was quite the guy, got so he would eat 'human food' people gave him. Then he got kinda ornery. That was actually him, stuffed, we saw inside the visitor center."

"Ornery, how?"

"I was parked in this very place several years ago in Unc's old Chevy pickup. I had walked down to the river to fish and when I came back, Bam Bam was grazing at the edge of the trees over there. Guess he was in a bad mood that day. When he saw me get into the pickup, he came running, smacked his head into the passenger side of Unc's Chevy and dented it pretty good before I could get it started and drive out onto the road."

Dana was chortling by the time Jax finished his story. "He wanted something to eat!"

"I don't think he was the least bit interested in anything but protecting his territory that day."

"With a name like Bam Bam, you probably weren't the only one he got mad at."

"You're right, he had quite the reputation."

CHAPTER 16

It was mid-afternoon when Jax parked at the trailhead where Dana normally left her vehicle. Instead of taking the canyon trail, he led her across a bridge that spanned the river to the north-facing side. The lay of the land was more open, flatter, still sagebrush and grasses but they were able to clamber over and around rocks and under the occasional tree limbs extending over the pathway.

"This is the area Unc told you about. The plants and animals here are much the same as you'd find higher up in the canyon," Jax said. "It's drier and easier to access the river, however. One of my favorite fishing holes is a small ways down-river."

"It's like the two sides of the river transpose each other here as opposed to the upper canyon."

"Yeah, you find that to be true in canyons like this where one side is protected by the wall, as well as the path the river takes through the canyon."

Jax took his fishing rod from the metal transporter he had carried slung over his shoulder. He attached the reel, placed a container of his favorite bait, squirming worms, within easy reach and started walking along the path, downstream.

He had gone only a few feet when he stopped and motioned for Dana to look up the hillside. On a slight promontory three buck deer were feeding. One of them was the obvious mentor of the two younger deer, with a rack of at least ten points.

Dana waved to Jax that she had seen them and watched for several minutes as the deer warily observed the two trespassers into their territory before returning to their feeding.

After that interlude, Dana moved off the trail into the bushy undergrowth and aspen saplings, seeking her plants. The day was stifling hot, with not the slightest breeze to offer a cooling draft. Even after the recent rain, the sun-exposed ground in the area was arid. Cicadas in the larger aspens communicated with each other with a heavy buzz. She would have to ask Jax if he ever used them as fishing bait.

She poked around for several minutes before finding anything that looked like a possible habitat for her *dicentra*. As she approached the lee-side of a large gray, flattened, limestone boulder her heart skipped a beat as she got a glimpse of what she was certain was a good-sized cluster of her plants.

She bent over and reached out her hand to examine the leaves and the stem system. But just as she did so, she heard a menacing hiss off to her right.

Dana froze. Less than a foot away a beady-eyed prairie rattlesnake lay coiled, with its rattles pulsating and its split tongue darting in and out. Only yesterday, Jed had warned her to be aware of rattlesnakes in the lower canyon. He had said if she ever came across one, to be completely quiet and to back away slowly. That thought flashed through her mind now. The only problem was, how was she supposed to keep calm and back away slowly when her heart was beating as fast and loud as a drum?

She slowly took a deep breath, withdrew her hand very deliberately, then shifted first one foot back and then the other. Once she was a few feet away, she stood upright, thankful she had not tripped over a root. All the time she kept her eyes on the snake. The rattler leisurely uncoiled its body and slithered under the edge of the large rock.

Dana remained where she was for several seconds, fanning her face. She must have cried out at some point, as she was still trying to gain her equilibrium when she heard Jax hurrying up the trail towards her.

He looked at her and did a double-take as he propped his fishing rod against one of the aspen saplings. "What happened to you? You're as white as a sheet."

"S-snake," she stammered, pointing a shaking hand toward the large boulder.

"He didn't get you, did he?" Jax asked, grabbing her right hand and examining it, front and back.

Dana shook her head back and forth.

Jax pulled her trembling body into his embrace. She crumpled against his chest.

"No, he r-rattled and warned me." *Oh, how good it felt to have his arms around her.* "Your uncle warned me about them, j-just yesterday. I really need to be more vigilant, especially around these rocks."

Jax lowered his head to hear what she said, just as she lifted hers to speak the words. His lips brushed her cheek.

"I'm surprised you haven't run into any rattlers before this."

She suddenly stiffened, pulled herself together, and stepped back. "I-I'm sorry," she said.

"What's wrong? What're you sorry about?" he asked.

"I mean, about… you know, being so shaken."

"Damn. I would have been jolted, too." He gave her a small smile at her awkwardness. "Guess I thought you needed holding up."

They stood, eyes fixed on each other, until she hesitantly broke the contact.

"You sure you're okay?"

Dana nodded her head as a tear slid down her cheek. Why had she pulled away from him? It was a harmless hug. He was only trying to steady her. It took her several moments to realize it was her habitual defense mechanism kicking in.

Jax stepped around her and walked up to the rock, kicked his hiking boot into a dead root, but the snake had disappeared. "Sometimes when there's one, there's two," he explained, looking back at her and noting the bewildered expression on her face.

Dana felt her cheeks glowing with embarrassment at her reaction.

"Maybe we should call it a day and just go back to town," she said quietly.

CHAPTER 17

Dana was silent as they drove back to Lander.

Glancing her way, Jax seemed to come to the conclusion that it was best not to disturb her. Dana guessed he assumed she was still shaking inside from the close encounter with the rattlesnake. Perhaps he thought she was angry with him for trying to hug her. She huddled into herself as if she was cold, arms folded across her chest and a pensive look on her face.

As they entered the outskirts of the town she stirred from her reverie. "You can just drop me off at my place."

But he drove past Dana's street. "Thought we'd get a bite to eat."

"You don't have to feed me again. I'm not very good company right now. I think it might be best for me to go home. I'm just in a bad mood."

Jax seemed not to hear and did not stop until they arrived at The Bronze Spoon.

Once they were seated and had ordered, he gave her a quizzical look. "So... what happened out there?"

"I know you were just trying to reassure me. But since Jeremy, I haven't allowed myself to get close to another man, either physically or emotionally. Your comforting me threw me for a loop." What she didn't say was that she was still experiencing the same confusion, nor how good it had felt to have his arms around her. *I'm such a ninny*, she scolded herself.

She shook her head, attempting to clear the cobwebs.

"Guess I shouldn't have hugged you," Jax responded, frowning.

"No, it's not you. I have a problem with trust. I'm trying to put the past behind me but I still struggle, particularly when it comes to men. I felt truly close to Jeremy... and believed in him." She took a deep breath before continuing. "When I learned about the drugs, I felt he had betrayed my trust, and my confidence has suffered. Being away from campus this summer has been good for me. I don't see Jeremy's friends or go to the places we used to frequent."

"I can understand that."

She looked him in the eye. "I really appreciate that you took me along today and helped me find a new area to study."

"So," Jax interrupted, swinging a straw back and forth over his glass of iced tea, "thanks for the ride, the history lesson, and the introduction to a rattlesnake, but I don't need your help anymore, is that it?"

Dana ducked her head before answering, trying to smother a sudden giggle that threatened to escape her throat at his description of what had happened. "No, not at all. I'm just trying to explain why I froze," she explained. She grabbed her napkin with its enclosed set of cutlery, and started toying with it.

"Hey, relax then. We're just friends, okay?"

A slow smile crept over Dana's face as she breathed a big sigh of relief.

"Besides, what would I tell Unc if he asks why you're upset with me?"

"Maybe that I pushed you in the river?"

"He would never believe that. He thinks you're the best thing since he discovered his first crystal geode rock."

There it was. The perfect opportunity to tell Jax about his uncle's fall, which she had promised not to say anything about. But how was she to explain the accident without compromising her promise to Jed?

Fortuitously, their food arrived just as Dana was seriously thinking about breaking that pact and they both sat back away from the table as the waitress placed their plates in front of them.

"Did I tell you about the seasonal workers for the forest service I've talked to a couple times along the trail?"

Jax finished chewing a bite before wiping his mouth. "I'm told it was some people from a clean-up crew who found the game warden, down along the river."

"That's odd. They never mentioned anything." If what Jax said was true, it couldn't have been pleasant for the young men to have come across the warden's body.

"It's possible they've been told not to say anything about it. As you know, it's still under investigation."

"Hmmm, you're probably right."

"I think I mentioned there were some unusual injuries to his body."

She looked at him with interest. "How do you know all these things?"

"Aw, one of the guys on my project has a cousin who works in the sheriff's office. She shouldn't have been discussing the details but guess she overheard some talk."

"What kind of injuries?"

"Something about an unusual wound on his upper back. Plus, the nasty head trauma. Anyhow, there were enough unanswered questions to have his body autopsied."

Halfway through their meal, Jax's cell phone trilled. He lifted it from the table and looked at the incoming call.

"I've got to take this."

Dana could hear his side of the conversation, obviously from someone at the hospital work site. As he listened, wrinkles furrowed his forehead and he rubbed the right side of his head, over his eye. He finished the call and returned to his meal.

"That was the construction foreman, Stubby. Seems there was some vandalism to some of our building materials last night. He's been trying to reach me all afternoon but cell service up in the canyon is spotty. I need to go check it out." He finished off his tea in one long swallow. "Want to ride along?"

As usual, Dana was preparing to decline when she remembered the words of their just-completed discussion. It seemed Jax wasn't going to be content to let their friendship slide. He had listened to her talk about Jeremy, and had even got a smile or two out of her. *Okay, Dana,* she told herself, *now is your chance to take a step forward.*

"Sure. I'll come with you. What happened?"

"One of the supply sheds was ransacked."

"That's too bad. Anything stolen?"

"That's what we need to figure out."

Jax finished his sandwich, wiped a napkin across his face and pushed his plate aside. He lifted his hand as if asking for her forbearance and placed a call. Dana nibbled on the last of her sweet potato French fries as he talked to the police department, asking an officer to meet him at the construction site.

"I forgot to ask if you got any fish this afternoon," she said as they drove up Main Street toward the hospital.

"Had a couple bites, but think they were just small fish nibbling at my bait," he replied. "Mornings and just before dusk are the best times to fish on the Popo Agie. The airborne insects the fish feed on are out and just above the water at that time."

"You've got this fishing down to a fine art."

"Just learning from trial and error and what my uncle's taught me."

He turned onto the access street to the hospital and drove past the entrance, through a large parking lot, to the back of the facility. Otherworldly steel beams jutted up from the ground, revealing the outline of the new extension.

Jax parked up beside another truck.

"You can come along, if you want."

"Are you sure?"

"I'll get you a hardhat," he said, grinning at her as he donned his own.

They picked their way around concrete abutments and toward a 30-foot metal trailer on the west edge of the property. This, it appeared, served as Jax's living quarters and office. Nearby was a stack of what appeared to be plumbing, chiefly sewer pipes and connectors awaiting installation.

A workman stood up from examining the door of one of the sheds and called out to Jax.

"Over here. Somebody's jimmied the lock on one of the storage bins."

Dana followed Jax over to join the short, rotund man as he removed his hat, revealing a head of dishwater blond hair cut into a bristly flattop. He was made to look even dumpier by the brown shorts he wore. These extended to around the knee, with just a few inches of hairy leg showing beneath, ending in leather sandals. He reminded Dana of a hobbit from *The Lord of the Rings*. She had to divert her eyes to keep from staring at his feet, though they were probably normal in size.

"Stubby," Jax said, "this is my friend, Dana Cameron. Dana this is Stubby, er... Elton King."

Dana extended her hand as the man whipped the glove off his right hand.

"Pleased to meetcha," he said.

The construction site was filled with neat stacks of plastic-covered materials, long lengths of steel rods, and large plastic containers of other structural supplies. The storage bin Stubby had been checking out was near two other containers, each about three feet across, five feet long and hip-high. The locking mechanism on the lid had been pried away. The plastic wrapping inside had been pulled apart and was now partially draped over the outside of the container. The damaged container, Dana gathered from listening to their conversation, belonged to one of the sub-contractors in charge of dirt work and concrete. He used it to store various supplies needed to accomplish his work.

While the two men discussed the situation, Dana surveyed the extension to the hospital building, which at this stage consisted of a concrete basement and the fortified beams intended to support the flooring for the main level, as well as a number of vertical steel beams.

She let her gaze wander farther to her left, taking in all the details of the site as the two men talked. Then she nearly squealed when she spied an old blue pickup-camper parked on the southern edge of the property under some large cottonwood trees. It was standing just beyond one of the tall stacks of building materials. Did the pickup belong to Stubby? She had assumed a newer pickup they had parked beside belonged to the foreman.

Jax saw the startled look that passed over her countenance.

"Something wrong, Dana?" he asked, as Stubby walked over to the tool shed to look for something they had been talking about.

"Who does the blue pickup belong to?" she asked, pointing it out.

Jax moved a couple steps to his right to see what she was referring to. "Oh, that belongs to a guy who's doing the masonry work on the project. He comes and goes a lot."

"Does he live in the camper?"

"I think Stubby says he has a place around town somewhere. Why the interest?"

"I've seen his pickup up at the trailhead in the canyon." Surely there weren't two rigs of the same color and vintage in the area? Dana took a deep breath. "I've seen it with a horse trailer attached and a couple horses."

Jax shrugged. "Like I say, he isn't here all the time. He works other places, too. I think he works some evenings and weekends. But I guess he still has some free time to spend up on the trail."

CHAPTER 18

Monday evening, Dana was sitting on her sofa, with Flag curled on the back cushion near her head. She had her laptop open, supported by her curled-up legs. It was dark outside but it was a warm, sultry evening and she had opened two of the casement windows that faced the street in the bay of her living room.

Every now and then an insect hit the window screen as it tried to gain access to the light inside the room. An occasional car drove by but, since the apartment was situated in an older, quiet part of town, the street was otherwise silent and deserted.

Yogi had promised Dana's car would be ready the following morning, for which she was thankful. She had felt like a butterfly with a missing wing without her wheels. Restlessness to get back out in the field, to test out her theory on the relationship between her plants and certain types of rock Jed had suggested, was making her antsy. Every day that went by was one more day that her plants might be in bloom, and she still had work to do before the blossoms faded. She had spent most of the day organizing her notes or snippets of paper on which she had jotted important information, such as names or types of rock she needed to follow up with Jed.

As she worked on entering data, new ideas and suggestions on the layout of her thesis that she would need to pursue once she returned to the university and could access their library, her mind kept wandering back to the day before, when she had spent time with Jax Ahrens.

It was clear he had a significant job as the architect of the hospital extension and that he took it seriously. It appeared he was well-respected by the people he worked with. Jax had told her the firm he worked for was small but growing, that he had been specially selected to work up the bid for the hospital job, then to supervise the project once it had been awarded to his firm.

Putting all her past emotional turmoil aside for a moment, she acknowledged that Jax was a strong, caring, athletic man who most women would be attracted to. And, she had to admit, through Jax's persistence, she had learned to relax in his company and to cautiously accept the friendship he had offered.

After Jax and Stubby had done an inventory of the vandalism and theft of the supplies at the construction site Sunday evening, Jax had invited them over to his small abode. As they climbed the two deep stairs to the trailer door, Jax picked up a gallon jug of sun tea from the wooden deck that extended along the front of the trailer. A wrought-iron picnic table and four chairs had been set up at one end of the deck, with a striped, green umbrella attached to the table. He handed the tea to Dana.

"There's ice in the fridge," he said, as he began rifling through files on his desk, looking for an invoice Stubby needed.

Dana surveyed his modest home. The living room of the trailer had basically been converted into his office. A small sofa and two side chairs remained, but a large oak desk now dominated the room and two of the walls were covered with architectural drawings of the project.

She found a small galley kitchen to the left. A bowl, spoon, and coffee cup were stacked to one side of a miniature sink, indicating he had had cereal and coffee for breakfast. The coffee maker held a half-full carafe of dark brown, hours-old liquid.

Beyond the kitchen, she glimpsed the bedroom, though only the lower half of the bed was visible, neatly made up. She smiled slightly at the idea that he took the trouble to make up his bed.

Dana began opening cupboards, looking for glasses and, on the second try, found a stack of large, plastic fast-food containers. The medium-sized refrigerator was filled with a large jug of milk, a container of juice and a selection of what she perceived to be bachelor food.

She opened the top section and found two ice-cube trays. The freezer was stacked with ready-made meals, mountains of frozen waffles, several foot-long packages in white butcher-block paper, and lasagna. Dana filled each glass three-quarters full with ice and poured the tepid tea over the ice, hearing it crack and split.

"Do you take sugar?" she asked as Jax pounced on the paper he had been seeking.

"Nope, straight up is fine."

Stubby tapped at the door and then entered. She handed one of the glasses to Stubby and he downed a good share of it in one gulp.

"Thanks, that's just what I needed," he said, smiling at Dana before addressing Jax. "Did you find the statement for the blasting caps?"

"I did and, just as I thought, it gives all the pertinent information, including the number of units delivered, the time, and where you signed for it, which is information the police will likely want."

"Didn't think to take any picture of the break-in," said Stubby. "That might be something the authorities will want."

"You're right," said Jax. "Let's not touch anything till the police arrive. Maybe they can get some fingerprints."

Dana handed the other glass of tea to Jax then turned back to the cupboard for another container for herself.

Then they had moved outside to the deck and each picked one of the chairs around the table as they waited for the police to arrive.

***

Without warning Flag lifted her head and stared at the window. Her ears perked up as if listening intently. Then a deep guttural yowl emanated from her body as she flattened herself on the sofa back and started creeping toward the end.

"What's wrong, Flag? Is there another kitty out there?"

A slight wind had begun to blow and an occasional branch brushed against the upper part of the pane in the tall casement window on the right. Flag had obviously been frightened by some unusual sound Dana hadn't heard.

The cat jumped from the sofa and crossed the floor to the window in a flash. She leapt up onto the ledge and crouched again as if stalking some prey. The primordial sound coming from her throat was like a throwback to her earliest ancestors.

Dana put her computer aside, stood, and walked to the window, expecting to see another feline outside. Instead, the distinctive odor of a skunk assailed her nose.

It was dark, but enough light filtered through the branches of an ancient maple in Aberdeen's yard for her to see the grassy area in front of her apartment. Nothing. She moved to the door, switched on the porch light, and peered out. An overwhelming stench of skunk blasted her in the face. She covered her mouth with one hand and with the other reached down to snag Flag who was frantic to get through the storm door and outside.

A skunk prowling the neighborhood was obviously what had disturbed the young cat. She was just about to close the door when she glanced down. And there it was, a dead skunk, laid out on her doorstep. It was bleeding from its mouth and a cord had been cinched around the dead animal's neck, as if it had been garroted.

Dana slammed the door shut, dead-bolted it, and turned her back to it. Where had the skunk come from? Had some animal dropped it there after killing it? Growing up, her family had had a big ginger tomcat that frequently left dead mice on their table on the patio. But a skunk?

Dana felt suddenly chilled. She picked Flag up and hugged her to her chest as she walked around the apartment, closing all the windows and pulling the blinds. Could a dog have killed the skunk and dragged it along before depositing it at her entrance? Would teenaged pranksters do such a thing? But the cord around its neck made no sense.

Flag's comforting purr eventually calmed her quaking nerves and she set the cat down on the floor. Not knowing what else to do, she called her landlady.

Aberdeen Calhoun answered on the second ring.

"The most disgusting thing has, er… happened," Dana spilled out. "I-I've just found a dead skunk by my front door!"

"Aw, lass," said Aberdeen, sounding appalled, "I'll come over right away."

Dana had just pulled on a heavy sweater when Aberdeen appeared at her door.

She had obviously been on her way to bed when Dana called. She was wearing a calf-length cotton nightgown with a pair of green polyester slacks she had pulled on under the gown. Her feet were in gray, high-top slippers and she had on a long-sleeved denim shirt Dana had seen her wear when she was out pulling weeds.

"What we got here?" she asked, holding a towel she had brought with her over her nose. She bent closer to examine the dead animal lying between them.

"My cat was very distressed," Dana told her, indicating Flag, "and when I opened the door, I found this."

"How could such a thing happen?"

"Do you think a dog could have done this, and just left it here?"

Aberdeen wagged her head back and forth. "Never seen such a thing."

Between them, they managed to wrap the skunk in the old towel Aberdeen had brought and Dana carried it around the carriage house, through the back yard, to the alley.

In the meantime, Aberdeen had returned to her house and came back with a bristle-brush and a tall container of tomato juice.

"I'll make sure my yardman disposes of the animal in the morning," she said as she dropped to her knees and set to work scrubbing the brick entryway.

"What's with the tomato juice?" asked Dana.

"My Ma used tomato juice for the dogs when I was a wee lass," replied Aberdeen. "It'll remove the skunk odor."

Dana tried to make sense of what she had said. Tomato juice? Dogs? Skunks? Then she dimly remembered that once her grandmother had given their brown lab a bath in tomato juice after he had had a run-in with a skunk.

Aberdeen soon had a gooey mass of the juice spread over a wide area of the front entrance. Dana went inside for warm water and together they worked at scrubbing away the skunk odor.

When they had finished, Aberdeen stood and looked at Dana. "Are you for being alright, then?"

"I will be. I'm just mystified as to how this happened."

Aberdeen was picking up the things she had brought over.

"Would you like a cup of herbal tea?" Dana asked.

"Don't mind if I do."

Inside, Flag circled Aberdeen several times before jumping up on her lap, purring, as the two women discussed possible ways the skunk had ended up at Dana's front entrance.

"I've noted your car hasn't been in the driveway."

Dana took a deep breath before replying. "It's having some repairs done on it. Actually, someone keyed the passenger side when I was parked at the trailhead up at Bruce's campground."

Aberdeen's dark brown eyes opened wider. "This keying? What do you mean?"

Dana explained that someone had taken a key to her car, scratching the entire length of the passenger side.

"Did you find the wrongdoer?"

"No, I was away from the car a good part of that afternoon so it's hard to determine what happened." She could think of no reason to tell Aberdeen about Jeremy and her qualms about him, but thought it might be a good idea to have another set of eyes watching out for her.

"That makes me a wee bit nervous, after what just happened this evening."

"Guess that thought occurred to me, too," said Dana pensively.

***

After Aberdeen left, Dana found it difficult to resume the work she had been engrossed with on her computer. She pulled her sweater more snugly around her as she stood and walked the perimeter of her small abode to make sure all the windows were closed and locked and the blinds shut.

Was someone trying to send her a message? She could think of no reason why. Had she unknowingly offended someone? *Could* Jeremy be around? She had not realized he might be disturbed enough to do such a thing.

Unable to settle down, she clicked on Arnie Watt's number in her phone. He must have been close by as he answered on the second ring.

"Dana? Everything okay? You usually don't call this late."

"Things are going pretty well here. But I have a favor to ask of you."

"You sure you're okay? You don't sound quite right."

She didn't wish to traipse through the bizarre things that had occurred in the last few days but knew she had to give Arnie some reason for her request.

"I've had the strangest feeling that Jeremy Vanderhoff may be about. I wonder if you could ask around quietly in Laramie and see if anybody knows where he is these days."

"You must have more than a feeling to go on."

"A couple small things have happened that make me wonder if he's here in Lander."

"What kind of 'small things,' Dana?"

"Well, someone keyed my car last week, and then tonight a dead animal showed up on my doorstep." There. She had said enough, if he wasn't willing to find out about Jeremy, she would call one of her female friends at the university.

"What kind of a dead animal?"

"A skunk."

"Damn it. You report these incidents to the police?"

She should have known it wouldn't be that easy.

"Actually, no, I was just hoping you would be able to help me find out where he is."

"Well sure, I'll do what I can from here," said Arnie, "but I strongly urge you to let the cops know about these events."

"My landlady knows what happened," she explained.

"My god, girl, isn't she an old bird? Think you said it's hard to make out what she's saying most of the time."

"Arnie, she is an older woman, yes, but sharp as a brass tack. Not much escapes her notice."

Dana could hear voices in the background on Arnie's end of the conversation. "Look, Corrine and I are just on our way out with a couple of friends and I need to get going, but I'll be in touch on this Jeremy thing. In the meantime, get the police involved."

"Thanks Arnie," said Dana, dejectedly shutting off her phone.

She returned to the sofa with a half-cup of tea and picked up her computer. Her scattered thoughts made it difficult to concentrate on her work so she shut the laptop down and mulled over the chat she had just had with her advisor.

Was she just being paranoid, blowing things out of proportion, or should she be talking to the police? After all, the damage to her car had been costly, and now this dead skunk throttled outside her front door was definitely distressing.

As she sipped a second cup of the soothing tea it calmed her thinking and she decided to see what the morning would bring. Besides, Yogi had promised she could pick up her car in the morning. She would be able to go back to the area she and Jax had walked on Sunday and examine the plants she had found before the rattlesnake spoiled that excursion.

CHAPTER 19

Back on the lower, south side of the Popo Agie, Dana pulled a walking stick Jax had loaned her from the back of her newly repainted Honda. He had called it his snake-poker and had suggested she use it while working in that area and to be wary of places where the heat-loving reptiles sunned themselves.

The morning was bright with light reflected off the sheer cliff across the river. Above the tree line, sagebrush covered the hillside. The pungent, piney smell of cedars and lodge poles filled the air and she inhaled deeply. An occasional mosquito buzzed around her head. Odd, she hadn't noticed the annoying insects before… then she reasoned it was her proximity to the water that attracted them.

She came to the large rock where the snake had interrupted her work and carefully prodded thick, low-growing junipers before stepping off the path. Except for the occasional pine tree, the area was open and exposed to the sunny morning and she was rather surprised she had found a sample of her shade-loving *dicentra* in this location. But there they were, in the shadow cast by surrounding vegetation, in full bloom, nestled up against the large boulder.

Before kneeling beside the plant, she carefully checked once more for any snakes. As she recalled how close she had come to virtually sticking her hand into the hissing mouth of the venomous serpent, she started thinking that perhaps it would be wise to move farther along the trail to look for other specimens. For all she knew, the snake made its home under this particular rock. One the other hand, she was equally likely to encounter one of the vile reptiles at other sites nearby, so she reached for her field notebook and a pen and began recording the layout of her latest find. By now she had a list of points she liked to verify when recording a new find:

Photograph the plant: check.
Surrounding type of rock: check.
Location in relation to rock: check.
Bloom size: check.
Leaf and stem structure: check.

Soil type: check.

After spending some considerable time studying all aspects of this individual plant and the flat limestone rock it was growing near, she stood up. Picking up her backpack, she swatted a mosquito off her arm and prepared to move on.

Back on the trail, she moved slowly, examining both sides of the path as she went. Surely this single specimen was not the only one to be found in this particular area? Maybe she would need to get up away from the trail to have further success.

While she had been bent over her plant, she realized a slight breeze had arisen, stirring the nearby grasses. At least it helped to discourage the annoying mosquitoes from buzzing around her face. A pungent, disagreeable odor wafted through the air, riding on the breeze. Was her sense of smell still attuned to and recalling the dead skunk? But this stench was different. She turned slowly, trying to determine which direction the unpleasant smell came from. It seemed to be coming from farther down the trail. Jax had told her that fishermen sometimes tossed unwanted catches like carp up on the bank for carrion-eating animals to eat.

Dana came to a small rill that had been created by the spring thaw higher in the mountains and crossed over it by means of two logs before continuing along the path. The unpleasant odor became stronger. A small flock of crows seemed to be interested in something off to her right. A couple of them circled overhead, while a raucous commotion erupted near a chokecherry bush up away from the trail.

Dana prodded the low-growing shrubbery at the side of the path and tentatively stepped into a small space clear of growth, but covered with small rocks. As she approached the bush, three crows that had been brawling on the ground flew into the air. The crows had apparently been attracted to something below the bush. The chokecherry, which was approximately ten feet in circumference and nearly as high, was filled with strings of small green berries that would eventually mature into dark maroon fruit come late August.

She pulled a couple of large branches aside near where the crows had been. Then she jerked back in astonishment and disgust at what she saw.

A deer's carcass was partially hidden by the chokecherry bush. The crows and other animals had been attacking the body and parts of it were shredded.

Dana pulled a lower branch aside to examine the remains. It had been a large deer, a buck. In addition to its battered body, the buck's head had been removed just above the shoulders. She looked around nervously, thinking a large predator might have dragged off the head. She knew a pack of coyotes could sometimes bring down a deer. That usually happened in the wintertime, though, and usually the victim was old or sick, but this animal appeared to have been a robust, healthy specimen.

She slipped her backpack from her shoulders and bent over the re-mains, holding a tissue over her nose and mouth because of the odor. She leaned closer and was shocked to discover that the head had been cleanly cut from the body. Sitting back on her heels, her mind reeled with the idea that someone had probably killed the buck and taken the head that, in all likelihood, had sported a good-sized rack.

Dana thought back to Sunday afternoon when she and Jax had been in the area. They had seen three deer feeding higher up on the hillside. She wondered if this was the older buck with the elegant rack. If it was, the animal must have been killed later on Sunday or yesterday. With the advancing summer, the temperature was reaching into the eighties and it didn't take much time for a body left exposed to the elements to start to deteriorate. Small animals and birds helped along the process.

Rising to her feet, Dana stepped away from the dead animal, feeling nauseous and thoroughly sickened with the idea that anyone would kill such a magnificent creature and just abandon the carcass. The fact that it wasn't the hunting season compounded her revulsion. She swallowed and took a couple of deep breaths, letting her stomach settle down.

Once she had returned to the trail, she retraced her steps back up the path to the trailhead. It was difficult for her to get the slaughtered deer out of her mind. It obviously hadn't been killed for its meat but for a trophy. She just couldn't get to grips with the thinking of someone who would do such a thing. She didn't know the exact cir-cumstances of the killing, but her fertile mind had enough notions to keep her occupied for several minutes.

The parking lot was nearly filled with vehicles, as people prepared to walk up into the canyon or to claim one of the tables in the nearby picnic area. Fishermen were donning waders and preparing their rods and reels to try their luck in the Popo Agie.

Since she had her camera with her, Dana decided to return to the area on the up-slope where she had found her first *dicentra*. The plant would now be in full bloom and at the height of its growth cycle. It was nearing the end of June and she presumed the hot summer sun would soon inhibit any future blooming if these plants were anything like other wild bleeding hearts, or even the domestic variety.

Sure enough, the blossoms on her original find were already beginning to fade and drop off. The next stage in her research would be to follow the plants themselves, to see how well they survived the summer, how they coped with the heat, and at what stage they went dormant.

After photographing the site, she walked a bit farther on, to the large rock from which she could observe the fox's den. Three young kits were frolicking on and around the burrow, nipping and chasing each other around the opening. The vixen lay on a nearby rock, sunning herself. Dana breathed a sigh of relief at finding the little family intact.

***

Returning to town, Dana drove to the game and fish department offices to report the plundered deer carcass. She approached the information desk, where a middle-aged woman with a blond, bob haircut sat. She looked up from her computer where she had been pecking away with bright red, ridiculously long fingernails.

"How can I help you?"

A question that had nothing to do with the situation popped into Dana's mind. *How do women type with nails like that?* She looked down at her own grimy, chipped, uneven nails and lowered her hands from the counter before the woman could see them.

"I just returned from doing some research up in the canyon," she said, "and I came across a buck deer that had been killed and had its head removed."

"Are the remains on the main road? Carrion can get after a downed deer very quickly."

"No, it's off the main road, across the river. What I mean is, its head was removed just above the shoulders. It was very plain to see."

"Did you take any pictures?" asked the woman.

Dana realized that, in her rush to get away from the unpleasant odor, she had been remiss in not getting a couple of pictures. "I didn't. I encountered a rattlesnake in the same area a couple days ago and I just wanted to get out of there. That, plus the stench of the dead animal…"

"I understand. They can get downright rancid in a very short time."

"I thought maybe you had somebody who could pick up the carcass." Dana thought it might be a job for the clean-up crew she had chatted with, but then she remembered they worked for the forest service and the two agencies might not share responsibilities.

"We like to do that, not only to examine the remains and the surrounding area where an animal is killed, but to keep the area clean."

"A friend and I were along the same trail on Sunday afternoon. We saw three deer in the area, one of which had a nice rack, so I'm thinking this buck must have been killed in the last day or two."

"You're probably right," said the clerk.

Dana nodded her head at what the woman said. But had she understood the animal had likely been killed for its head and rack? Or was it such a common occurrence it was no longer disturbing to her?

"However, we're short-handed right now," the woman continued. "As you may know, we lost one of our game wardens for this area."

"I was very sorry to hear about that," said Dana. "I had a chat with him for a few minutes only a day or two before his accident. Do they know yet what happened to him?"

"Not officially," whispered the woman, "but between you and me and that fence post out by the entrance, I think he was beaten and was dead before he was pushed off into the brush."

"Why do you say that?"

Before she could answer, a door behind the information desk opened and a man in the standard game and fish department uniform of red shirt and blue jeans walked out. He glanced at Dana before looking around the room as if searching for something. Then he sauntered over to a kiosk that held pamphlets on game and fish rules and regulations and began leafing through them. Dana's informant straightened up and plastered a smile on her face.

"Now, where exactly did you come across the animal?" she asked.

Dana gave her directions in terms of the approximate distance from the trailhead.

"We'll be sure to send someone out there as soon as possible," the woman said, with another smile. "We certainly make it a priority to dispose of any dead animals in the valley."

As Dana left the office and walked out to her vehicle she was wishing the man had not shown up just when he did. If he hadn't, she might have been able to learn more about the game warden's death.

***

Back at her apartment, Dana fed Flag, vacuumed her living room, and was running a dust cloth over the oak tables at each end of the sofa when her cell phone rang. She answered, but no one responded. She could tell someone was on the line, however. Looking at the screen of her caller-ID, it showed an out-of-state number. She slammed the phone down, deciding it had probably been a robocaller, but her phone rang again almost immediately. She ignored it and went back to her dusting. When her phone continued to ring, she rushed across the room and grabbed it, ready to ream out the person on the other end.

It was Jax.

"I was just leaving you a message."

"Were you the heavy breather who just called?"

"Excuse me?"

"I just had a hang-up call," she explained. "I thought it was the same person calling back."

"You get that kind of thing frequently?"

"I've had a couple recently."

"Maybe you should report them."

That seemed to be the mantra Dana was hearing a lot lately. She hesitated for a moment. "Actually, they're probably just wrong numbers."

Wrong numbers, or Jeremy? Maybe she should take the advice she had been getting and report the calls to the police.

"Hmmm. I wondered if you want to take a run up to South Pass City with me. Thought I might drop a line in one of my favorite streams."

"When?"

"Soon as I can pick you up, if you want to go?"

"You mean, this afternoon?" Dana had planned on organizing her project into some semblance of order, but the temptation to see the historic gold mining town on South Pass that Jed had told her about was enticing.

"Yeah, I'm leaving the project right now."

"Would we be late getting back?"

"We would leave up there by dark. So probably 9:30 or 10:00. Who knows, you might even come across some of your plants. Or we could stop and get a fishing license for you."

"What's the topography like?"

"Mostly arid, much flatter up on top, big rocks in some places, but nothing like the canyon, although the altitude is probably about the same."

Hearing she could possibly locate some of her *dicentra* in another, completely different site sealed the deal for Dana. "Think I'll just watch you fish this time."

Ten minutes later, Jax pulled into her driveway.

CHAPTER 20

It took them forty minutes to reach South Pass City. The route out of Lander led them steadily upward into the foothills of the Wind River Range past Red Canyon.

As the highway followed the rim of the canyon, Dana's attention was captured by a wide, deep gorge notable for its red rocks and soil. It made for an amazing change in terrain.

"Unc has told me this canyon was created by uplift when the mountains were formed millions of years ago and then was further eroded by a stream that runs through it."

"And the soil is red because of the iron in it?"

"Yep. This area is part of the Chugwater Formation. The color comes from oxidization of the minerals in the sedimentary sandstone rock."

"I'm somewhat familiar with the Chugwater Formations. I believe there are several in this area of the west."

Jax nodded in agreement. "If you look closely, you can see the creek that meanders through the area. It eventually feeds into the Popo Agie."

"That looks like a big ranching operation down there."

"Damn!" Jax suddenly applied the brakes as three yearling deer ambled across the highway. He reached out and grabbed Dana so that she didn't slam against her seat belt.

The deer crossed the road and Jax returned his hand to the wheel.

"Settlers moved into the valley and did some farming in the mid-1850s. Because of the secluded nature of the area, they were able to grow some great fruit. It's like a mini-climate down there. Of course, there were Native Americans in the area, as well. Unc says they used the valley to access the cut through the mountains, farther up."

"Which tribe?"

"Shoshone. I think Chief Washakie was around then. The Nature Conservancy owns much of the land down there today. That's the big ranch you mentioned."

Dana looked down to her right toward the area of red clay that looked like it had been picked up somewhere else and plopped down in the midst of this mountainous terrain. She could see a large building surrounded by smaller outbuildings and a road that meandered in a switchback manner up the side of the canyon to access the highway.

"I can imagine your uncle's interest in this area."

"He told me once that the main reason he decided to return to the old family homestead was because of all the geological options in this area for him to study, plus the adjoining formations."

"That's true of several regions in Wyoming, don't you think? And I've visited a ton of places around the state where there are intriguing petroglyphs on some of those formations."

"Intriguing in what way?"

"Oh, the history of the peoples who carved them is so evident from the animals they hunted, the things they observed, even the style of their early artwork."

"Well, when you consider much of the land in this state has been undergoing uplifts from the get-go, it makes sense there would be unusual rock formations. The petroglyphs I'm not so familiar with, but I've heard they're interesting to study."

"Many are thousands of years old. Yet they're still visible today."

"Makes one wonder if others have been worn away by the elements."

"Then, of course, there are the modern scribes who like to leave their names and initials on everything from trees to public restroom doors."

"Ah, yes, the true arteests," Jax replied with a French accent.

***

They were soon past the beautiful canyon and traveling between forested hillsides, following long, wide curves that wound up the mountains. Once they reached the summit, the land leveled out, the trees disappeared, and the sagebrush became more abundant. Meanwhile, Jax continued to tell her what he knew about the area.

"South Pass City is located on the site of an old, deserted gold mine, situated between the Wind River Range, the Oregon Buttes, and Great Divide Basin. The once-abandoned ghost town has gained notoriety in recent years, as various individuals have restored some of the old buildings and people have actually moved back into the area. They seem to be captivated by its history. The community sits in a scooped-out spot near the continental divide. It got its name from travelers on the Oregon and Mormon trails who traversed the three ranges on their way west during the mid-1800s. Compared to the rocky, uneven trail the early settlers traveled, the area surrounding the mining town is flat as a flitter. It's covered in sagebrush but because of the recent rains the wild flowers have grown rampant this year. Just getting to this area was the difficult part for early travelers. You saw how steep some of the road coming up here is. If it hadn't been for the trappers and explorers who found a pass through these mountains, it would have been impossible for them to make the trek."

"Some of those explorers must have had some eye-opening experiences."

"How's that?"

"Wild animals... the weather... getting lost and have to retrace their routes to find a way through, over, or around obstacles."

"Well, some of the routes we're using today were first laid out by them."

"Wonder if they were aware, at the time, that they were carving history?"

"If I recall an American history class correctly, some of the exploratory expeditions that first investigated and mapped the area were sent out by the government, and even some private enterprises."

"Bet you can't say that three times in a row without getting your tongue twisted."

"Wanna bet? Exploratory expeditions, explorashree expedishuns... exploring trails."

"Oh, you're a dandy, Ahrens. So there were private endeavors to find a way over the mountain, too?"

"There were companies who organized and led some of the big wagon trains, led by wagon masters, who probably had information acquired from earlier explorers or even their own scouts. The coastal west was opening up, so it had to have attracted people."

Once Jax turned off the highway onto a dirt road, Dana keep a careful eye out for any sign of a likely habitat of the *dicentra* plants for her study. There were no boulders in this area, just an occasional football-sized rock, and what she did see was mostly shale. Small whirlwinds of dust were blowing along the road in front of them.

As Jax drove slowly on the two-track road through the old mining town, he pointed out various buildings from the past.

"Here we have the Carissa Saloon," he said, stopping in front of a weatherworn, dilapidated building. The cover over the front entrance sagged down on one side and glass was missing from the two windows.

"Must have been a popular place at one time," Dana mused as they moved on. "At least, judging by the old western movies."

Jax chuckled. "I imagine the gold miners were good customers. At one time, there was a small hospital here, a butcher's shop, the Idaho House, which I think was a hotel or a rooming house, an ice house, a school, and another saloon I don't know the name of."

"No mercantile?"

"Probably blew away."

"And these little huts were inhabited by the people who lived here, I guess," Dana said as they wound around a series of very small, ancient, sod-roofed hovels. In many places, pieces of old iron equipment lay half-buried in the ground. In addition, probably one of the first and oldest trucks in Fremont County lay covered by wind-blown soil, along with rigging for horses and bent and crushed mining cars.

Dana could only imagine what dreams had caused people to leave their homes, pack up their families, basic household goods, and a few animals and join a wagon train that passed through the cut in the mountains. Some may have had their eyes set on making a fortune on the west coast. Or, as they drew close to the area, perhaps they heard about the gold mining and made the choice to stay, staked out claims, and eventually built one of these small cabins.

However they got there, she could envision tumbleweeds blowing down the dirt main street, with people hurrying from one establishment to another, swept along by the incessant wind.

In many places across the west, small abandoned communities such as the one they were driving through had once been vibrant settlements. Regrettably, when the mineral they were mining was depleted the people moved on, creating yet another ghost town.

"This was called The Pit," said Jax, as he stopped near the remains of a large, weatherworn, wooden structure. "At one time this building housed a rotary elevator and winch to drag the gold and detritus up out of the ground."

"Given the size of this thing, gold mining must have been quite the operation here at one time," Dana ventured.

"A lot of hits and misses from what I know," Jax replied. "At the time this area got built up, in the mid-1840s, lots of people were on their way out to California to dig for gold there or to Oregon and Washington where affordable land was becoming available. Then a few miners found some veins around here and, of course, rumors flew and everybody and his burro came up here to make their fortune."

Dana was thinking Jax must have read her mind, as she had compiled a similar list in her head of the various possible reasons people had headed farther west.

"Close to one thousand people lived here at one time," Jax told her. "But you have to remember this was also Indian Territory, and the Indians took exception to having their land settled. So there were some skirmishes between the miners and the Arapahoe and Cheyenne tribes. As a result, the Army had to patrol throughout this area."

"It sounds as if a great deal must have been invested in this place if the Army sent soldiers in. And The Pit appears to have been quite an operation."

"Not sure how much gold went out of here, but the boom only lasted a couple years before people moved on to other places or were discouraged by how little gold was being mined, plus the Indian attacks had to have been hard on families."

They passed an older, nattily dressed gentleman, walking along the road with a handsome golden retriever at his heels. The bottom of his jacket was flapping in the wind. His status as resident or tourist was unclear but he lifted an arm in greeting as they drove by.

Several cars were parked around one of the rehabbed buildings and the sign on a post outside indicated the enterprise was that of a potter. Well-tended window boxes were filled with vivid flowers and vines, providing a bit of color and cheerfulness in an otherwise drab environment.

After making the rounds of the historical site, they turned south toward the headwaters of the Sweetwater River. Jax turned the pickup from the main dirt road and they drove a couple of miles before winding around some low-growing pines down to the waterway on a narrow one-lane sidetrack.

Lush, green grasses covered the hillsides, waving in a slight breeze. The sun was beginning its downward arc by the time they parked and Dana followed Jax as he picked their way around the willows growing on the banks of the stream.

Instead of the mosquitoes that had troubled her in the morning, small flies and gnats now buzzed around Dana's face and in her hair and she was kept busy swatting them away.

She watched as Jax assembled his fishing rod, attached the reel, and chose his favorite lure from his tackle box. He fished silently for a half hour, pulling in several eight to ten inch trout from the stream, but he released them all. She followed him slowly along the bank as he cast his line once more, noting the difference in flora from what she was used to seeing in the canyon.

There were a couple of places Dana thought might be conducive to her plants, but she found nothing when she looked. The more she learned about the *dicentra*, the more convinced she became that they were very picky about where they put down roots.

Eventually they came to a point where a large boulder was embedded in the ground, forcing the stream to curve around it in a hairpin bend. The rock was flattened on top and Jax climbed up, then reached down for Dana's hand and pulled her up beside him.

"This is one of my favorite spots," he said as he squatted on the rim, looking six feet down to the water.

"I'm beginning to think one of many, Ahrens," Dana said, smiling as she looked around for a place to settle.

She found a comfortable position off to one side, with her back against an even higher rock, and relaxed, watching as Jax cast his line out and it settled gently into the water of the deep hole below them. She leaned her head back and breathed in the clean, earthy smells of their surroundings. The water moved quietly around them, with an occasional gurgle as it rippled over rocks farther upstream.

The sparse clouds overhead drifted slowly, changing from one form to another, and Dana found herself identifying what looked initially like a whale but then morphed into a roller-coaster. *Almost like my life,* she mused, *first a monster of an emotional problem to contend with over Jeremy, and then the ups and downs that had occurred more recently.*

She glanced back up at the clouds as the carnival ride transformed into vague flat stepping-stones. Smiling wistfully, she roused herself from her reverie, wondering what the meaning behind the stepping stones might be.

They had been on the rock for a few minutes when Jax yelled, "In-coming," and he flipped a nice-sized trout up beside Dana. She grabbed the squirming fish, unhooked it from the lure, handed it to Jax, and he tossed it back into the water.

"Oh, sorry," he said as he saw the squeamish look on her face. "There are wet wipes in my tackle box."

"Am I supposed to be quiet?" she asked, pulling out a moist towelette and wiping her hands.

He turned and looked at her quizzically, as if to say "why would you ask such a thing?"

"I was with my brother and one of his friends once, while they were fishing, and they told me I talked so much I was scaring the fish away."

"I don't think they can hear you from up here. Besides, I've never noticed you being overly talkative."

"Why do you even bother fishing, when you always throw them back?" she asked.

"Just the fun of snagging them. I've got my freezer filled with trout," he responded. "I'll be glad to get a couple nice ones for you if you'd like, though."

"No thanks. I'm not a real fan of trout."

Jax jerked his fishing rod up and another fat fish landed on the rock between them. Again, Dana unhooked the fish and passed it over to Jax.

"Hope you're not snagging the same fish over and over."

"Don't think so. Been my experience that when a trout is hooked, he's pretty mistrustful of the same bait when it comes swimming along again."

Jax eventually got his fill of his catch-and-release routine. Dana watched as he put away his gear, taking care to return all his equipment to its proper place, cleaning a couple of items, as well as his own hands, before settling beside Dana.

"I'm betting you've got some interesting items in your tackle box."

"Oh yeah? And what might they be?"

"I was thinking probably a razor, some batteries."

"What? You think I shave the fish I catch?"

"No, I just thought you might need to clean up and make yourself presentable before returning to work, or headed to a meeting with the hospital trustees."

"And batteries? I don't have an electric reel, yet."

"You mean there is such a thing?"

"Well, kind of. Okay, Smarty-Marty, let's hear about the things you carry in your backpack, huh?"

"Just the normal things I need doing my research."

"Like?"

"Well, my field book, camera, flashlight, plenty of pencils, and, until recently, a set of binoculars."

"No personal items?" he asked, with a wry look on his face.

"Such as?" she asked, wondering where this conversation was going.

"Well, I was thinking, maybe a manicure set."

Dana exploded in laughter. "Oh sure, when I take my lunch break, I whip out files and brushes and lie around blowing my nails while the polish dries."

Jax captured her left hand, as she flipped it around demonstrating her talent in nail-polishing and, without taking his eyes from hers, slowly brought her hand to his lips. Turning her fingers over, he nuzzled her palm.

"Dana…" he said, then stalled. Any other words he had in mind remained unspoken.

It was several seconds before Dana responded by curling her thumb and fingers around his chin and gently stroked his cheek with her index finger.

***

The sun was descending into the western sky off to their right. The few clouds that hovered were tinged in orange and dark blue, reminding Dana of a sunset painting she had recently seen in an art gallery. It had sold for hundreds of dollars, and here she was getting the same effect for free, courtesy of Mother Nature.

"Have the police found any leads into the items stolen from your job site?"

"They stopped by this morning to clarify some information we gave them. Guess you probably heard Stubby and me talking. It was dynamite detonators that were taken. But no, I haven't heard about any leads."

"Why would someone steal detonators?"

"Who knows? Why would someone key your car or leave a dead skunk on your door step?"

"Guess I thought my problems were a form of revenge."

"Or a sick mind."

"How do people get like that? I mean, say with Jeremy, what made him think it was okay to buy meth and sell it to college students? I can't tell you how many times I've questioned my involvement with him in the first place."

"Don't be so hard on yourself. Be thankful you didn't marry him and have a kid or two," he said, dipping his head to look her in the eyes. "I suppose psychologists would say the society we live in makes it okay to do what Jeremy did, or the genes he was born with. Not to mention the money."

Dana was picking at a loose thread on her shorts. "But when do people's morals come into the picture?"

"I'm not sure everyone has morals, Dana. Or at least they are pretty choosy in justifying what is right and what is wrong. And some people's definitions of right and wrong are definitely out of kilter."

"So you don't think, for instance, the theft at your job site was a robbery of convenience? I mean, somebody must have known which storage shed to look in to get what he wanted."

Jax was sitting with one leg bent at the knee and pulled up against his chest, facing Dana as they spoke. "I think the police had that same thought. Anyhow, they seem to be checking out all possibilities. You know, if you're not careful, you could solve this case before they do."

"Speaking of solving cases, I came across a buck deer carcass on the south side of the river earlier today, along the path where we were on Sunday. Its head had been cut off."

"Whoa. What are you saying?"

"Somebody killed the deer and removed its head, probably because it had a nice rack. I'm wondering if it's the bigger one we saw on Sunday? I reported it to the game and fish people when I got back to town."

"What did they say?"

"Just that they would send someone out to clean up the remains and look for any clues."

"Had it been shot?"

"I didn't see a bullet hole, but I didn't look, either."

"Hmm."

"Doesn't it seem bizarre that some of the big fish down at the pond, where the river rises, have gone missing, and now this deer? Not to mention a dead game warden thrown into the mix."

"Yeah. You think they're all connected?"

"Possibly."

"So, you got any suspects?"

Dana thought for a moment before replying. "With the number of people who are in and out of the canyon area, it could be anyone, or some person who thinks he doesn't have to abide by the laws."

A mass of gnats swirled around Dana's head and she swiped her hand through the air, chasing them away.

"They must think you're sweet," Jax said, holding her gaze once again with his intense brown eyes. Then he wiped his hand on his jeans and lifted a thumb to capture a gnat that had become entangled in one of her eyelashes.

CHAPTER 21

It was nearing 10:30 p.m. when Jax parked his pickup in Dana's driveway. Before starting the drive back to Lander they had dined at the top of the mountain on bratwurst and corn chips from a small convenience store.

After their pleasant evening, Dana was torn about inviting him inside. She had made big strides as far as their friendship was concerned and wanted to keep it that way, so she resolutely thanked him and turned to exit his truck. He caught her left arm, stopping her progress, then leaned over and kissed her on her upper cheek before she bounded out of the truck with a smile on her face.

Dana removed her house key from the pocket of her shorts and inserted it into the lock but before she had a chance to turn it, the door opened by itself. *Hmmm, I mustn't have locked the door as I was leaving*, she mused. She reached inside the doorjamb and flipped on the entry light, turned, and waved a hand at Jax as he waited to see that she got inside.

She could hear him backing down the driveway as she entered the apartment and turned on the table lamp at one end of her sofa. She hung her jacket on a peg just inside the door and called for Flag.

A slight odor of cigarette smoke hit her nostrils.

That's interesting, she thought. *Flag usually meets me at the door, demanding attention, and entwining herself between my legs...*

"Flag?" she called. "Are you upset at me for leaving you alone this evening?"

She walked over to the counter that separated her dining area from the kitchenette. She looked behind the counter, thinking the young cat might be eating. She checked the small alcove off the kitchen where she kept the litter box. She gave the bedroom a cursory look, then the bathroom. No Flag.

She went back to the front door, opened it, and looked outside, thinking that if the door had been ajar, just possibly the young tabby cat had ventured out. But the storm door had been shut.

She called the cat's name and pulled aside the branches of the shrub just outside the door. Still no Flag.

A brisk wind had begun to blow, swaying the branches of the large tree in Aberdeen's yard. Dana rubbed her forearms and gave a slight shiver as she turned to go back inside. She ran her hand lightly over the latch, and the tip of her middle finger caught on a sharp edge. She brought her finger to her mouth to remove the drop of blood that appeared and then bent to closely examine the latch.

Where the key was supposed to go, she found one end of the keyhole widened as if it had been jimmied. It was strange she hadn't noticed it before. And hadn't the whole residence been recently refurbished? Everything should be in excellent working order.

Then, with stunning comprehension, she realized she hadn't noticed the damage before because it hadn't been there before!

She quickly looked around her, her eyes scanning up and down both sides of the street, to see if there was any unfamiliar vehicle parked nearby. Nothing. She slipped inside her apartment, then closed and locked the door.

Had someone been inside during her absence? She knew Aberdeen had a key and wouldn't have needed to damage the lock to get in. Aberdeen didn't appear to be a busybody landlady like that, anyway, and Dana felt sure she would have left a note of explanation if she had come inside for any reason.

Dana went quickly through to the bathroom, double-checked behind the shower curtain, then went back into the bedroom, where she got down on her hands and knees and tentatively looked under the bed skirt before opening the closet and pulling her clothing aside. What was she looking for? Was Flag sick, or had she been injured so that she had crawled into some dark, quiet place? The apartment wasn't that big. Flag had to be hidden somewhere, or else she had gone outside. Was it possible she had been snatched?

Dana turned slowly around in her bedroom, even looking up at a narrow ledge high up on the wall, looking for a place the cat might have retreated to. Then she realized how silly she was being. How would Flag have been able to get up there?

Then Dana remembered the hang-up call she had received earlier in the afternoon, before she and Jax had left to drive to South Pass

City. Did that have something to do with it? Was there a connection between the call and Flag's disappearance? This thing with Jeremy was beginning to get out of hand.

She grabbed her cell phone and called Jax.

"Hey, didn't expect to hear from you this soon. Everything okay?"

"Jax, could you come back to my place? My cat has gone missing and I think someone broke into my apartment while we were gone."

"Are you alone?"

"Yes," she said, tremulously.

"I'll be right there."

Five minutes later, he was parked in her driveway. The beam of the truck's headlights scattered the shadows around the entrance to the carriage house. Dana flew out the door and ran straight into Jax's arms as he stepped down from the vehicle.

Jax held her for a moment, stilling her shaking body and rubbing the outsides of her arms in a calming manner.

"Have you called the police?"

"No, I'm more concerned about Flag."

Jax got a flashlight from his truck and together they searched the exterior perimeter of the apartment as Dana continued to call Flag's name in an enticing voice. He put one arm around her and they returned to the door. There he examined the lock and agreed it looked like it had been tampered with.

Back inside, Dana stood in the middle of the room, trying to gain reassurance from the familiarity of her quarters.

"Is anything missing?"

"Everything looks normal." She was trying to think. The small flatscreen television was there and her laptop computer lay on the counter where she had left it.

Dana had brought very few items with her from Laramie, only summer clothing, a few textbooks, and a minimum of cooking and eating utensils. She had acquired a couple of pots of African violets since coming to Lander and she walked over to the small dining area and the north-facing window where they had sat on the windowsill.

"Darn," she muttered as she realized one of the plants had been knocked off the sill and was in disarray on the hardwood floor beneath the window.

Jax saw what she was looking at. "Did Flag do that?"

"She must have. She sits in this window quite a bit, but she never bothered the plants before." She knelt, picked up the plant, and stuffed soil and plant back into the small metal container, which she replaced on the ledge by its mate.

"Oh, nooo," she moaned.

"What?" Jax asked as he walked around the table to her.

She was pointing at the plant that had not been damaged. A cigarette had been stubbed out in the soil and the butt remained.

"You know, I thought I smelled cigarette smoke when I first got home. I thought it had drifted in from outside, though," she muttered.

"I smelled smoke when I walked in, too."

Dana looked at him, the fright obvious in her eyes. "He's been inside my apartment," she said, disheartened, with no emphasis on any of the words. It was as if her subconscious had acknowledged what, for some time, she had suspected. Jeremy, or even "the poacher," was responsible for all her troubles. Now she had expressed that fear verbally. Where had that come from?

"He?"

"It has to be Jeremy, or the guy I've been telling you about up in the canyon with the foxes. My car being keyed, the dead skunk, on and on..." Listening to herself, it sounded as if she were grasping at any name that came into her mind.

"Okay, Dana, enough of this stuff. It's time to get the police involved. At the very least, the police need to be aware of your suspicions."

Dana lifted her head, tears hanging on her eyelashes. "What if it isn't Jeremy?"

"Who, then?"

"Like I say. This character up in the canyon keeps turning up almost like he's lurking in the shadows," she sputtered. "And why does he take a packhorse into the back country?"

"Good question, but there could be any number of reasons."

"There are just too many unanswered questions about him."

"If it's the same person," Jax went on, "his name is Leon Archileta. You said the truck you saw at my job site is the one you've seen at the trailhead? I don't know that much about the guy. As I mentioned before, he was hired as a sub-contractor to do the rock work on my project."

"I'm sure it's the same truck."

"So you think he's a good possibility?"

"Yes… no… I don't know. On the other hand, I can't get away from the idea it could be Jeremy." Then, almost immediately, "Is this Leon Archileta working every day at the hospital?"

"We're not that far along on his part of the work yet. He's been around talking with Stubby occasionally. They've been getting his supplies ordered. Truthfully, I'm not sure why he's even here yet, but Stub made some kind of deal with him to park his rig at the work site. I'll ask Stubby more about him."

"That would explain why he has time to be up in the canyon."

"Describe your guy."

"He's a large man." She tried to recall details about "the poacher" from the one time she had actually exchanged words with him. "He's bald, has a dour face. The day I encountered him he was wearing an Aussie Outback hat."

"That does sound like Leon."

Jax pulled a cell phone from the pocket of his shorts.

"What are you doing?"

"Calling the police."

CHAPTER 22

Dana's initial reaction was to reach out and stop Jax from placing the call but commonsense niggled its way into her brain. Besides, it felt good to have someone be her advocate for a change.

When his call was answered, Jax gave Dana's name and address and briefly explained what had happened. Dana paced the floor while he spoke, as she tried to calm the body-wide trembling that had overtaken her once she realized someone had been inside her apartment.

After a couple of minutes Jax signed off. "They're sending an officer by."

Jax raised his head and looked across the room. "Well, look who we have here," he said, folding down and sitting on his haunches.

Dana turned and saw Flag's head tentatively peeking around the corner of the utility room. She hurried over to the small space.

"Flag," she crooned, "here, kitty, kitty."

To her surprise the cat withdrew.

Jax led her back to the sofa. "She's obviously traumatized, Dana. Let's just sit here for a minute. She'll come back in her own time."

"But what happened to her?"

"It's okay, it's okay," he said, pointing toward the area where the washer and dryer were. "You'd be traumatized, too, if some stranger invaded your territory."

"She must have gotten up behind the washer. I didn't think there was enough room for her to get in there."

"My experience with cats is that they like to have secret hiding places, and that is obviously hers."

Sure enough, as they sat quietly, Flag soon poked her tri-colored head back around the corner. Jax laid his hand on Dana's knee in an effort to keep her calm. The cat crept around the wall and slunk behind the opposite end of the sofa beyond their sight.

Soon, Dana felt the cat jump up onto the back of the sofa and walk along the edge of it. She sniffed around Jax before moving to Dana and nudging the back of her right shoulder. Obviously now over feeling threatened, Flag jumped down onto the seat of the sofa then onto the floor, licking first one paw then the other, as she nonchalantly bathed her head and cheeks.

"Looks like she's cleaning up after an unpleasant scare," said Jax. He watched the cat for a moment. "Doesn't look like she's been physically harmed."

"Poor baby," cooed Dana as she sat watching Flag go through her ministrations.

***

Two police officers arrived shortly afterward. The older of the two introduced himself as Officer Morgan and his partner as O'Brien. They listened as Dana explained about being gone during the late afternoon and evening and about returning home and finding her apartment had been broken into. After both officers had been down on their hands and knees examining the lock, opening and closing the door a couple of times, and clicking the lock on and off they agreed it looked as if the locking mechanism had been pried open.

"Anything else damaged?" asked Officer Morgan, a small, trim man, with a bushy brown and gray mustache.

Dana showed him the cigarette butt sticking out of the soil of her African violet. "This is what got my attention, plus the smell of cigarette smoke when I stepped inside."

"I take it you don't smoke? Or you either, sir?" he asked, addressing both of them.

They both shook their heads.

The policeman pulled a chair away from the table and motioned for Dana to have a seat. He then made a couple of notes in a small notebook he took from his shirt pocket.

The younger officer, O'Brien, was a lanky, thin-faced man, with a mass of curly black hair. He walked into the kitchenette, tentatively lifting a newspaper from the counter and peering under it. Then he went into the bathroom and bedroom, evidently looking for anything out of the ordinary. A moment later he re-emerged then pulled a heavy-duty flashlight from a carrier on his belt and went outside to look around the yard. Dana could see the light flash under the front windows and through the branches of the tree.

"Do you have any reason to believe this forced entry was done by someone you know, or are we shooting in the wind as to the identity of the suspect?"

Dana hesitated before answering. "I've had a run-in with an individual up in Sinks Canyon where I'm doing some research."

"What kind of a run-in?" asked Morgan.

"Well, while working on the hillside above the trail, I found a red fox den with kits in it. Later, I came upon this bozo that appeared to be digging the kits out of their den and I stopped him. He was using a digging trowel and had a gunnysack with him. It seemed to me he intended to take the kits."

The officer raised an eyebrow.

Dana pressed on. "Prior to that, I had met Game Warden Trig Henderson on the trail. We chatted, and he talked specifically about not disturbing the wildlife in the area."

"Henderson, huh?" The policeman tapped his pad thoughtfully with his pen. "So, you confronted this fellow with the foxes. And he what, just walked away?"

"He was belligerent."

"Don't suppose you know who this guy is?"

Jax spoke up. "Dana has described him and we believe he's a sub-contractor on a project I'm working on. His name is Leon Archileta."

Officer Morgan turned to Jax, "And you are, sir?"

"Jackson Ahrens. I'm the project manager on the hospital extension."

The policeman looked Jax up and down and made a note in his book. "Thought you looked familiar. Think we have an on-going robbery investigation up there."

Jax nodded.

Officer Morgan turned back to Dana, "And this research you're doing that takes you up to the canyon… you doing a count of animals? You work for the game and fish?"

"I'm a botany student at the U, doing research for my thesis along the trail to the falls."

"I see. Is that one incident the only time you've encountered this Archileta fellow?"

"Yes," she said, realizing it might be only a half-truth.

"Well, Dana," the officer said, "anybody else you can think of who might have broken into your apartment?"

Dana hesitated. "I'm not sure, but I may have seen my former fiancé downtown a few days ago."

"And would he do something like this?"

She cleared her throat. "Um, when we broke up, he said he would get even with me, for ending our relationship, I guess."

"How long ago was that?"

"Two years. It happened while we were both in Laramie, at the university."

"So he's not from Lander?"

"No, sir."

"And his name?"

"Jeremy Vanderhoff."

Officer O'Brien returned from his foray outside and indicated to his partner that he hadn't found anything. Officer Morgan nodded an acknowledgement.

"Is there anything else you can tell us?" Morgan asked Dana.

"Well, yes. A dead skunk was left on my doorstep a few days ago."

"You report that?"

"No, I didn't."

Flag jumped up on Dana's lap, demanding her attention. When Dana stroked her she began purring.

"Well, it looks like we've got some different things going on here," said Morgan.

Dana exchanged a look with Jax and decided to clear the board of all her woes. "I guess I should add that while I was parked at the trailhead last week, my car got keyed."

Morgan scratched his head as he looked up from what he was writing. "Don't suppose you reported that, either?"

"Only to my insurance agent. It was damaged all along the passenger side, and it's already been repaired."

O'Brien wandered around the room, checking the windows and peering out into the night as Morgan continued his conversation with Dana.

"Please tell me there isn't more."

Dana shook her head, then remembered something else. "I don't know if you even want to know about this, but I did come across a buck deer up in the canyon that had been killed and beheaded. I realize that has nothing to do with me personally but, before you ask, I did report it to the game and fish department."

"Now we're making progress," said Morgan.

O'Brien tried to keep a straight face, but failed.

"You are either a magnet for attracting messy situations or someone, or more than one someone, has it in for you, Miz Cameron," he said, looking at her with curiosity. "I hesitate to ask again, but are there any more incidents we should know about?"

"No," she said, breathing a sigh of relief.

"Have you checked thoroughly to see if anything is missing from your apartment?"

"I have. Nothing is missing. Other than the damage to the door and the cigarette butt in the plant, everything is fine."

Morgan read over his notes, then flipped his book closed and stood. "You don't happen to have a Baggie, do you? Think I'll take this cigarette butt in and see if we can raise any DNA."

"Sure," said Dana and she went to a cupboard and extracted a sandwich-sized plastic bag. She felt that the officers were ill-prepared as they did not have an evidence bag for the investigation.

"Don't know what our person of interest was thinking by leaving this," said Morgan as he donned a latex glove, plucked the butt from the flowerpot, and deposited it in the bag. "We'll see if we get a match to anyone on our system."

Dana and Jax exchanged a confused look.

"Is it possible the cigarette is just a plant?" asked Jax.

"Sure, it's possible. Likely, even."

"And yet we both smelled cigarette smoke when we first came into the apartment," added Dana.

"We'll check out both of the names you've given us and go from there. Should any other confrontations occur, please notify us immediately, okay?"

Dana walked the officers to the door.

"I'd let your landlady know about this forced entry. She may want to have new locks installed."

"I'll do that."

CHAPTER 23

June, with its achievements and its troubles, had come and gone and the first weekend of July was upon Dana. Jax and Jed Ahrens had been speaking of the Pioneer Days' parade and rodeo that consumed the entire community during the Fourth of July weekend.

Jax told her he planned on staking out a shady spot along the parade route so that his uncle could attend, and he invited Dana to go with them. He also told her Sinks Canyon would be crawling with recreationists over the holiday so she agreed it would be a good time to avoid the heavy traffic on the two-lane road to and from the trailhead. Besides, the rodeo was touted as one of the longest continuing rodeos in the area.

On the morning of the fourth, Jax picked Dana up a couple of hours before parade start time.

"I've got a place reserved for Unc under the awning at Picklesimer's Drug."

"How did you accomplish that?"

"Got down there about six this morning and set up a couple chairs, along with a golf umbrella in case the parade lasts an extra long time and the sun gets to us."

"Aren't you afraid people will move your stuff?"

"Naw, they're pretty good about respecting the need to reserve places for the handicapped. Of course, Unc doesn't see the need. But he's been coming to these parades for years and I don't dare break with tradition."

"My landlady says to expect a mob of people."

"Oh yeah, all the old farmers and ranchers from throughout the county will be here. Usually with every member of their families."

"Do the Native Americans come?"

"They do. You'll see a lot of them in the parade, as well."

***

An hour and a half later, all three of them were settled in front of Picklesimer's, sipping cool drinks to combat the heat that had descended like an invasive adversary by 9:00 a.m. Jed Ahrens wore a wide-brimmed straw hat, Dana had on a pink golf visor, and Jax wore a Rockies' ball cap.

People were packed three and four deep along both sides of the parade route by the time the procession kicked off. It was led by the usual color guard, made up of Boy Scouts and the American Legion, followed by the local high-school summer band.

Dana couldn't help but study the people across the street as well as those standing near them as the crowd shifted before them. Watching for Jeremy, she wondered what she would do if she spotted him. At least she wasn't alone this time.

She could hear the thrum-thrum of drums heralding the arrival of an Indian dance contingent. They included people of all ages, from children of about six or seven, Dana guessed, to elders dressed in their native finery. They wore beautiful headpieces made of bird feathers, beads, and fur, as well as buckskin dresses and tunics with elaborately woven patterns of beads and conches. Most of them wore matching moccasins with incredible designs made, again, of beads.

As they made their way down the street, they stopped periodically to perform a round of dancing. Most of the young women, and some of the men, wore their long black hair plaited and intertwined with beaded hair ornaments.

Following the Native Americans, a mounted group of the Fremont County Search and Rescue corps rode by. One of the riders pulled a heavy-duty gurney used for rescues from inaccessible places, as well as the ropes and pulleys required for such an endeavor. Then several decorated floats depicting life on the frontier, the Wyoming Beef Growers, and a local church group passed before them.

A lone horseman came into view next, leading a packhorse loaded with camping supplies.

Dana was clapping along with those around them when she took a second look at the person riding the lead horse. Large, dressed as a mountain man in a leather shirt, with a rifle sling hung over his right shoulder, leaving both arms free, he wore an outback hat with an eagle feather stuck in the band. He held the reins loosely in his left hand as he gazed around at those watching the parade. Something in the way he carried himself as he waved to the crowd caught Dana's attention.

She tugged on Jax's arm. "That's the guy who was trying to dig out the foxes," she hissed.

"You sure? No doubt, that's Leon Archileta."

Just as he passed in front of them, some thirty feet away, the man spied Dana and directed his right pointer finger at her as if he were cocking a pistol.

Jax felt Dana go rigid beside him.

"What the hell was that all about?"

Dana looked beyond Jax to see if Jed had noticed anything but he was deep in conversation with another man seated on the far side of him and probably hadn't seen the gesture.

"You okay?"

"I just don't ever want to cross his path again."

Dana tried to absorb herself in the festive attitude of the people on the street around her as she watched other Indian units and children's groups process before them. Her mind kept returning, however, to the silly gesture Leon Archileta had made, as if pointing a gun at her. How had he picked her out of the crowd? Certainly, they had a front-row view of the parade, but there were others sitting on the curb in front of them so it wasn't like they stood out.

As the parade wound down with the usual display of firefighting trucks tooting and the crowd beginning to disperse, Jed gave Jax a broad smile. "Well, that's another one under my belt, but the day's not complete till we have some barbecue. Lead the way, lad."

Jax gathered up their folding chairs and Dana carried the umbrella, as they negotiated their way along the sidewalk through the throng of people. Jed's motorized wheelchair ground along between them. The smell of spiced cooking meat wafted through the air, luring them toward the enticing aroma.

Neither Dana nor Jax mentioned to Jed the obscene gesture Archileta had made toward her during the parade.

They came to a side street that was completely blocked off to traffic and filled instead with food vendors offering everything from BBQ ribs to Indian tacos and fried bread, burgers and hotdogs, ice cream, and a wide variety of side dishes. Tables and chairs lined one whole side of the street.

Jax got Jed and Dana seated then made a quick trip to his truck to stow the items he had brought, instructing both of them to think about what they wanted to eat. When he returned, Jax and Dana strode along the various vendors, getting barbecue for Jed, an Indian taco for Dana, and a burger and fries for himself, along with cold beers for all three of them.

Dana had noticed from the moment she awoke that morning the occasional round of firecrackers, though mostly in the distance. However, once they had their food and began to eat, that all changed. In the alley that bisected the street where they were sitting, groups of young boys were occupied with placing small packages of firecrackers under tin cans, lighting the stems and watching with glee as the cans flew into the air when the crackers exploded.

"Damn city council," muttered Jed. "Don't know why they allow fireworks here in town."

"They're loud, but look how much fun the kids are having," offered Dana, watching the youths in the alley.

"Lander may be one of the last hold-outs for fireworks," said Jax. "Most towns find them too much of a fire risk, but the sale of fireworks is actually encouraged here. Several stands around town sell all kinds of pyrotechnics. It draws people in from other towns."

"At least the fire department should be geared up," muttered Jed, reflecting on the string of equipment on show at the end of the parade.

"It didn't seem to be that much of a problem in the past," recalled Dana. "As kids, my siblings and our cousins used to have bottle rocket battles each Fourth, with several of us hiding behind bunkers of some kind and actually aiming at each other. Of course, we came inside afterwards with our clothing riddled with burned spots."

"You don't even want me to get started on the things some of my crazy friends and I did with firecrackers back in the day," said Jax.

"Like blowing up the old outhouse?" suggested Jed as the two men shared a chuckle.

"Unc, you know you're the one who instigated that little caper. I seem to recall you said it was going to be torn down anyhow."

"Yep, that's true. Just remember, we had no trouble finding kindling wood that winter when we wanted to start the fireplace. Of course, it was probably more work than it was worth, picking up all those pieces of splintered wood."

"Which you made sure we picked up and stacked so it was easy for you to get to," said Jax, poking his own chest.

"Hey, Day-na!"

She recognized a familiar voice and turned to see Edeen from the clean-up crew and a couple of other young Indian men approaching their table.

"Hi, Edeen, you enjoying the day?"

"Wouldn't miss the parade. Did you see us in the Indian dancers?"

"No, I didn't," she admitted guiltily. "Had I known you were going to be in it I would have paid more attention."

"Probably because of our headgear. You're not used to seeing me in a war bonnet or a tail sheath. We just changed," he said, noting the look on Dana's face.

"I'm familiar with war bonnets and headbands, but I'm not sure what a tail sheath is."

"It's another head dress. It used to be worn into battle and for dancing. It's smaller and usually falls farther down the back," Edeen explained, turning to demonstrate how far down his back one might fall.

"Your clothing is very colorful."

"Our grandmothers make our dance costumes. By the way, did you see the ol' mountain man?"

Dana didn't realize who he was referring to until she recalled that he and Adam had referred to Leon Archileta as such. She glanced at Jax to see if he had heard what the young man had said. Jed was still complaining about the firecrackers to the couple sitting across the table from him.

"Yes, actually I did recognize him."

"Surprised he's not up in the canyon doing his usual thing."

Jax had been listening to their conversation and interjected.

"I take it you've come across him out on the trail?"

"Jus' what I told Day-na a while back," replied Edeen, looking around anxiously. "He comes and goes a lot."

Hmmm. The question seemed to make Edeen uneasy, Dana noted.

She sensed that he was sorry he had mentioned Archileta. She recalled the last time she had talked to the guys on the clean-up crew. They had been hesitant to say much about the mountain man then, too. But what had he meant by "doing his usual thing"?

"We need to get goin," the young man told Dana. "Just wanted to say hi."

"Good to see you, Edeen."

The three young men disappeared into the crowd.

"That ended rather abruptly," said Jax. "Guess I shouldn't have asked him anything."

"It's not you. I thought he seemed a little nervous, talking about Archileta's comings and goings. I wish he had said more."

"I'm thinking it's time to get moving," said Jed, as he reached for his hat and replaced it on his head. Clouds had hid the sun that had been beating down earlier. As they were finishing their food a loud clap of thunder boomed overhead.

"Doesn't bode well for the rodeo," Jax said as he began gathering up their paper plates and napkins to dump in a nearby trash receptacle. "Glad we decided not to go, Unc."

"Just our usual afternoon shower, I hope," said Dana.

"Uumph."

***

The storm that had threatened earlier moved on, leaving very little moisture. As Jed put it, the amount of rain wasn't enough to make an earthworm curious. Back at Jed's after their downtown lunch, they relaxed in the coolness on his large patio.

"What did you think of the parade, Unc?"

"Same old, same old," Jed responded. "Don't know why I bother to go anymore. They trot out the same danged things every year."

Across the table from each other, Dana and Jax chuckled quietly.

Jed's housekeeper, Hildy Gullickson, brought out snacks and cool drinks for them to enjoy and set them on the table.

"Dana, have you met Unc's housekeeper?"

"I haven't."

Hildy was a tall, stout, no-nonsense woman with frizzled salt and pepper hair. She was dressed in denim culottes, a cotton blouse, and neon green Croc shoes. The stature, looks, and mannerisms of Hildy reminded Dana of her own German grandmother, who had been so instrumental in her life.

The two women smiled and nodded at each other.

"And for you, Mr. Jax, I made your favorite caramel brownies," she said, setting a plate of delectable-looking goodies on the table and nudging them toward Jax.

"Got any of them dill pickle potato chips?" asked Jed, grinning up at Hildy.

She stood with her hands on her hips, glaring down at him. "You know what the doctor said about your salt intake, Jed."

"Yeah, but this is a special occasion."

"Unc, you better heed what Hildy says," Jax warned. He turned to Dana. "Hildy is an ex-policewoman from Los Angeles and was known to be a pretty tough cop in her day. Plus, she apparently won some awards for her marksmanship abilities."

Hildy tossed her head and went back inside, grumbling.

"You probably don't want to cross her then, Dr. Ahrens," said Dana. "How did she get to this part of the country?"

"Think she has family here, a daughter maybe," said Jax. "Isn't that right, Unc?"

"Uumph."

Minutes later, Hildy returned with a bowl of Jed's favorite chips.

Jed winked at her as she tidied up the table of napkins and crumbs and left them to resume their conversation.

"Jax tells me he showed you the Sinks," said Jed.

Dana nodded. "We saw all of it, including the Rise. I was impressed by the size of the fish in that pond."

"Oh, yeah," responded Jed, as if people speaking of the fish was common to him. "There seems to be some mystery about that grotto where the Sinks go underground."

Jax, who had been tilted back on his chair with an ankle over the opposite knee, abruptly put both feet on the floor and sat up straight. "You got me hooked, Unc. What kind of mystery?"

Jed rolled his head to one side, as if trying to recall some facts. "There have been a couple people who have disappeared from Lander and the area surrounding the canyon."

"Just recently?" asked Dana.

"No, no, nothing recent, I'd say over the last twenty-five to thirty years. Some think it's possible the victims were done in and their bodies disposed of in the sink hole where the river goes underground."

Jax looked at his uncle with curiosity. "You're kidding, right?"

"I'm not kidding, I'm just saying."

Dana frowned. "But from what Jax told me, the water breaks up into very small rivulets once it goes subterranean."

"That's what we've been told, but to my knowledge nobody has been able to penetrate the waterway far enough to be sure."

"If such a thing has happened, I'd think there would be some way to determine if there is a body or bodies in there," said Jax, "especially when the water recedes by late summer."

Dana cringed at the thought.

"Of course, it's all speculation," Jed conceded. "Some have even suggested the bodies could have been, you know, dismembered before being disposed of in there."

"I think it's idle gossip, Unc," said Jax, resuming his relaxed position, with his right leg hitched up and his ankle resting on his left knee.

"Crazier things have happened. If those folks who've gone missing haven't been found, where do you reckon they are?" Jed posed.

"Maybe they wanted to become missing," suggested Jax. "You know, like, become anonymous."

"You mean like starting a new life elsewhere or with someone else?" asked Dana.

"Sure. I don't think it's that unusual."

"Uumph."

"Or, in deeply forested areas, like up on the mountain, I can imagine people could dispose of somebody they had killed by burying them up there or pushing them into deep ravines. Their bodies might not be found for years," Dana offered. "Not that I'm thinking of doing anyone in," she added quickly, as the expressions on both their faces turned to surprise.

"Besides," said Jax, "stuffing parts of a body into the Sinks would be too gruesome."

"I can imagine the reaction if a deceased's foot or something suddenly showed up in the pond with the trout," said Jed.

"Now that would get the gossip going," Jax agreed, winking at Dana.

Jed's facial expression remained staunchly serious and it was evident to Dana that he firmly believed the hearsay about the Sinks. Recognizing her respect for the geologist's knowledge of local lore, a slight shiver ran up her back at the idea that people could actually have been disposed of in such a manner.

"Say, are you two going to take in the street dance this evening?" asked Jed suddenly.

Dana and Jax exchanged a look.

"Haven't talked about that yet, Unc."

"Well, maybe you should," said Jed, with a sly look at the pair of them.

Street dance? Dana had seen something in the list of festivities to be held on the Fourth but hadn't given it a second thought.

"Are you inclined to go, Unc?"

"I think not," Jed said, in an affronted tone.

The topic of conversation moved on by mutual agreement. By the time Dana and Jax left in the early evening, however, Jed remained fixed in his opinion that the Sinks had not given up all of its secrets.

CHAPTER 24

As they drove down the lane away from Jed's place, Jax shot Dana a look. "So, what do you think? Want to check out the street dance? They always have a couple of pretty good bands. There will also be some nice fireworks after dark."

"Is it actually held downtown?"

"Yep, in the same area where we had lunch."

Dana's first thought was, *What if we go and run into Jeremy? Or Leon Archileta?* And then her saner self gained control. So what if they did? There would be others there, and Jax would be close by. She could handle either of them.

"Sure, sounds like fun," she told him.

"Hope you don't think Unc's mind is starting to wander," said Jax, "what, with all that talk about people's bodies being stashed in the Sinks."

"I take it you hadn't heard anything about that before."

"I imagine Unc and some of his old cronies got to talking and one thing led to another."

"You think it's a case of 'I can tell one better than yours'?"

"Wouldn't be surprised."

"It's awful to think of such a thing happening. In any case, your uncle is pretty sharp. I find it hard to think he would pass on idle chit-chat."

"I know," said Jax pensively.

They rode in silence the rest of the way back into town, each trying to make sense of Jed's conjecture.

***

Jax found a parking space two blocks from the site of the street dance and they joined others moving along the sidewalk in the same direction. Many of them were dressed in brightly colored shirts, jeans, boots, and, in many cases, cowboy hats, having apparently attended the rodeo, which had just finished. As they neared the roped-off area, the sounds of a western band warming up could be heard.

They arrived at the site for the event and saw that several couples were already romping around in the street below the stage. Others were standing on the perimeter, clapping, hooting, and cheering. Several of the food vendors were still in business, and several new beer stations had opened up.

Jax and Dana made the rounds of all the stands before picking out a table at the edge of all the activity. They had just got seated when Stubby King and a short woman built much the same as him strolled up to them. Stubby's lady friend was dressed in a knee-length bouffant skirt, a coordinating blouse, and strapped slippers. Stubby's shirt was of the same fabric as her skirt, and he wore jeans cinched around his waist with a belt and a large buckle depicting a long-horned steer's head.

"Hey, Stub, how was the rodeo?" asked Jax, standing and shaking hands with his foreman.

"Wild, like always."

Jax turned to Dana. "You remember Elton? And this is his wife, Teresa."

"I do remember you," she said, smiling at Stubby. "Good to meet you, Teresa."

"Have a seat," suggested Jax.

Stubby and Teresa looked at each other and slid into seats on the opposite side of the table.

"Yeah, the bull riding had some wild stock," said Stubby. "One of the riders got thrown into the fence but he was up and walking around in a few minutes, so I guess he was okay."

"Think that was one of the Tarkington boys, wasn't it?" offered Teresa.

"Yep, one of the local ranchers," added Stubby. "Those guys cut their teeth on horses and wrangling cattle so it's pretty regular stuff for them."

"I noticed your belt buckle," said Dana. "Did you do some rodeoing?"

Stubby looked down at his buckle and rubbed it. "Matter of fact, I did. I've ridden a few mean bulls in my day. Traveled the circuit for a few years all the way down to Texas and up to Calgary and a lot of places in between. 'Course that was a few years ago."

"That's how we met," said Teresa, giving Stubby a lingering look. "I was a barrel racer and we ran into each other at one of these street dances. He was such a bashful guy; it took me quite a while to get him to ask me to dance."

"Now, Teresa," Stubby chided, as if downplaying what she had just said.

"Stubby, shy?" said Jax, blinking his eyelashes. "That's a hard one to believe."

Stubby smiled broadly as he ran his hand over his bristly hair. "I just do the best I can."

Jax chuckled. "Did you see the parade this morning?"

"We were standin' up by the bank. Lots of kids chasin' the candy," Stubby said.

"Including you," his wife said, with a whimsical smile on her face.

"Hey, did ya see ole Leon?" asked Stubby.

Dana and Jax shared a questioning glance. "We did," Dana said, remembering the eerie feeling she had had that morning as she saw Leon Archileta ride by.

"How did that guy happen to get a job on our project?" asked Jax.

"Not sure. I've never worked with him before. Know he's from somewhere in Idaho, lined up by the general contractor. Heard some talk he might have been associated with one of the Aryan Nation groups at one time."

"I thought those radicals had been pretty much brought under control."

"Suppose they have, but there're always holdouts."

"They prefer to live off the land in isolated places, don't they?" asked Dana.

"Wouldn't be surprised."

As they sat chatting, the acts on the stage changed and a group of fiddlers, a base viol, and a tall, rangy speaker with a deep, melodious voice took over.

"Okay, all you hoe-downers, grab your favorite filly and git over here."

"That would be us," said Teresa, sliding out of her seat and motioning to Stubby.

"See you folks later," said Stubby, following his wife away from the tables and over to where squares of four dancers were forming.

Many of the ladies were dressed similarly to Teresa in knee-length, flouncing skirts, with numerous multi-colored petticoats. The tall man on the stage, known as a cuer began calling over the sound system, "bow to your partner, bow to your gal," and the dancers began swinging their partners, as they followed the cuer's directions, then exchanging partners as the square dance proceeded.

"Cute couple," said Dana, as they watched Stubby and Teresa move through the dance steps.

"Never would have envisioned Stub dancing."

"Or riding a bull."

"Oh, that kind of makes more sense than him dancing."

"What do you make of the thought that Leon Archileta was or may still be associated with one of the Aryan Nation groups?" Dana asked in a low voice.

"It kind of fits his actions, but I think we need to let the police check him out. Being an Aryan isn't a crime, unless a crime is committed. But, having said that, I think his gesture during the parade was completely unwarranted."

"It still makes me shiver."

After several sets, Stubby and Teresa returned to their seats, both of them huffing and Teresa waving a handkerchief in front of her face, creating a soft breeze.

Although the street was well lit, they were aware that the sun had gone down and darkness was settling in around them. Several of the younger attendees were beginning to feel their spirits, joking, laughing, and dancing, even though the music of the hoe-downers had ended.

The original band returned to the stage and began playing a popular upbeat country tune. Jax caught Dana's attention by raising his eyebrows in a quizzical expression. He reached out a hand to her and they left their seats and walked toward the dance floor.

Jax led her through an upbeat two-step, with an occasional dip and interlocked arms that put them back-to-back and side to side, as he twirled her around amongst the other dancers. They were both laughing helplessly as that particular piece ended and segued into a slow rendition of "Keeper of the Stars," made popular by Tracy Byrd. Jax pulled Dana close and she placed one hand on his shoulder as he took her other hand in his. She raised her head slightly as he held her gaze with his eyes.

Gradually, Jax let go of her hand and encircled her body with both his arms. Slowly, both of her hands crept up over his shoulders and locked behind his neck. They glided fluidly through the crowded dancers and were still swaying slightly long after the music had ended. Then Jax placed a hand on each side of her face and kissed her lightly on the lips.

As if on cue, the street lights went dark and with a loud boom, a large blossom of red, white, and blue pyrotechnics burst high overhead and slowly dispersed, followed closely by a splash of green, another of yellow and white, and on and on.

Dana looked around at the people sitting at the tables and standing around the perimeter, some cheering roundly, their faces filled with rapture and delight, others ignoring the fireworks and deeply engaged in conversation. Then she looked over at their table and saw Teresa leaning into Stubby's shoulder as he slipped his arm around her. She smiled softly and slipped her own arm around Jax's waist.

Chapter 25

Officer Morgan of the Lander Police Department called Dana on Tuesday afternoon to see if she had an address for Jeremy in Laramie or anywhere else he might have lived. She reiterated that since he had left her apartment two years before she had no idea where he had lived. He told her the police were following up on both names she had given them but there was nothing new to report. Likewise, there were no results yet on the cigarette butt.

The thought crossed Dana's mind to tell Officer Morgan of the gesture Archileta had made toward her during the parade the day before. Would he think she was paranoid? But Jax could corroborate what had happened? She convinced herself to let it pass, and to avoid any future contact with the man.

***

The headline in the Lander newspaper on Wednesday afternoon read, "LOCAL GAME WARDEN'S DEATH A PROBABLE HOMICIDE." Dana sank onto one end of the sofa as she unfolded the paper and read the story.

"Officials have released the findings of an autopsy done on Trig Henderson, Fremont County game warden, whose body was found on June 14th along the path to the falls in Sinks Canyon. The autopsy performed by doctors in a facility in Longmont, Colorado, showed blunt-force trauma by a sharp instrument that had fractured his skull plus a gunshot in his upper back. Authorities do not believe the warden sustained life-threatening injuries from the fall he evidently took from a rock approximately twelve feet in height. Warden Henderson's death is being investigated by the Fremont County Sheriff's Department."

Dana frowned as she read the account, then she put the paper aside as she absorbed the information she had just read. From the results of the autopsy, there wasn't much doubt that the warden had been murdered. How was that possible? That kind of thing didn't happen in an extraordinary place like Sinks Canyon, where hikers, families, young children, teenagers, a whole cross-section of people, spent time enjoying the beauty of the region. And yet Jed seemed to think people did die and disappear from the area.

Why? Why would someone kill the warden? He had seemed like a friendly, outgoing, caring man. True, she had only spoken with him once but he had seemed knowledgeable, well acquainted with his area of responsibility and, according to others she had spoken with, was well liked in the district. Did someone have a grudge against him? She knew it wasn't always easy enforcing game and fish regulations. But to kill an officer?

Dana spent several minutes thinking about the game warden and the family he had left behind, upsetting thoughts that distracted her mind from her own troubles. Eventually, however, while acknowledging it was a stretch of the imagination, she wondered again if the strange occurrences in her own life could in any way be linked with the warden's death.

If Jeremy was involved in her recent mishaps, though, she could think of nothing that linked him with the game warden.

The niggling feeling that there was a connection between all the bizarre happenings of the past few weeks—the man digging out the fox kits, the keying of her car, the eerie feeling of being watched the day she was at the falls, the dead skunk on her doorstep, the mutilated body of the buck deer, and the realization that someone had been inside her apartment—wouldn't go away. They had to be related. They wouldn't let her mind rest.

Her thoughts were interrupted by her cell phone's familiar jingle.

"Any more suspicious craziness happening in your life?" asked Arnie Watt.

"Hi, Arnie."

"I wanted to let you know that I checked on Jeremy."

Dana held her breath, not knowing what to expect.

"Seems he was arrested for DUI about ten months ago. He was involved in an accident that caused bodily damage to another person but the case was thrown out when it was discovered the other person had alcohol in his blood, too."

"Did this happen in Laramie?"

"No, down in Fort Collins, Colorado."

"Is that where he is now? Fort Collins?"

"Nobody seems to know. I talked to the police department down there and he's disappeared off their radar."

"So he could be anywhere."

"If you haven't actually seen him, Dana, I doubt he's your trouble-maker."

"Well, that's the thing. I think I did see him one day when I was downtown."

"That's a different breed of cat, then." Arnie was quiet for a moment. "You just think you saw him? If you're not sure, and he hasn't approached you directly, I kind of doubt it."

Was he just trying to make her feel better or did he know something he wasn't saying?

"Oh, and Arnie, I did get the police involved in some of the things that have happened and they're checking into Jeremy and the guy I stopped from digging out the fox kits."

"You know his name?"

"Yes. He's a sub-contractor on the new hospital extension here in town."

"Be sure to keep me posted. How's your project coming?"

"Good. I've found several pockets of my plants and am beginning to build a case for the relationship between the minerals in some varieties of rocks and the *dicentra*. Many of them are in the final stages of blooming, so I'm watching them closely."

"By the way, I've got you scheduled for your final exams in mid-April. The actual date may change by the time we get into the spring semester."

"That sounds fine. Will there still be a panel of three?"

"As far as I know. I'll be interested to see how long your plants last after they finish blooming."

"Me, too. Hey, thanks for checking on Jeremy, Arnie."

After speaking with Arnie, Dana felt more confused than ever. If Jeremy was in the area and still held a grudge, she could imagine him doing the skunk, entering her apartment, and maybe even scratching her car. But what had he hoped to accomplish by breaking into her home? Just to let her know he had been there? Several of the incidents had been so personal, and Jeremy had made that promise... Why hadn't he shown his face? Why hadn't he confronted her one-on-one as Arnie would have expected him to?

If it wasn't Jeremy, was it someone she didn't even know? Was Leon Archileta behind it all? And if so, why did Archileta have a grudge against her? Because she had stopped him from digging out the foxes? A strange sensation zipped up her spine as she recalled the threatening gesture he had made toward her at the parade on the Fourth.

The foxes were still in their burrow. She had seen them just a couple of days ago. He hadn't returned another time when she wasn't around and completed what he had started. Probably because he knew she'd report him to the authorities if the animals went missing. But how many other creatures had he been successful in trapping?

Taking that train of thought one step further, one colossal step farther, Dana began to conjecture that Archileta might also have been responsible for the game warden's death. Surely not... It was one thing to harass her, possibly even cause physical damage to her car, but to kill a game warden?

Now she remembered that he had made some comment, that day at the fox den, about *the interfering game warden*. Yet she had a difficult time accepting the two incidents could be related. Was it possible she had two, or more, unstable people ticked off at her?

Dana picked up her keys and her small over-the-shoulder handbag, stuck her cell phone inside, and locked her front door with the new security device Aberdeen had had installed following the break-in.

***

Jax had left for a quick trip to Denver that morning to consult with an HVAC supplier and planned on returning the following evening. He had warned Dana to be extra vigilant, especially if she was out on the trail, and to call the police if she saw or sensed anything out of the ordinary.

In her car, Dana turned off South Fourth Street onto Main and turned up the street, heading for the hospital and the construction site. Jax had told her Leon Archileta was doing the masonry work on the remodeling project and worked around the regular crews mostly on weekends and evenings.

If the man was a mason, didn't that explain why he was up in the canyon so much? Perhaps he had found a place higher up on the mountain where he could mine the rocks he used in his work on the hospital project. That would be reason enough for him to take two horses on his excursions into the upper areas. But then, she reflected, it was probably illegal to quarry up there.

When she had left the trailhead parking lot earlier that afternoon, Archileta's rig wasn't there. It was approaching 6:00 p.m., and Dana reasoned the regular crews would be finished for the day. It was possible he could be at work on the extension.

What she really wanted was to talk to Stubby. After failed attempts to reach him by phone, her hope was that Stubby might still be at the construction site so that she could quiz him privately about Leon Archileta and find out why he took horses into the high country.

Dana had resolved to give Archileta a wide berth and had planned on just driving to the hospital to see if Stubby was still there. She slowed her Honda to a crawl as she approached the hospital complex. Her eyes scanned the parking area off to the west side, searching for the blue pickup-camper. Not seeing it, at the last moment she turned into the construction site lot.

Stubby's pickup wasn't in the parking area either. In fact, there were no other vehicles at all and the whole construction site appeared to be deserted. Dana sat for a few moments, tapping her forefinger on her steering wheel, before driving slowly forward a few feet and parking on the outer fringes of the workers' parking lot. Maybe Stubby had parked somewhere out of sight. She left her vehicle, cautiously walking parallel to the small grove of cottonwood trees. The only sound was the chirping of birds as they flitted back and forth between scrub bushes at the back of the site and their nests in the cottonwoods.

Additional construction materials had been moved nearer the trees and stacked since she had been there several days earlier with Jax. The new extension had progressed considerably since then as well. The steel frame was now enclosed on three sides and was beginning to take shape. Two large concrete supports had also materialized to handle the weight of the planned second story.

Stubby's pickup was nowhere to be seen. As Dana walked closer to the building, the peacefulness of the place was disturbed. She could hear a faint chipping sound coming from inside the structure. Thinking it was a flicker, she stopped and listened intently. The birds were known to peck away at any object that would sharpen their beaks. There was no evidence of anyone else at the site so what else could be causing the noise? She moved past several tall stacks of brick, pausing every few steps to listen again.

A flash of color between two of the pallets caught Dana's attention. She peered around the stack of bricks and gasped. Archileta's blue pickup was parked under the cottonwoods, just twenty feet away. The camper had been parked at an angle behind the stacked supplies, which explained why she hadn't seen it from the parking lot. She took a couple steps backward then stopped again and listened. The chipping sound continued. It seemed possible Archileta was inside the hospital extension doing some masonry work.

Dana moved back up to the plastic-wrapped stack of bricks and slowly peeked around it again. The back door of the camper was open, with the step-down extending out. Was Archileta inside the camper or working on the project? She listened closely, but could discern no sound coming from the camper. Her jumbled mind was telling her it was madness to be anywhere near where Archileta might be, but what if she could find evidence that he had some illegal poaching operation going on?

Jax had said Archileta kept his horses at another location, and the horse trailer didn't seem to be on the site. If the man was trapping animals or, even worse, taking trophy heads, would there be evidence of that in the camper? Most likely not. Dana's hunch was that he wouldn't be stupid enough to have them in his possession at this work site, especially since the police had been around more than once since the robbery.

She listened cautiously again. Hearing no sound from the camper, she approached the open door and very cautiously peered inside. She could still hear the chipping sound coming from across the parking lot. She caught the scent of fried meat and paused for a moment, then climbed onto the step and up into the vehicle.

Dana found herself in a compact space, with miniature appliances arranged in one corner and a two-seater table occupying another. There was a small closet just inside the door. She eased the closet door open and found it was jammed full of clothing, mostly on hangers, but some articles stuffed on a shelf above.

The table was strewn with paper. There were small pieces with notes on them, full-size sheets with printed matter, magazines turned inside out and left where the occupant had stopped reading. On one corner of the table sat a plastic plate with the remains of a recent meal, the fork and knife hanging over the edge of the rim.

On the two-burner cook-top was a skillet with a thick rime of fat and crackling covering the bottom. The sink was filled with mud-encrusted, metal work tools.

At the back was a single bed with storage drawers underneath and, above that, a three-quarter sized bed that extended over the cab. The smaller bed was covered with yet more publications, books, a roll of butcher-block paper, and hunting supply catalogs. She flipped quickly through a couple of them, trying not to disturb the order in which she found them. Thankfully, there were no animal parts visible anywhere.

Dana scanned the papers spread over the top of the table, but nothing stood out. There were numerous outdoor publications, and something on taxidermy. *Wait.* Taxidermy? Why was he interested in taxidermy? Unless he was gathering information on how to do it. Or maybe he was looking for places to sell taxidermy items?

She could see nothing to implicate Archileta in any wrongdoing. She put her hand to her forehead as if attempting to gain a clearer understanding of her own aberrant behavior. She turned around, looking for anything in the small space that might give her a clue as to what the man's interest in the canyon could be. Dare she open any of the drawers to see what they might hold?

Suddenly, she realized she could no longer hear the chipping noise from the construction site. She moved back to the doorway and saw Archileta brushing off the sleeves of his green canvas shirt as he walked across the parking lot towards the camper.

Heart beating wildly, Dana immediately darted down the steps of the camper and slipped around the corner of the vehicle, where she crouched, holding her breath.

The man's footsteps crunched over the gravel as he strode purposefully nearer. Then the footsteps suddenly paused and there was a short silence before they resumed in a new direction. Dana was close to the front fender and risked a look. Archileta was now walking toward the outer parking lot and her Honda. Dana ducked down behind the front of the camper and peered past the rim. She saw Archileta walk right round her car, then bend to look inside. He even tried the driver's side door, only to find it locked.

Dana retreated quickly from the camper and into the trees behind her. Once concealed by the foliage she moved swiftly between the huge cottonwood trees until she had removed herself some distance from Archileta's campsite. Finally she reached the street that ran by the hospital and she took a deep breath before she started walking openly up the sidewalk toward her parked vehicle.

Archileta was leaning with his back against the front of her SUV, gazing first in one direction and then another as if trying to see where the owner might be.

Dana approached casually, as if coming back from a leisurely walk. Her insides were in a tangle, but she made an attempt to appear cool and unflustered.

"Were you looking for me?" she called out as she came nearer.

Archileta whirled around. Then he raised the index finger of his right hand and wagged it at her. "Just what do you think you're doing here?"

Dana lifted her shoulders in a shrug. "Walking."

Archileta's eyes narrowed. "Quite the coincidence, you decidin' to walk around my place of work. Would have thought you got enough exercise on the trail."

"It's a nice, quiet street. I enjoy it here." She folded her arms over her chest. "The work I do up off the trail is beside the point." Her mind was racing, trying to figure out how she could get into her car and speed out of the parking lot. "I'd appreciate it if you'd remove yourself from my car," she said curtly, stepping toward the driver's door.

"What's wrong with walkin' your own neighborhood, anyhow?"

"What would you know about my neighborhood?" she asked. "Unless you've been there?"

Archileta stood upright. A low whistle escaped through his teeth, his sunburned face turned a deeper shade of orange, and his hands clenched at his sides as if he was holding in his fury. He moved a couple of steps toward Dana and she thought for a moment he was going to shove her. But then he seemed to think better of it.

"Git in your car and git out of here, Missy," he said, through gritted teeth. He turned and stalked a few feet away, then gave her a parting glare before continuing in the direction of his camper.

Dana removed her keys from her pocket, clicked the door open, slid inside, and locked the doors. Now that she was in her car and he was walking away, she found she was shaking. She started the Honda, backed out of the lot, and drove slowly out onto the street. After a couple of blocks she pulled over to the curb. She gripped the steering wheel as waves of emotion and shakiness washed over her.

What had she been thinking by getting out of her car in the first place, let alone going into his camper? What if he had come back while she was still inside? She could only imagine what might have happened. And what had possessed her to say anything about the possibility of his being in her neighborhood?

Slowly she calmed down. Her jingling nerves somewhat composed, she shifted the car back into drive and drove past the hospital out to Main Street. Fearing what she might see, she checked her rear view mirror every few seconds to make sure he wasn't following her.

CHAPTER 26

That night, once again, sleep was a long time coming and then only fitfully. Before going to bed, Dana made sure all the windows were secure and that the front door was locked, with the security chain in place.

She couldn't get the insanity of her foray into Archileta's camper out of her mind. She kept telling herself that had she seen the camper as she drove by the hospital she would never have driven onto the construction site in the first place. But it had been concealed by the stacks of brick and parked in such a way that it was impossible to see from the street. With horror, she kept seeing herself approaching the small RV and then actually stepping up into it.

It took her jumbled memory some time to remember all the contents of the camper in detail. If only she had thought to take a closer look at the taxidermy publications. She had seen nothing to do with Aryan Nations, but didn't know what that might entail anyway. What was the roll of butcher-block paper for? The only thing she could think of was to wrap meat in. Or bones? Or animal parts, such as a buck deer head?

Dana turned over onto her other side and looked at the digital clock on her nightstand. It was 1:30 a.m. and sleep still eluded her, even with Flag cuddled against one of her legs.

She realized she hadn't given the tools in the small sink much attention, assuming they were masonry implements. But now that she re-visualized what she had seen, she remembered there had been a small, jagged-tooth saw, an ugly pair of clippers similar to what gardeners and landscapers use, and, now that she thought about it, a knife with a serrated edge. They didn't look like the sort of tools a mason would normally use. Perhaps they had a more nefarious purpose…

The comment Archileta had made when she returned to her car after flitting through the cottonwood trees, about why she didn't walk in her own neighborhood, still concerned her. It may have been a stab-in-the-dark comment but it suggested he knew where she lived. And how had he found that out? Had he followed her home at some point? If he knew where she lived, then it seemed he was the most likely person to have entered her apartment and left the cigarette butt in her plant. But she hadn't seen Archileta smoke. On the other hand, she knew Jeremy definitely did.

But she still had no evidence for anything. What if it was all her wild imagination? There was still the possibility that Archileta was simply an eccentric bird. Jeremy could be lurking in the shadows, or he could be hundreds of miles away.

The last time Dana checked the clock, it was going on 3:00 a.m. Then, finally, she slept, not awakening until after 8:00 the next morning.

***

Dana yawned wearily as she padded out to the kitchen in her bare feet to start coffee. As the coffee machine went through the motions, she fixed two pieces of many-grained toast before she puttered from the kitchenette to the living area to catch the news. After her restless night, it took two full cups of high-octane coffee to get her moving. It took a bit longer to get her walking-legs under her, not least because she was still in a state of shock after her run-in with Leon Archileta the previous evening.

She took comfort in the fact that Officer Morgan appeared to be following up on the information she had given him and hoped he would soon be able to bring relief from her qualms.

If all went well, within the next two weeks, she could wind up her field research and begin the process of giving her thesis some organization. She was beginning to look forward to being gone from Lander and away from all the drama. She knew that once she was back on campus in August, the semester would be upon her, full of graduate-level courses and a practicum with a botanical garden in Cheyenne. Following Christmas break, the spring semester would include a continuation of her internship at the garden and the final two courses in her curriculum, plus the presentation and testing of her thesis.

She believed Arnie Watt had prepared her well for what would be expected in the spring, and those thoughts encouraged her to look forward to the final days of her research.

∗∗∗

Dana's plan was to make yet another trek along the trail. She had taken good notes as to where to leave the main path to revisit each of the specimens she had found. Jed Ahrens had encouraged her to photograph the rocks and even to bring him samples, so that he could evaluate them to see if his results matched any of the data she had accumulated.

So, on this Thursday morning, her thought was to document specifically the kind of rock one of the more robust clusters of *dicentra* had been growing near.

By 11:00 a.m. she was above the trail, crouched on the ground near a large mass of her plants. She was attempting to get a different perspective on the plant itself and the large boulder it grew near. At one time, based on the proximity of yellow yarrow she had found growing within feet of her variety in a couple of areas, she had even considered that perhaps the two plants exchanged root nourishment and thrived in proximity to each other. She had also discovered in one of her internet searches that yarrow had some of the same healing qualities as her *dicentra*. But as she found further specimens, they weren't necessarily accompanied by yarrow nearby.

Her "to do" list of "matters to research" before leaving behind her field studies was growing as she added a big question mark regarding the relationship, if any, between the two species.

Dana knew she was breaking one of the cardinal rules of not removing anything from the park. Nevertheless, she selected three peach-sized, different stones in the immediate vicinity of the plants she was studying and slipped them into one of the side pockets of her backpack. One had obviously calved off the huge boulder that offered protection for her plant but she wasn't sure about the other two. She took several photos of the larger rock itself, and the *dicentra*, in addition to several similar smaller rocks nearby. She wanted Jed Ahrens to see the actual setting for her plants.

Standing to look farther afield and to stretch, she looked up the valley and tried to pinpoint where another cluster of her plants was growing. On hearing the sound of a hiker's boots crunching over the rocky surface below her, she pivoted on her heel, surprised as she hadn't noticed anyone on the hillside as she worked.

"Well, if it isn't Miz Nosy Parker."

Leon Archileta was standing not ten feet from her, with a sneer on his sunburned face. Dana felt as if her heart was flipping over in her chest at his close proximity. In his right hand he held the unfolded shovel she had seen him with earlier in the summer when he was attempting to dig out the fox kits.

"What are you talking about? I don't appreciate you following me."

"I'd say you're more likely in the wrong place at the wrong time, aren't you, Missy?"

Dana chose not to respond. Instead she leaned over to pick up her backpack and placed her camera inside. Beside the fact he was confronting her openly and had scared her by his presence, she had no way of knowing what he had in mind. The fact that Archileta was on the trail today meant she would have to delay her plans to visit the other plants, but that felt like a trivial inconvenience just at that moment.

He advanced a step up the incline. Dana edged to her left to make room for him, thinking he intended to climb farther up the hill past her.

"Not so fast, Missy," he said, leering and taking another large stride toward her. "You're not gonna git away as easy this time."

What was with the "Missy this" and the "Missy that"?

Archileta came even closer, looming over her and blocking her way past him. He stared at her, evidently awaiting her next move.

Dana irresolutely clutched her backpack by one strap and juggled it for a moment, attempting to distribute the weight evenly. Her insides were doing flip-flops as she tried to work out what his intentions were. She didn't like the smug way he was looking at her.

Okay, if that was the way it was going to be, then so be it. She didn't hesitate a moment before turning to her right and swinging the pack at him with all the strength she could muster.

Her laden backpack, which included the stones she had just picked up, hit Archileta full in the belly. Caught off guard, he fell to his knees, bent over and obviously in pain. Her powerful thrust had caught the shoulder of the small shovel with the other strap, pulling it out of his hand. Now it clanged against a nearby rock as it fell to the ground. Gasping, Archileta pulled himself back to his feet and bent over to retrieve the tool.

Dana seized the opportunity to escape. She bolted around the edge of the boulder and was met by a small rivulet of gravelly rock that had slid down from above. Changing direction, she bounded over the rock onto more stable soil, barely missing a mass of prickly pear cactus.

She was several yards up the hillside by the time Archileta emerged from behind the shed-sized boulder, shovel in fist. She awkwardly wriggled the straps of her backpack over each shoulder, freeing up both her hands as she scrabbled to get a foothold on another stream of scree.

What to do? Ahead of her was more of the same terrain. If she climbed, she was faced with a steep slope and the blank cliff of granite towering over her, blocking any further escape in that direction. She turned to look over her shoulder. Archileta was steadily clambering after her.

Though Dana was in good physical shape and weighed far less than Archileta, he appeared to be gaining on her. She angled farther up the valley, climbing as she did so. However, the higher she climbed, the more scree there was, with less sagebrush to grab onto and fewer handholds and places to safely put her feet.

Should she stop and make a stand? She looked down toward the main trail. Earlier, there had been several groups of hikers headed up the trail toward the falls. Now she saw no one and, even if she did, they would be far below her and unlikely to hear her cries. Just what were Archileta's intentions? Would he actually do her bodily harm? The look on his face when he had first accosted her had been one of fierce anger, his eyes glaring and full of rage, with a large vein protruding on his forehead.

Dana threw a glance up along the face of the canyon wall on the off-chance that a group of climbers, or even one climber, might be within sight. But the cliff face was empty.

Where would she go when she got to the foot of the precipice? There were only two choices—follow the base farther up the valley, or turn to her right and follow the base downward toward the trailhead. The only problem with the second alternative was that Archileta would very likely cut her off, due to the angle of their ascent. There seemed no choice but to continue up through the scree. Surely, when she reached the base of the cliff, the going underfoot would become firmer?

Dana turned back to the task of keeping on her feet in the loose pebbles. One wrong step and she could easily fall and slide a considerable way down. If that were to happen, she feared Archileta would be on her instantly.

She heard a curse from behind her, looked over her shoulder, and saw Archileta scrambling to get a foothold. He had apparently slipped in the gravel and looked like an overweight Ichabod Crane, with both arms flung out in opposite directions as he attempted to stay upright.

The hand that held the shovel lost its grip and the tool dropped to the ground just as Archileta's feet went out from under him.

Dana increased her efforts to put some distance between them. Ahead of her, she could see some of the rocks in the scree runnel were beginning to get larger. She reached out her arm to get a hold of such a rock, thick and about a foot in length, jutting out of the ground. It offered a good handhold and she put all her strength into pulling herself forward.

Unfortunately, the rock was not deeply embedded in the ground and her grasp on it caused it to slide toward her, taking her feet out from under her. The rock broke loose and landed on her right foot and ankle. She cried out in pain, then fell to her knees to try to push the weight off her ankle, which was turned in an uncomfortable position.

Further down the incline, Archileta was wallowing around on his side after coming to rest against a larger outcrop. Dana knew her respite would be short-lived and that he would soon be back on his feet and again in pursuit.

Though the piece of granite pinning Dana to the hillside was not that large, it was heavy and she found herself in a serious predicament. She had to stretch back to her right in order to reach the rock but in doing so, twisted her ankle farther at an awkward angle.

After twisting around in different positions, she managed to extract her left leg and foot from under the injured foot. That left her reclining on her elbows, against her backpack. With her feet encased in leather hiking boots, she was finally able to push the rock away with her left foot, but she did so slowly, not wanting to loosen any other rocks and cause a bigger problem.

She pulled herself back up onto her bare knees. She felt a knifing pain shoot through her right ankle and into the arch of her foot. No question now as to whether or not she had sustained an injury. Now what was she going to do?

The palms of her hands were raw and bleeding in several places from having wrangled with the sharp edges of the rock. Both her knees were scraped, bleeding, and smarting from her fall.

The temperature had to be in the nineties, she thought as she looked overhead at the cloudless sky, and the heat reflecting off the face of the sheer cliff looming nearby only added to her discomfort. When she fell, her sunglasses had sailed through the air but she couldn't see them anywhere. She felt a slow trickle of perspiration run between her shoulder blades and wiped the back of her hand across her brow, wiping away an accumulation of grime and moisture.

Slowly, Dana stood upright and took a faltering step with her left foot. She gritted her teeth as she placed her right foot into a small space left by the errant rock. Not too bad. She looked over her shoulder to see how close her pursuer was. He was back on his feet and gingerly picking his way through the field of stone, about twenty-five yards behind her, apparently unhurt.

She hoisted her backpack onto her shoulders and took another tentative step. This time she winced when she put weight on her injured foot. She took another step and nearly went down again but was able to remain upright by grabbing hold of a pocket in a large limestone boulder. Hanging onto the handhold she had found, she pulled herself upward a couple of feet. The only problem, she was thinking, would be if she dislodged another of the bigger stones and went tumbling down the slope.

Another glance backward and she could see Archileta had gained a few feet on her. She had to put more distance between them. At the rate she was going, he would soon overtake her and she had no means of defending herself. She lunged forward for another larger stone and cautiously pulled herself up beside it, gritting her teeth as she applied weight to her right foot.

Tears of frustration trickled out of her eyes as she realized the seriousness of her situation—her injured foot, the stifling heat, and Leon Archileta steadily gaining on her. This could only end badly.

She had to find a means of getting away from him. She looked around where she stood. She couldn't begin to heave a rock down the incline towards him with any hope of disabling him. And ahead of her was only the sheer, shining cliff face, rising up and up and up. At the very base of the wall, juniper and deciduous shrubs hugged the earth. If she could somehow make it there, perhaps she would find easier going.

She heard a loud snicker and knew her pursuer was getting closer.

To her right, the skeletal remains of a small lodge pole pine tree that had grown between two good-sized rocks caught Dana's eye. Standing on her left foot and balancing her right foot on a flattened stone, she reached as far as she could for one of the branches that protruded closest to her. Her reach fell short and she nearly lost her balance but she steadied herself at the last moment by means of the rock she was wedged up against. She repositioned herself slightly and it was enough to grab the stiff branch. She tested it for stability and when it didn't break off but showed some sign of flexibility, she pulled herself farther up the grade. With her remaining strength, she bent the branch back and forth in an attempt to break it off. It wouldn't give.

She tried a smaller branch, five feet long, higher up the trunk. It snapped off with one yank and she turned to face her adversary. He was almost on her.

She pointed the jagged end of the branch at him in a jousting move, back and forth, with small lunges in and out. Caught by surprise at her confronting him with such a poor excuse for a weapon, it deterred him momentarily. Then he grabbed the end of the branch as she whipped it past his face and ripped it out of her hands with a malicious laugh.

However, in doing so, Archileta stepped backward, lost his balance and stumbled. Both of his arms flew out wide again and he went down, cursing like a brigand, onto a wide rock scree that began to slide downward with Archileta entangled among the talus. He reached out with one hand to grab a low-growing pine, trying to gain a hold and stop his descent, but it slipped through his grasp.

Dana didn't linger to see what became of him. She didn't even look to see if he had been injured or was moving. Instead, she snapped another, sturdier, branch off the dead pine to use as a support and hobbled on upward to the base of the cliff. There she paused for a few moments, trying again to decide what her best course of action would be. The sun had just passed its high point and was now hidden beyond the cliff face, giving her a respite from the glaring brightness. Another positive change was that the stones at the foot of the precipice had dwindled to mostly pea-sized gravel, with an occasional larger piece. Now was her chance to put some distance between herself and her attacker.

CHAPTER 27

Leaning against the foundation of the cliff base, Dana set her back-pack down, leaned over and loosened the lace of her right hiking boot. Pain soared up her leg as she did so and she realized she should have left her boot tightly laced, giving support to her injured foot. The foot and ankle had already begun to swell, and redness was extending above her cotton sock.

Below her, Archileta was thrashing around, attempting to regain his footing on the untrustworthy shale scree he had landed in. She hoped he could not see her as she stood partially hidden by a thick juniper. Which way to go? The foliage along the base of the cliff was sporadic, especially back down the basin to the east. To the west, the canyon wall eventually joined the apex of the elevation.

Archileta was now back on his feet, supporting himself with the branch he had snatched from her. He brushed dirt and gravel from his clothing, removed his Outback hat, swiped his hand across his forehead, then looked up the incline in Dana's direction.

Could he see her? She reclaimed her pack and slowly, painfully, made her way along the base a short distance. Her progress proved dis-heartening. She would never be able to get away from him at this rate.

She attempted to squeeze behind a serrated-leaf shrub she was un-familiar with and bent to clear out some accumulated twigs and leaves from behind it, wondering if she could hide herself between it and the cliff wall. To her surprise, the scrabbling revealed a small indentation in the granite.

Were there rattlesnakes up this high? *Just what you need*, she chided herself, *another thing to be concerned about*. Pushing that possibility to the back of her mind, she used the branch to scrape more detritus aside. Could she possibly conceal herself within the shrub's foliage? The more she dug the more debris she was able to pull away.

She leaned farther to examine what she had uncovered. It was a small hollow, maybe three to four feet in diameter, which had been worn away in the base of the cliff. Dropping to her knees and digging with both hands, she frantically pulled fragments of rock, dried weeds, twigs, and grasses away. She looked over her shoulder, knowing Archileta had to be getting closer.

Dana peered inside the niche she had cleared and found it was a larger space than she had originally thought. Cobwebs with insects entangled in them hung along the sides of the opening and she brushed them aside with a grimace. She dug inside her backpack, located her Maglite and swung it around inside the hole. It was definitely large enough to conceal herself and her belongings. Laboriously, she crawled inside.

Setting her pack aside, she began pulling the debris she had just removed back into the entrance, hoping Archileta would not discover the disturbed material around the bush.

She could hear him huffing, and knew he must be getting close. When she heard his boots crunching on the small pebbles a short distance away she stopped what she was doing and knew he was trying to locate her. She shrank back farther into her hiding spot, wishing him to keep moving along the cliff base. Her back was pressed up against the rock wall and she held her breath, fearing to move. It sounded as if her pursuer was poking the tree branch into the shrubbery as he moved slowly along the base of the cliff.

Dana quietly took in a long breath, sagging against the side of the den. Gingerly she felt around, trying to discern how much space she had. Little light penetrated the thick undergrowth covering the entrance.

Given that she had cleared away spider webs, she questioned just what other creepy-crawly creatures might be sharing her space. This might be just the place scorpions would seek shelter from the hot mid-day sun as well. She decided one crisis at a time was all she could deal with and extended her right arm, trying to determine how far back into the cliff face her hideaway went.

It met only open space. Did she dare turn on her flashlight again? She couldn't tell if Archileta was just outside or if he might simply be waiting nearby for her to make a move, so he could grab her. To be on the safe side, she resisted turning on the light. Gradually, she moved onto her hands and knees and felt along the wall she had been leaning against. The surface felt smooth as she trailed her hand along. She flinched as she moved her right foot and another pain shot up her shin.

Her hand found open space once again, and she frowned, trying to get a mental image of the layout. She turned slightly toward what she thought was the back of the hole and moved forward. It was difficult to see anything inside her space because the large shrub that covered the opening blocked any light. Once more, her hand came into contact with the wall, which seemed to jut out before opening into a larger space.

She was alerted by the sound of small rocks sliding down the incline just outside. It sounded like Archileta was just feet away. Throwing caution to the wind, she grabbed the tree limb she had used to pull herself upward, dug one end into the ground and maneuvered herself quickly around the protruding wall, dragging her pack behind her. Now she could hear him once again poking his stick into the bushes outside, getting steadily nearer to her sanctuary.

As Dana retreated deeper into the hole, it became truly dark. Her pursuer had stopped moving and she could hear him stirring the branches of the shrub aside.

"Soooo, our Nosy Parker has found a place to hide, has she?" he jeered.

Dana didn't say a thing.

She heard Archileta brushing the debris away from the opening and pulled herself onto her knees, ignoring her right foot, which complained at any movement.

Now he got his flashlight out and moved the beam around the inside of her den. Dana pulled herself as far back behind the jutting wall as possible, not wanting to get caught in the beam.

She followed the path of his light as he traced the inside wall of the opening. The ceiling appeared to be higher than she had originally thought, as well as the floor space just inside the cavity. But now she could hear him grunting as he got down on all fours and the small amount of natural light diminished considerably as his large frame filled the opening and he struggled to look farther inside.

It became obvious to Dana that she hadn't thought out her plan to hide in this small cavern well enough. She had imagined she would be safe there until he got discouraged and moved on. What was she going to do if he was able to get to her in this confined space? No one knew exactly what part of the canyon she had planned to explore today. And, even if they did, Jed wasn't expecting her to stop by, and Jax was likely just starting back from Denver. Aberdeen knew she came and went most days, so she wouldn't be concerned if Dana wasn't around. Besides, it was Thursday, and Aberdeen would either be hosting or attending her afternoon bridge club. She hadn't seen any sign of the clean-up crew for several days now. They were probably working farther up the mountain. What she wouldn't give to hear Edeen call her "Day-na" now!

There was no way she could get away from Archileta, even if she could get past him. Her foot was pulsating with every breath she took, giving her little hope of getting back down to the trail, even under the best of circumstances.

She crab-walked as far back into the cavern as it went, feeling around on the ground as she moved, all the time fearful of touching a reptile or insect she had no desire at all to encounter.

CHAPTER 28

Archileta had somehow folded his sizeable body inside the opening to Dana's hiding place. He was just feet away from her, inching forward. She could smell his disgusting body odor and could imagine the drool hanging from his mouth.

She guessed he had determined that the grotto extended beyond the partial wall she had found and was trying to figure out just where Dana was. She tried to think of anything she had in her backpack that could be used as defense—but all she had were the rocks she had picked up earlier. And there was no room in which to throw one and do any damage.

She grabbed the limb that had been so useful in getting her this far, positioned herself on her knees, and poked the sharp end of the stick toward her adversary. It must have hit his mid-section from the way she felt it give when it struck him with a whump.

He howled. Good. She hoped that would slow him down. She backed up against the wall. The poke she had just given Archileta had most likely just made him angrier, but it had stopped him briefly. Then she heard a *skitch* that sounded like Velcro being pulled apart. What was he doing now? He had turned his light back on and it sounded like he was searching for something in one of his vest pockets. Did he have a weapon?

Dana could tell she had reached the backward extent of the cavern and knew she was cornered like an animal in a pen. She reached behind her, feeling along the wall. It was all smooth rock as high up as she could reach and curving slightly around her. She scooted farther to her right, continuing to feel her way along the wall.

Just as she had about determined she had explored everywhere, her hand found a small opening near the base of the wall. She quickly changed her position and felt around the hole with her hand. Time was running out. Archileta must be readying to make a move.

Another flash of his light and she could see the hole was maybe sixteen inches high and maybe a yard in width. She couldn't see how far into the cliff wall the opening extended. Dare she try to get inside?

Dana realized she had no other options. But what if the space ended with no alternative but to squirm out backward, or she became wedged inside and unable to move? Knowing she had to keep going, she shoved such thoughts out of her mind. She pushed her backpack inside the passageway ahead of her, then pulled the knobby limb in beside her, realizing it was the only means she had to defend herself.

She was on her stomach, facing forward while clawing at outcroppings in the wall to pull herself farther away from Archileta. At this point, the tunnel was quite broad but very low in height. She tried not to think about claustrophobia. Pushing any thoughts of confinement aside, she concentrated on the task at hand.

Again, Archileta flashed his light around the opening. Lowering her left shoulder and looking backward, Dana could see him nearly flat on the ground behind her. So he had discovered the tunnel and was trying to see inside the cranny she had crawled into. He had something in his hand. The wall closed in around her on her left side. Was the space going to simply shrink in size and leave her stranded and at Archileta's mercy? With her right arm out in front of her, she explored that side, finding more open space. Quickly, she inched to her right.

Suddenly, she felt a sharp prod on her left calf. Her pursuer had poked his stick inside the cleft and was trying to reach her. Could *he* get inside this opening? She didn't see how that was possible, given his size. She would be well and truly in a fix if he could. She had seen a knife in a sheath on his belt. What if he had a gun?

Frantically, she clawed forward as fast as she could. In places, the height of her crawl space dropped to a little over a foot and she wondered what kind of madness had driven her to make the choice she had. She could hear the point of his stick hitting the wall behind her, as he struggled to reach as far inside as possible. She stopped for a moment to catch her breath, apparently out of his reach.

If her thinking was correct, the crevice she was in ran parallel to the cliff face. Would she eventually come to another opening that would allow her to escape? Or would the space turn deeper into the granite rock or simply peter out? She had to keep telling herself Archileta would be unable to follow her into this part of the cave. She had barely managed to squeeze herself through a couple of places and, unless

Archileta could transform his body, she felt confident he could not get to her, but if he had a handgun she had no doubt he would use it. Plus, she felt sure he would be waiting for her when, or if, she emerged from her underground hideaway.

Abruptly, the tunnel seemed to end. Her backpack was wedged tightly against the wall ahead of her. Trapped like a wild dog, with fear and anxiety taking control of her body, she groaned in despair. She laid her head on her forearms, stretched out in front of her, and tried to calm her spiraling thoughts.

At least she was seemingly out of Archileta's immediate reach with the stick. Slowly she realized she could no longer hear him moving around behind her. What was he up to now? Had he withdrawn from the cavern to lie in wait for her to struggle out?

She began groping around with both hands, and discovered the small, confining space felt like what she had always thought the inside of a coffin would be—smooth, cold, unyielding. *Think, Dana,* her mind kept reiterating, *don't do anything without thinking it through. You have to be smart, now more than ever. Just rest for a moment and you'll figure this out.*

Extended flat on her stomach and taking deep breaths, her heart rate gradually slowed and she began to think logically again. She stretched out both arms as far as she could reach on each side around her backpack, feeling along the wall blocking her way. Suddenly, her fumbling left hand found open space. She raised her head expectantly and explored farther in that direction. The passageway continued with a sharp turn to the left.

After struggling for a few moments, pushing her backpack ahead of her, and figuring out how to get her body and the cumbersome limb around the curve, she stopped. Was she foolish to keep crawling forward? Would this crevice in the cliff face eventually shrink, making it impossible for her to continue? Looking back over her shoulder again, she could see Archileta pointing something at her. There was just enough light from the flashlight he held in his mouth to see the metallic gleam on the barrel of a handgun.

A split second later he fired it. The boom was deafening in the small space. Dana's ears rang. There were flashes of fire as the round hit the granite wall off to the side and ricocheted around the small space she was in. Shrapnel hit her in the right temple. She felt a sting, reached up, and felt a smear of blood.

Before he could fire again, she clawed frantically around the sharp curve, to put as much space between her and her pursuer as possible.

Not having any sense of how long the fissure was, she kept moving forward, stopping only briefly to rest when she needed to. She heard Archileta cursing once he realized she was still moving forward.

The floor beneath Dana was seemingly the same smooth granite as the walls, with an occasional pocket of dirt or small gravelly pebbles. She winced when the debris grated on her raw hands and knees as she inched forward.

Had anyone else been through this cleft in the cliff? More worrying was what animal might account for the occasional grime she encountered.

All sense of time escaped her as she crawled deeper into the crevice. All she could focus on was pulling her body forward a foot, then another and yet another.

Ever so slowly the crevice expanded in size. Her neck was weary from the constant lifting and lowering of her head. It was some time before she realized she could hold her head up without hitting the upper surface of the crevice. Encouraged, she rotated her backpack until she could pull her flashlight from one of the pockets.

She ran the beam around her surroundings. The space was definitely expanding. She was able to get up on her hands and knees and crawl ahead gingerly.

Then, almost without warning, she began sliding downward into what seemed to be a bottomless pit.

CHAPTER 29

Dana shuffled farther into the cave. Her stomach had been grumbling for some time now. Normally, she ate a good-sized lunch, as tramping up the trails ate up many calories. She needed protein to keep her energy level high. Many times she stuck an apple or a banana in her backpack for a mid-morning pick-me-up, but she hadn't done that today.

She clicked her flashlight on again and pointed it around the cave. Was it her imagination or was its beam getting dimmer? She quickly shut it off and chastised herself for not checking the batteries last night as she had intended.

The blackness she was surrounded with was all-consuming and she felt as if its tendrils were creeping into her being. The chilliness of her surroundings only added to her feeling of being isolated from the rest of the world.

Unless Jed had a new suggestion for her to follow up on, or Aberdeen stopped in to see how the new lock system was working, or Jax called her when he got home, it could be a day or two before she was missed. That thought was unnerving. How long could she survive in this environment with no food, very little water, and scant clothing? She was dressed in khaki shorts that fell just above her knees and a short-sleeved cotton tee shirt that offered little warmth.

Dana pushed thoughts of her immediate plight and the pain she was in aside and concentrated on pleasant thoughts of Jax. All this just when she was learning to feel comfortable in his company, she mused with a faint smile. She took pleasure in his sense of humor, loved his affection for his uncle and that he listened with an open mind about her shattered relationship with Jeremy. On top of that, when she had shared her concerns about the strange happenings in her life since she had started her research in the canyon, he had proved a valuable resource to help her figure out the best course of action. Truth be told, she had come to rely on Jax, his instincts, his get-it-done attitude, and, more importantly, she realized—like a warm fire in her soul—she trusted him.

Jerking back to reality, Dana realized there was no longer any doubt who had been stalking her over the past few weeks. She should have put it all together much earlier, except the possibility that Jeremy was around had kept popping up. The idea that she thought she had seen him had confused the issue even further.

The fact that her car had been damaged while parked at the trailhead, with Archileta's truck parked at the other end of the lot, should have made it obvious who was after her. The dead skunk on her doorstep, with a garrote around its neck, certainly made sense after she had been in Archileta's RV and seen his array of strange tools. Granted, it was only by chance that she had come across the buck deer—however, the hunting paraphernalia and the taxidermy magazines in his camper fit all too perfectly.

Archileta's trips into the high country now made sense as well. He clearly took a packhorse to carry out the animals he'd been poaching higher up on the mountain. She only knew about the buck deer and the missing trout at the Sinks, but who knew what other animals he had taken? The gunshots she had heard on the day she encountered the cougar now made sense as well. But for her standing her ground with him at the fox den he would certainly have taken the kits.

Dana shook her musing aside, knowing she must keep moving. Back on her feet, she put her left arm out and slowly moved along the wall, feeling its smoothness until it was broken by a rough patch. Her right hand felt raw and stiff from the jagged rock she had grappled with on the hillside, yet she relied on it now to lean on the tree branch.

She limped along bit by bit for a distance, taking very small steps. She dared not risk stumbling on the uneven floor and going down again.

How far did this cavern go into the canyon wall? And how had this space been formed? Water? Volcanic action thousands upon thousands of years ago? She realized she had more questions than answers.

A shiver ran up Dana's arms. She stopped and rummaged in her pack for her fleece pullover. Surely, she hadn't forgotten to bring it? When her fingers sank into its well-known softness, she gave a sigh of relief before pulling it on over her head. A familiar sense of warmth and protectiveness surrounded her. In a pocket of her backpack, her fingers touched a bottle of water that she withdrew and opened, taking a deep drink.

Every ten minutes or so, she switched her flashlight on fleetingly to check the layout of the cave. The room she was in appeared to be larger than she had first realized, not so wide but the length going on farther and farther and the ceiling appeared to loom high overhead.

Did it make sense to continue going farther into the darkness in the hope of finding an exit? For all she knew, she could go on like this for hours, even days. The twisting and turning of the narrow tunnel had completely disoriented her and she was no longer even sure in what direction she was going.

If only she hadn't crawled into the small opening in the first place. If she had stood stalwart against Archileta, she might have been able to reason with him, to work out some kind of strategy whereby they could each go their separate ways.

Stop it, Dana told herself. *That would never have happened.* Reason again told her that her worst suspicions about him had been confirmed. He was an evil person and would not have allowed her just to walk away.

All the same, was she going to be able to get out of this cave? She was still worried that the animal that occupied the sett she had come across earlier might return. She was several yards beyond that area now, but animals had a keen sense of smell and might come to investigate who had come into their domain.

Not likely, though, if Archileta was still hanging around at the entrance. But what if there was another opening she hadn't come across? She shook herself mentally, trying to rid her imagination of all the "what ifs."

She sat down again to rest her aching foot. It was beginning to feel like a useless leaden block. Her back was wedged against her pack and her arms were entwined, wrapped around her for warmth with her hands tucked under her armpits.

The cool penetrated her body through her bare legs and Dana soon found herself shivering. Was there anything she could use to build a fire? She was sure she had a waterproof container of matches with her. She mentally scoured the contents of her backpack for anything that would burn and give off some warmth.

She risked switching her flashlight on again. The beam flickered dimly then died altogether. She gave it a quick shake and it came back on weakly. She could see no wood or debris of any kind, save for the tree limb she had been using as a walking stick. She refused to give that up, although, she reasoned, there might come a time in the coming hours when she'd change her mind.

Slowly, Dana struggled back to her feet. It was best to keep moving at least some if only to keep her body from getting stiff.

The floor of the cave was beginning to slant upward. In one place the ground was covered with grit on which she could easily have slipped backward if not for her staff.

She clicked on her watch to display the time. It was nearing 4:00 p.m. Was it still a blistering hot day outside or had an afternoon rain shower moved through? Perhaps thunder was what she had heard earlier but this deep inside the granite she doubted it.

She knew a tornado could have passed through the canyon and she would have had no way of knowing.

CHAPTER 30

Dana had once read an article about well-known caves around the world. The one that intrigued her the most was the Hang Son Doong cave in a national park in Vietnam, which was enormous compared to where she was presently.

It was deep within the Vietnamese jungle and had only been found a few decades before. Explorers were only now beginning to map it out. Portions of the cave were open, with access to light from above and vegetation growing inside. It was a far cry from what she was experiencing here in Sinks Canyon.

Dana knew of a couple of caves in western South Dakota. The very long passages of Wind Cave and Jewel Cave had intrigued her, making her seek out further information. The Wind Cave had mineral outcroppings in honeycomb patterns with bridge passages, called three-dimensional mazes in some parts. She also learned that new passages were still being found every year. She had planned on returning to learn additional information about it when she could spend more time on her own, and perhaps become a part of the mapping team, but life at the university had intervened.

Jewel Cave acquired its name from the calcite prisms found in it. Another anomaly of the cave was the hydromagnesite balloon-like bubbles that formed on the walls and ceiling when a pale, pasty material of dampened salt was inflated by some unidentified gas in the cave. Finding out more about them remained on her "to do" list as well. Could a similar anomaly be present in this cave, causing the unusual odor and, even more frightening, was it dangerous to breathe?

Was this cave commonly known? She wondered if Jax had ever come across it. Doubtful, as she had found it quite by accident, secluded behind the shrubbery growing at its entrance. Perhaps only she and the creature who used it as a den had discovered it.

As she limped along, she recalled that Arnie had said he would check on her this evening to get a progress report. But was that definite, or was it just her mind playing games? If he became busy, he might wait until tomorrow to call. And even if he called and didn't reach her, he would just think she was late returning from this latest excursion.

Dana remembered telling him she had to check on the air tempera-ture near a couple of clumps of her *dicentra* plants. Arnie had said something about needing to schedule a time with her to go over the entire outline of her thesis once she returned to the university. But right now, the hum-drum of the hoops to be jumped through in com-pleting her degree seemed like a distant memory.

Dana decided to try sitting again for a while in hopes of easing the pain in her foot. Perhaps if she propped it up on her pack it would ease the throbbing. Again, she settled against the wall and situated herself so her foot was more comfortable.

Early in the summer she had carried a fire retardant blanket in her pack in the event she got caught in a forest-fire storm but she had removed it several weeks ago in order to make space for something else she deemed more important. *Now*, she was thinking, *it would feel good to have something to cover my legs.*

Huddled in the pullover, she stretched the sleeves of her jacket down as far as they would go over her hands and tried to concentrate on something besides the situation she found herself in. It was so quiet.

Surrounded in deepest darkness, she had never felt as isolated as she did at that moment. She had, many times, imagined what it would be like to be blind, and now she was experiencing that very thing. Had it not been for her flashlight, she would have virtually been stumbling along with her hands out in front of her, not knowing what awaited her.

She wondered what the temperature was in the cave. It probably wouldn't get any colder at night than it was right now, maybe forty to forty-five degrees, but how long would she be able to survive these conditions?

Stop it, she chided herself. *What would Grandma have done in this situation?* Probably let loose with a string of curse words in German. She certainly wouldn't have sat around feeling sorry for herself. Dana thought about the early settlers of the west and the hardships of hunger, sickness, loss of loved-ones, Indian raids, and harsh weather they had faced. Yet they had persevered. They had gone on to establish homes and businesses, break, till, and farm the land. *And*, she reminded herself, *you're a descendant, several times removed, of one of those stalwart women.*

Her grousing stomach roused her from her thoughts and reminded her again that she hadn't eaten in several hours. She did have plenty of water and there should be two or three energy bars in her pack. When she got up she would dig one out.

She pondered the alternatives open to her. Dare she retrace her steps back through the cave and through the wriggle-room-only passage? What if she were to meet up with the animal whose lair she had come across? *When I get up*, she thought somnolently, *I'll think about going back out to the entrance.* Even assuming Archileta was gone, she'd have a treacherous trek down through the scree-field to the main trail. But she could scoot down through the worst part and would likely come across others on the trail who would help her.

It felt good to have a plan.

***

Dana jerked upright. Had she actually dozed off for a moment? Her body was cold and shaking again and she realized it was too unpleasant to sit still. She had to keep her body temperature up so she wouldn't run the risk of hypothermia.

Stiff and sore, she slowly regained her feet and, leaning heavily on the tree branch to protect her injured foot, she turned her flashlight on again to get her bearings. The light was very dim and barely made a dent in the darkness surrounding her.

Okay, she thought to herself, *even if there is only this one large chamber she could conceivably wander around it for days.* That thought helped her make the decision to go back to the opening. Having made her choice, she took a deep breath and turned around, determined to follow the wall as she retraced her steps to her point of entry.

She would have to take her chances with Archileta, and whatever that might entail. She dug two energy bars from her pack and wolfed them down, followed by a long drink of water. That little nourishment seemed to revive her and she started shuffling back, bit by bit, in the direction of the small crevice.

It took some time for her to make any progress but she gritted her teeth and persevered. Several times she came close to stumbling over formations that projected out of the uneven floor. Eventually, however, she sensed the ceiling of the cavern was much lower and her surroundings more enclosed. Another quick flick of her flashlight and she located the opening to the small passageway. Back on her hands and knees, she crawled into it, slipping and sliding backward from the slightly elevated opening. Then she got a handhold on a rough outcropping and pulled herself up into the fissure she had come through earlier.

When she could no longer navigate on hands and knees, Dana pushed her backpack ahead of her and crawled and wriggled through the confined space. Was it her imagination or had the space shrunk? Perhaps she had been so intent on escaping from Archileta that she hadn't noticed. Surely, there couldn't be more than one of these crevices and she had crawled into the wrong one?

Dana kept going, crawling forward slowly, a few inches at a time. The zipper on her pack was on the opposite side as she shoved it along, and there was no room to maneuver it around to reach her light.

She couldn't recall how long it had taken her to traverse this section of the passage earlier when Archileta was poking his stick and firing the gun at her. It had meant nothing to her then as she had attempted to escape the fiend. Now, pulling herself forward, she realized just how sore her knees were and probably scraped raw by the floor of the passageway.

It was exhausting work, making slow, repetitious movements to push her backpack the length of her arms ahead of her, then drag her aching body forward after it. She paused for a moment and reached out her right hand, feeling to see how far to her side the crevice extended. She couldn't feel the wall, but the ceiling was lower. She tried the same with her left hand and found virtually the same.

She moved forward again. The next shove of her backpack jammed it against the wall. She pushed harder, but her pack wouldn't budge. Then she realized she had returned to the sharp bend in the passage and maneuvered the pack around the corner to her right.

Her confidence returned as she deduced she was in the same fissure as before and would shortly be nearing the entrance. The floor became gravelly which tortured her knees. The darkness as black as midnight still enveloped her.

Suddenly, the space surrounding her enlarged and she was able to struggle into a sitting position. Now she could reach her flashlight in her backpack. She ran the feeble beam around the small enclosure. Yes, there was the wall that jutted out a few feet from the cave opening. She crawled around the barrier, pulling her pack behind her.

No light seeped in from the entrance. Was her watch wrong? Was it already dark outside? Had she been inside the cliff that long? With her anemic Maglite still on, she crept closer to the entrance.

But the entrance was no longer there.

Dana switched the beam off and could see no light where the access had been. She searched around the small area, feeling for the edge where the opening should be. All she could feel as her hands explored the area was a mass of variously sized, mostly sharp-edged rocks where none had been before. A large heap of stone filled the entrance.

A cry of panic escaped Dana's lips. She frantically pushed against the obstruction. But it was solid, nothing budged. On hands and knees once again, she threw her shoulder against the blockage. That only resulted in her being jolted backward and hurting her shoulder on the sharp edges.

She sat for a moment in frustration, trying to calm her racing mind. Had Leon Archileta actually enclosed her inside the cliff face? How had he been able to move a mass of this size? What a shit!

She felt around for her stick and pulled it up beside her. Wedging the smaller end of the branch between two rocks, she tried to force it through the barrier. But it was only met with more rock. Though she tried to use it as a lever to force some movement, she was unable to make even a slight impact on the obstruction. The blockage at the entrance was too complete, and she was afraid of breaking the precious stick if she put too much pressure on it.

She turned off the light and moved up against the wall of rock, trying to see if she could perceive any light through it. Nothing. A glance at her watch and she could see it was going on 8:00 p.m. It would still be daylight outside. She listened attentively but no sound penetrated—no birds, no insects, no wind.

Dana slumped down against the wall of the cavern. At least her attempt at trying to move the mass of rock had generated some warmth in her body. She pulled her fleece pullover off and stuffed it back into her pack.

She felt physically exhausted, mentally defeated, and spiritually disheartened by her situation, not to mention her aching body parts. The recent effort had put extra strain on her foot, and pain was pounding from her ankle all the way up her leg. She didn't know what to do next.

There seemed to be some silty matter covering everything around her, clinging to her clothes, her hair, her face, her lips, and clogging her breathing. She sneezed. Instantly, as if the sneeze had dislodged some thickness in her brain, she recalled the unidentified sounds she had heard earlier in the larger cavern. Suddenly it all made sense.

Archileta had obviously set a couple of charges and blown them to cause enough rock to dislodge from the face of the cliff to cover the opening. And who had access to explosives? Obviously, Leon Archileta! Jax had told her the ransacked supply shed at his work site was missing, among other things, some detonator caps. That simply confirmed her suspicions about him setting off some kind of explosion.

What on earth caused a man to become like Leon Archileta? He was seemingly a loner, working on the hospital renovation from out of state and, in all probability, had no local links. If he had ties with one of the white supremacist groups, as Stubby had said, how did that play into his actions? As she had presumed earlier, with his forays into the upper canyon and further up the mountain, he was collecting wild animal trophies and clearly came prepared for any eventuality. It was quite obvious he was a predator of both man and beast.

Dana sneezed again.

Sitting up straighter, she acknowledged to herself the reality of what had previously just been wild ramblings.

She sneezed again, then reached for her pack and fumbled around inside until her hand grasped a bottle of water. She took a sip, swished it around her mouth, then spat it back out in disgust after feeling the gritty silt grind against her teeth. Then she took a long, second drink that tasted and felt wonderful.

Her thought process, just minutes before, about Archileta being a predator of man and beast now coalesced with her opinion that he was also responsible for Warden Trig Henderson's so-called accident. And who knew how many others?

She slumped forward at the thought. She could only imagine the game warden had come upon Archileta in the process of capturing or killing some animal. Angry words had probably been exchanged and either at that time or later, when he didn't know Archileta the predator was around, the game warden had met his demise.

Dana's mind preyed upon her own culpability in the situation she now found herself in. She should never have gone up to the hospital in search of Stubby. That episode had only made a bad situation worse. Had she not felt the need to make one more trip to her plants in the canyon, this incident would not have happened. At least, not today. She had been close to completing her research on the *dicentra*, so why had she felt the need to make this foray along the trail today? Why? She had the information she needed to begin forming her thesis. But there had been one troubling issue with the length of flowering time, and she had wanted to revisit some of the specimens she had found, and recheck the air temperature around her bleeding hearts. Her plants were nearing the end of their bloom time and each day that went by she lost an opportunity to study them. To be truthful, the work she had accomplished today would clarify her research, but look what it had cost her.

In hindsight, she acknowledged she had been headstrong in thinking she could handle Leon Archileta. She also realized her mistake in not informing law enforcement officials earlier about the damage done to her car, the dead animal left on her doorstep, and the forced entry into her apartment. Jax knew of her concerns about the man, of course. If she didn't make it out of the cave, the law would connect the game warden's death with her own disappearance, especially since they had both occurred in the same vicinity. But, enclosed in the cave as she was, her body might never be found. She'd become just another person who had disappeared into the Sinks.

Dana shook herself and straightened up. She wouldn't let her circumstances defeat her. There was no sense sitting there at the now-closed entrance and rehashing the events that had led up to this. That wouldn't change anything. It would be getting dark outside in an hour, and if she had any hope of finding another way out of the cave while it was still light she needed to move.

She could only imagine there was going to be one very pissed-off animal that wouldn't be able to get back to its lair, at least not from this access-point.

***

With new resolve, Dana crawled to the back of the smaller cavern. Back on her hands and knees once more, she realized crawling through the crevice was going to be torture again. She rummaged inside her backpack and found her small first-aid kit. Inside it were a couple of good-sized, square gauze pads. Fumbling in the dark, she opened them and applied one to each of her knees. Then she shoved her backpack and her stick into the passageway and began wriggling her body from side to side behind them.

The second time through seemed shorter. She came to the sharp curve with little sense of the anxiety she had experienced the first time, knowing she could twist around it. Then, about halfway along the tunnel, she realized she had lost the bandage on her right knee. Fortunately, she was over the rough stuff by then.

When she neared the opening into the main cave she remembered the tumble she'd had there earlier, so she emerged slowly and turned her body so that she slid feet first back into the cavern. She sighed with relief, though knowing one major bridge had been burned behind her.

Past experience prepared her for what lay ahead. Dana retrieved her jacket from her backpack and pulled it on. The coolness of the open cave closed in around her once again. Stabs of pain shot up from her injured foot when she struggled upright, but she determinedly moved forward, groping along the wall with her left hand. With the aid of her flashlight, whose beam was merely a dull halo of light, she could see only a couple feet ahead.

She skirted the animal lair, shuffling forward. Her mantra became *take one more step, just one more step, then you can rest*. The only sounds were her breathing, her occasional gasp of pain, and the sound of her stick on the floor. Eventually, she could tell she was back to the gradual incline in the floor of the cave where she had rested before.

CHAPTER 31

At last, allowing herself to rest with her foot elevated, Dana's thoughts returned once again to the huge Hang Son Doong cave in Vietnam. As she recalled from the article she had read, in places where the ceiling had collapsed, sunshine penetrated and vegetation thrived. She desperately wanted to feel the life-giving sun on her arms and legs and knew, without thinking it consciously, she would never complain about the heat again. If only she could see and get some clearer sense of the overall dimensions of this cave, it would help her to understand what her options were. The nagging, dank, odor remained a constant as well, though she had yet to find its source.

She could empathize with those chained in dungeons for days on end and how helpless it must have felt not knowing what was in store. Would her foot become infected without medical attention? How long could she go on without nourishment and adequate water? She attempted to force herself to think of something other than her own demise.

How caves were formed still astounded her, especially this one in a piece of granite whose overall size she couldn't begin to imagine. As a student of the planet's evolution, however, she knew there had been some explosive upheavals in the earth's development that had caused a variety of anomalies. Jed had also mentioned that geologists were constantly learning more about the controversial magnetic center of the planet that he opined might have caused some of the turbulence. Scientists, geologists, and oceanographers would someday find the answers to these mysteries.

Dana suddenly jerked herself upright. She had been dozing again, though it seemed impossible in the context of her predicament.

She became aware of a slight rustling overhead and dragged her thoughts back to the present, moving the paltry beam of her light around over her head. Though the flashlight was fading rapidly, the ceiling high overhead appeared to be teeming with movement.

Now what? Adrenaline raced through her system, reviving her. She grabbed her stick, pulling her body erect as her heart lurched with anxiety and bracing herself for whatever this new challenge might be.

She flashed her flimsy light overhead once more. It was bats! Had they been there before? *Oh, my god!* Had the light she'd been turning on periodically awakened them? She didn't recall using her flashlight much when she was in this space before, but they must have been hanging above her all along.

Finally, she could identify where the sourish odor was coming from. A shiver ran through her body at the idea and she wrinkled her nose involuntarily.

The bats were beginning to disconnect from their footholds and some were flying about. She glanced at the face of her watch. It was nearing nightfall and they were probably stirring for their nightly feeding outside the cave. There was a flurry of swishing and a chorus of barely audible squealing.

She shuddered. What if one or more of the bats flew into her? She had heard of them getting tangled in people's hair. She pulled her ball cap down tighter and ensured the collar of her jacket was turned up to protect her neck.

Surely the bats didn't use the opening Archileta had dynamited shut to get outside? If they did, they were in trouble, and so was she. On the other hand... a tiny hope surged in Dana's soul at the possibility of another way out.

Dana knew bats communicated through echolocation and through that same ability found their way back to their nesting sites. Most bat species subsisted on insects, small bugs, and even pollen from flowers. At higher altitudes like this canyon, most species hibernated in the winter due to the lack of food.

Still, she was uneasy at the thought of them dangling overhead all the while she had been groping around in the cave. Now that she was aware of their presence, the uneven floor of the cave made sense—she had been walking on heaps of bat guano.

Dana pulled her backpack over her shoulders, ready to move out of their way. Would they stay close to the ceiling or would they organize to fill the large space?

She stood and tried to think what to do as she stabilized her stance. Now she knew that there was guano everywhere, she only touched the wall of the cave when it was absolutely necessary to keep her balance. She preferred not to dwell on the fact that she had rested several times leaning against these very walls.

She switched her flashlight on once again but the light was weak and emitted only a faint glow. She gave it another shake. It was enough to let her see hundreds of bats turning loose from the ceiling. They appeared to be flying in a thin stream ahead of her, like a wispy cloud. The movement of their wings and their sporadic communication reverberated thinly through the space.

Okay, at least they aren't going in the direction of the opening that has been dynamited shut. That means they must use a different access to get outside.

Would it be foolish to follow them? It didn't take Dana long to realize she had no other choice. She limped forward, attempting to keep the bats in sight as they swished and swooped ahead of her.

The floor of the cave was very bumpy as it inclined slowly upward and she used her stick more than once to keep herself from slipping. Another flick of her light and she could see the bats veering to her left up ahead. Following their lead, she soon came to a branch in the cave. Should she follow them or stay in the main cavern? Her gut feeling was to follow the small mammals, but she hesitated, not knowing if they would veer off yet again and lead her in circles deeper inside the canyon wall.

Then she shrugged and resolved to press on after them. She knew that in nature the fittest of the animal kingdom had survived by following the lead of those who preceded them. She turned into the left-branching passage and followed the sounds made by the little creatures.

She found herself entering a smaller chamber. Even without the weak beam from her flashlight, Dana was able to sense that the bats were disappearing somewhere. She stared around in all directions. Was her mind playing games with her or was there a faint light coming from somewhere? *Yes.* She reeled with the possibility that the bats had just led her to another opening.

She moved in the direction from which the faint light seemed to be coming. The closer she got, the lighter it became, until she found herself staring up at a large round channel that almost looked like it had been cored out of the granite. Scrambling upward, and frequently sliding back, she tried to force herself up into it, but failed to gain a purchase on the rounded walls.

In the very dim light, it was tough going. If only she could see her surroundings more clearly... With that thought in mind, she sat down and pulled her flashlight apart, trying to determine if it was damaged or could be jury-rigged. Her fumbling fingers came into contact with the "D" batteries and found one of them had lost direct contact with its neighbor. More than likely, it had been jarred loose when she swung her backpack at Archileta earlier. She realigned the batteries and screwed the end back on.

Holding her breath, Dana clicked the switch. A strong beam of light bounced off the opposite wall. Overjoyed, she didn't even think to chastise herself for not checking it earlier when the beam had started to weaken.

Ahead of her, she could now distinctly see the last few bats disappearing into the fading dusk of evening. Once free of the short tunnel in front of her, they seemed to disperse in all directions. Encouraged, Dana stood up, gathered her belongings and surveyed her surroundings. Now, all she needed to do was locate a handhold to pull herself up over the gravelly, guano-laced surface.

She tried to imagine how far she was from the original entrance. Was Leon Archileta waiting in the bushes outside to ambush her? She was thinking likely not. Since closing off the entrance she had used earlier, he probably thought she was no longer a problem and was long gone.

The passageway that led out of the cavern narrowed as she climbed and she found it increasingly difficult to make headway. Soon it was so small she was back on her hands and knees, crawling toward the dim light at the opening.

If she could just make it up over the last few feet of rock, it appeared that the base of the opening leveled off. Dana flashed her light around the curvature of the channel and managed to find a small pocket in the granite, about halfway up. She lifted her stick ahead of her, wedged the smaller end into the opening, and shoved it in as far as it would go. That gave her about two feet to use as a lever to raise herself up.

She just prayed it would hold her weight. Did she have the energy left to do this?

She hoisted her backpack above her shoulders and launched it up onto the lip of the ledge above her. Reaching for her stick, she hauled her upper body forward and upward. Her head and shoulders were elevated high enough now for her to see the opening itself and the twilight straight ahead.

The floor of the shelf was covered with granules of sand and rock. She leaned over onto the earthy particles and just as she placed her left leg to use her stick to boost her entire body over the edge onto the level ground, she heard the stick crack and knew it was about to break. Using all her remaining strength, she lunged forward. Bit by bit, she slowly pulled herself up and over the brink. Reaching for her backpack, she pulled it away from the edge to safety.

She lay curled in a fetal position for a moment, a keening moan escaping from her hurting body as she recovered her breath. Her injured ankle had banged against the wall as she heaved upward and her knees and hands were stinging with open wounds, but she could feel fresh air on her face.

CHAPTER 32

Dana slowly sat up and looked around her. Her greatest fear was that Leon Archileta would be watching for her to appear. She crawled toward what subdued light there was and cautiously neared the new opening. Touching the stem of her wristwatch to light the face, she could see it was 8:45 p.m. Keeping inside the tunnel by a good foot, she could see a dusky sky outside. In the distance, she heard the oh-so-welcome sounds of evening insects and frogs. Slowly, tentatively, she peered outside the hole, afraid of what she might see.

Nothing—not being pursued by Archileta, injuring her ankle, wandering through the cave system, the chilled temperature and hunger, the dynamited entrance he had trapped her in—none of her struggles prepared her for what she found before her. She was staring out the side of a cliff face, perhaps seventy-five feet above the base of a granite precipice.

***

Dana jerked back inside in astonishment. The opening was no more than a good yard across and slightly larger in height. She slumped back against the wall for a few moments in bewilderment as a chilling scenario appeared in her mind. She could easily have dropped out into open space had she not been vigilant. Night was advancing and she hadn't realized she was so high up.

Inside the big chamber underground, she had been unconsciously aware of a gradual incline in the floor, but it hadn't registered in her thought process that she could be climbing this far up. When she had reached the tunnel by which she escaped, there had clearly been an increase in elevation, given the effort it had taken her to gain that final hurdle. But, a third of the way up the cliff face?

She took a deep breath, stretched out on her stomach, and slowly eased up once again to the opening. Dark shadows were splayed out across the landscape below her. Trees and shrubs were shadowy apparitions left by a sun that had long since disappeared below the horizon.

SAGEBRUSH ALLEY

She looked down along the foot of the cliff, in both directions, as far as she could see. She could discern no movement, no Leon Archileta, no animals. She could see none of the bats that had led her to this opening. They had all disappeared to feed.

Dana pulled her flashlight up beside her and flashed it down and out over the scene below her. Boulders and rock scree extended down to the sagebrush alley. The trail she knew so well wound through the pines and aspen groves much farther down.

Were there still people on the trail, hurrying to return to the trail-head before full darkness overcame them? If she were to flash her light on and off would anyone be able to see it from the trail? It wouldn't hurt to try. But what if Archileta was still out there, lurking around? If he were to see the light, was there any way he could get to her? It would take some serious equipment for that to happen, and she doubted he had immediate access to gear like that.

It was worth a try. She tried to remember anything she had ever read about SOS signals. Was it dot, dot, dot, dash, dash, dash, dot, dot, dot, pause? Or was that too simple? She tried it for several minutes, listening carefully to try and pick up the chatter of human conversation far below her. Nothing.

She squirmed back into a sitting position. Her foot was screaming in pain. She loosened the laces of her hiking boot and could see her foot and ankle were both badly swollen. She unlaced the entire boot and gradually eased it off.

Each movement brought a new round of agony. When it was finally off, she realized her sock was soaked with blood on the right side and she could see she had suffered a jagged laceration on her ankle. She surmised something was torn when her foot had become twisted and wedged between the two rocks.

She rummaged through her backpack, seeking water. She was down to her last bottle and resolved to drink that sparingly. Would she be spending the night here in this hole in the side of the rock face? And tomorrow? People did not ordinarily climb up to the base of the cliff. She did not know if, when, how, or by what means she could be rescued.

She was suddenly alert. Was that voices she heard? She looked down the darkening hillside below, thinking she might be able to see where the sounds were coming from. Were her eyes playing tricks on her or was there actually a light flickering through the trees and underbrush down on the trail?

Yes. A light was definitely moving downhill from right to left along the trail. She could vaguely see the light as hikers moved in and out among the trees and shrubs. As she had noticed before, voices seemed to carry long distances along the trail.

She shouted, hoping her call might be heard, but her yell seemed to be lost in the small opening and she wasn't sure it reached out any distance. She picked up the flashlight, swiping it back and forth, from one side of the opening to the other.

Was it possible the lights she saw moving along the trail were people who had come to search for her? Not likely, she decided, as they didn't seem to be flashing their lights around off the path or calling out. They were apparently concentrating on nothing more than moving down the trail back to the parking lot. Anyhow, who would have summoned a search party?

Nonetheless, she continued shouting and flashing her Maglite on and off with the SOS dots and dashes she hoped would mean something to anyone who saw them.

It soon became evident the lights from the trail were just people intent on hurrying back to their vehicles. When the lights disappeared from Dana's sight, she leaned her head against the edge of the opening in frustration, tears welling up in her eyes.

She looked down to the ground, many feet below her, to the boulders and rocks that had calved off the cliff face. There was nothing she could use to lower herself down, even part way. Was there any way she would survive jumping that distance? Her injured ankle was already making her nauseous. What additional damage would she do to her body with a fall from such a height? The picture she imaged in her mind dissuaded her of that notion.

Then she sat upright abruptly. She had just spotted some more lights, and this time they were moving up the trail. Could someone actually be looking for her? They were moving at a steady, determined pace. She couldn't imagine why they jerked about the way they did, but then the thought occurred to her that the party below her might be on horseback. But why were they headed up the trail at this time of the evening?

What if it was Archileta?

The party eventually passed out of her sight around a hill that extended down to the trail. Dana told herself she might as well resign herself to spending the night inside her little cavern. At least she was no longer cold, though she knew the overnight mountain temperatures usually dipped into the high forties.

She searched her mind for anything she knew about how long bats fed each night but came up empty. What would happen when they completed their feeding frenzy and returned to their sleeping quarters? She shivered at the thought.

She curled up on one side of the opening, trying to make herself as small as possible, and arranged her backpack over her legs and feet for some semblance of protection from the bats when they returned. It also might provide some warmth when it cooled down. She had long ago slipped her fleece pullover back on and now stretched the sleeves out over her hands and tried to get comfortable.

She would get through this. She could, so she would. She must.

CHAPTER 33

Jax returned to Lander in the late afternoon. The interstate north of Denver was crowded, but once he got back into Wyoming the traffic thinned out and the miles slipped away. He drove immediately to his job site and checked in with Stubby King.

"You're back earlier than we expected," said Stubby.

"Yeah, well, everything clicked into place. I was able to work out the problems with the air conditioning unit and the parts we need are in the back of my pickup."

"I'll get the HVAC crew back up here in the mornin' then."

"And tell them we'd appreciate it if they can expedite getting that unit in place. It's already held us up for two days."

Stubby nodded. "Say, we had a little excitement here earlier today."

"Don't tell me our thief returned."

Stubby looked at him quizzically before continuing. "A couple of the sheriff's officers were here lookin' for Leon."

"The sheriff's department is involved now?"

"Seems like it."

"Was Leon here?"

Jax frowned as he said it. If Archileta wasn't working here at the construction site, he might have gone up Sinks Canyon. And Dana hadn't answered her phone when he tried to call her. She was usually home by this time of day when she had been out in the field... and hadn't she said something about staying around home for a phone call from her thesis advisor?

An uncomfortable notion bugged him. He knew Dana's concerns about Leon Archileta, and he had seen the gesture the horseman had made toward her during the parade. If Archileta was up in the canyon, he only hoped he and Dana hadn't crossed paths.

"Naw, haven't seen him since yesterday afternoon," Stubby told him. "His rig wasn't here this mornin' either. The deputies talked to most of the concrete crew. None of them had seen him around today."

"They say what they wanted to see him about?"

"They was as tight-lipped as a sow's purse."

Jax shook his head and chuckled at Stubby's slaughtering of the term "you can't make a silk purse out of a sow's ear". "Hmmm, didn't you say he keeps his horses somewhere west of town?"

"Told 'em about that, but I'm not sure of the exact location. They said they'd look into it. The deputies spent considerable time lookin' at Leon's rock-cutting tools, his saws, and measuring equipment. Don't rightly know what's goin' on, but they also took pictures and measurements of tire tracks where his truck and camper were parked."

"Keep me updated on that, Stub."

"Sure 'nuff."

After helping Stubby and a couple of the crew unload the air conditioning parts he had brought back, Jax walked to his office and checked for messages on his answering machine. There was a call from the sheriff's office asking him to call and clarify a couple of questions they had, plus a hang-up with no identifying number. Instead of returning the call to the sheriff's office, he returned to his truck and tried calling Dana again on his cell phone. The call went straight to her voice mail. He didn't like the idea that Archileta hadn't been around, and now Dana wasn't answering her phone.

But there was also Jeremy. He wished he had a better handle on that character, and whether or not he was actually in Lander. When he talked with the sheriff's department, he would ask them to check on what police officer Mason had learned of Jeremy's whereabouts.

These thoughts churned in Jax's mind as he made his way to his uncle's home. It was possible Dana had stopped by to discuss some matter with his uncle.

He tried Dana's phone once again. Still no answer.

If Leon Archileta was responsible for the scratch on Dana's vehicle and the other bizarre occurrences she had experienced, he would feel like kicking himself for not looking into the matter himself, especially now that the sheriff's department was looking for him. What was that about?

He found his uncle in his workshop, dozing in his chair with a magazine open on his chest and his head tipped sideways. Jax gently removed the copy of *Geology Today* and laid it aside. In doing so, he brushed against his uncle's shoulder and Jed jerked upright with a start.

"Unc," Jax said, laying his hand on his uncle's arm. "Sorry to disturb you."

"Wha-what's going on?"

"Have you seen or talked to Dana today? Did she happen to stop by here? Do you know if she was going up into the canyon?"

"Dana?" Jed was having a hard time awakening and adjusting to Jax's salvo of questions.

Jax walked around in front of his uncle and knelt down to look him directly in the eye. "Dana is usually home by this time of the day when she goes to the canyon, but I thought she was going to work at home today and I can't reach her."

"Suppose she could be out running errands," said Jed as he righted himself in his chair. "When did you get back? You worried about her?"

"It's probably nothing. Just got back about a half hour ago."

"Say, I did get a strange phone call today," Jed said, putting his glasses back on. "Some man called, guess it was around ten this morning, asking if Dana was here. Guy was pretty rude when I asked who he was. If he'd been here in person, I would like to have kicked his butt."

"Who was it?"

"Don't know, he wouldn't say."

"You didn't recognize his voice? It wasn't her advisor from Laramie, was it?"

"Arnie? Hell, no, I'd know his voice. This guy was somebody else."

Jax sat back on his heels as he listened to his uncle describe the earlier phone call. As he listened, he tried to put together what he was hearing. Then he stood up, frowning.

"Think I'll go by her place. If she isn't there, I'll make a run up to the canyon."

"You think she might have had an accident?"

"Probably not, but I just want to see if her car is up there."

"Anything I can do in the meantime?"

Jax stood and patted his uncle on the shoulder. "You let me know when you hear from Dana."

"I'll do it."

***

Dana's car was not in the driveway at her apartment. Jax walked up to the front entrance and moved into the shrubbery below the window fronting her living room. Through a space in the blinds, he could barely see inside. There were no lights on. Dana usually kept a light on when there was no natural light from outside. He spotted Flag curled up on the sofa and concluded that Dana wasn't home.

He hurried to the side door of Aberdeen's house and rang the bell enough times to attract her attention if she were in the far reaches of her Victorian home. She obviously wasn't home, either, and her yellow Volkswagen convertible wasn't parked in its usual place in the port-co-chere adjoining her side entrance.

Jax sat down on a bench beside Aberdeen's house. If Dana didn't return home shortly, he would go looking for her. He tried to calm his increasingly anxious mind. Was he overreacting? Perhaps Dana had taken the day off and was out scouting some area other than the canyon. But she had said she wanted to revisit one particular clump of her *dicentra*, and that probably meant Sinks Canyon. In his limited experience, he knew that when she focused on something she usually stayed on track.

He thought back over the weeks he had known Dana. She had impressed him as a friendly and forthright person, albeit having a difficult time warming up to him. Her previous relationship with Jeremy the sleezeball drug dealer had damaged her self-confidence and her ability to trust men. He thought, with a slight smile on his face, that he had made some inroads in that area. Truth be told, he had come to care for Dana a great deal. She and his uncle had connected from the beginning and he knew they had a mutual respect for each other. He shared that respect for her.

No longer able to sit still, Jax stood and cast his eye over the area separating Dana's apartment from her landlady's house. Nothing seemed out of place.

Back in his truck, Jax looked over his shoulder into the back seat where he kept his climbing gear, wanting to make sure he had indeed left it there after his last excursion. The drive up the canyon seemed to take forever. More than once, because of his anxiety, he had to slow down as he found his foot pressing too hard on the accelerator.

When he finally pulled into the trailhead parking lot, his heart quickened. Not only was Dana's Honda there, but so was Leon Archileta's pickup-camper. Several other vehicles crowded the lot, so there were obviously a number of people along the Popo Agie fishing or hiking on the trail. That second thought brought him a degree of relief, to think that others were out and about. He parked next to Dana's SUV, checked the doors, which were locked, and peered inside. Nothing out of the ordinary.

Jax walked down the line of parked vehicles and looked in the cab of Archileta's truck. Moving to the back of the camper, he knocked on the door and then tried to open it. It, too, was locked.

What to do? If Archileta's pickup hadn't been there, he wouldn't have been so concerned. He had no way of knowing if Dana was up on the slopes or had gone farther up near the falls. Was she back off the trail in an isolated location or had she fallen and hurt herself somehow?

He might waste valuable time by hiking the trail. He raked off his ball cap and checked his watch with a grimace. It was after 8:00 p.m. He tried to call his foreman, but there was no reception in the valley. He needed to report the location of Archileta's vehicle.

Jax remembered the call he had found on his phone earlier from the sheriff's office. In his haste to locate Dana, he had neglected to return that call. No use wasting time trying to find a place for cell phone reception. That would have to wait.

He looked up at the canyon wall looming to his right. The sun had long since passed over the crest. He had, at best, a couple of hours before the valley became shrouded in darkness.

Jax sped back toward Lander, then took the two-rut dirt road that started in the foothills and wound continuously upward through pines, aspens, and scrub oak. It was slow going in places over rocks and roots. As he rounded a sharp bend, he encountered a pine tree that had blown over across the road since the last time he had been that way. He cursed as he was forced to stop and maneuver it by hand far enough off the road for him to drive forward.

It was over thirty minutes before he cleared the tree line and gained the top of the incline. From there he drove for another quarter hour, to the apex of the canyon wall from where he preferred to launch his descents.

He wasted another ten minutes scouring the valley spread out before him, searching with his binoculars for some sign of Dana. It was far too dark for him to be able to see anything distinctly. He saw a couple of groups of hikers on the trail and peered closely at them but it was too dark to make out individuals.

He tried once more to reach Stubby and was surprised when the call rang, and was then answered.

"Stub, I'm up in the canyon. Leon Archileta's pickup is in the parking lot at Bruce's campground. Would you call the sheriff's office and give them that information?"

"Yep."

"Uh, Dana's car is still up here, too. I'm concerned that she may have run into some trouble, so I'm looking for her."

Stubby sounded concerned. "Do I need to have the sheriff send somebody out to help?"

"I'm not sure. I'll try to keep in touch."

"Roger."

Jax's hope of being able to spot Dana from this height faded. If he couldn't locate her from up here, he had no idea where to begin a search. He stood at the edge of the canyon top and continued to look through his field glasses, moving from right to left, down through the valley.

Wait, what was that? Had he just seen a blinking light reflecting off a tall pine tree off to his left? He concentrated his attention on the spot. Nothing. He stood, motionless, watching to see if he had, indeed, seen something.

There it was again! And what was that indistinct sound coming from somewhere beneath him?

Jax wasted no time in pulling his climbing gear from his truck. He quickly changed shoes, donned his headlamp, and tied his anchor rope to the front axle of his pickup. It appeared somebody was flashing a light from somewhere below him.

If Dana was somewhere down there or, incomprehensibly, somewhere along the base of the canyon wall, he would have a better chance of seeing her from the elevation of the cliff wall. And he didn't want her encountering Archileta alone.

As he dropped his line over the face of the cliff and started to rappel down, he noticed how the deep shadows on the hillside below him were distorting the shapes of trees and boulders. It would be dark soon.

CHAPTER 34

Dana jerked awake. She had dozed off again for a few moments. Twilight was staring back at her from outside her opening in the cliff face. What had awakened her? Her foot still throbbed, but she had become familiar with that pain.

A faint tinkling sound seemed to be coming from somewhere outside the cavity. She knew there were cattle roaming open range in the valley below. It was probably one of them with a small bell feeding far below her.

She peered out from her small nook but the gathering darkness prevented her from seeing all the way to the ground. There the sound was again, like chains clinking together. She tried to make sense of what she was hearing.

She reached for her Maglite and flashed it around, trying to see if there were cattle grazing on the slope below her. Nothing was visible. Fearful of leaning too far out, she swung the light around the perimeter of the cliff wall outside the opening. Still nothing. She pulled herself back up into a sitting position, slouching against the wall and rubbing her aching leg just above the ankle. The pain was blinding.

There it was again. The jingling sound she had heard before. Perhaps the sound was coming from down on the trail. She repeated the dot, dot, dot, pause, pause, pause, dot, dot, dot attempt at an SOS communication with the flashlight.

It was probably useless. With a sigh, she switched it off and was immediately encircled in darkness once again. The moon, hidden behind a cloud didn't offer a bit of light.

Dana suddenly sat up straight. She had just seen a wispy light swing out over the opening of the cave. And it wasn't coming from the ground, but seemingly off to her right! Then, the jingling sounded again.

She crept up to the lip of the opening and shouted "here!" several times out into the night.

She heard more metallic jingling, then the sound of someone faintly calling.

"Daaana?"

She was startled beyond belief to hear her own name, indistinct though it was. Was someone calling from down on the trail? The strange thing was, and she didn't know how it could be, but it sounded like Jax's voice.

"Here, here!" she screamed.

"Turn—flashlight—again," the voice shouted. "I—locate you." It sounded like he was quite a distance away as his voice kept fading in and out.

Able to make out just enough of what he was saying, Dana readjusted where she sat just inside the mouth of the cave and flashed her light from right to left, up and down.

The sound of jingling metal became clearer now as he called to her again. "Dana? Dana?"

"Jax?" she shrieked.

"Hang on, Dana. I'm still a-ways above you and to your right."

How could this be? Was he actually climbing down this sheer cliff in this darkness? She hadn't thought he would even be back in town yet.

"How're you doing?" he called, closer now.

"I'm here."

She could hear him adjusting his climbing line and the jingling of the belays hanging from a clip on his waist. The strobe light attached to his climbing helmet moved back and forth as he worked on his gear to move toward her.

"Hang on, Dana, I'm getting close."

Too relieved to utter anything, Dana could only moan from deep in her soul, "Jax, oh Jax."

"Okay, Dana, I can see you now. Don't lean out too far." A moment later he sounded just feet away. "When I get down just a bit farther, I'm going to try to swing into the opening. You might want to move back some."

Dana scuttled back away from the entrance. Seconds later, Jax swung his body sideways and gripped a sharp edge of rock protruding from one corner of the entrance with his gloved hands. Dana found herself shivering with relief as she huddled to one side. His body soon filled the opening. He knelt and steadied himself.

With a cry halfway between happiness and grief, Dana crawled toward him. He reached for her and she melted into his arms, tears running down her cheeks.

"Dana, are you alright?" Jax wiped her tears with the open-tipped gloves he wore, kissed her face, then held her away from his body. "We'll be okay now, babe."

All she could do was cling to him and sob.

"What the hell happened? How did you get to be inside this cliff? In all the times I've climbed in this area, I've never even seen this opening."

"Leon Archileta," she gasped. "He chased me up the hill and into a cave, shot at me, then dynamited the entrance shut." Dana's body was shaking again and her mouth was crimped as she struggled to hold back more tears.

"He shot at you?" he asked incredulously. "That bastard. I'll do him in myself."

"I couldn't believe it. He threatened me down on the hillside. I hit him with my backpack and ran."

Jax stared at her, trying to process what she had just said. "It's okay, it's okay," he said, wrapping her in his arms again. "You're safe now."

"I-I didn't know if I would be found. I thought I was going to be here all night."

Jax noticed her hiking boot lying to one side and the way she was protecting her right leg. "What have we here?"

"I crunched my ankle."

"How did that happen?"

"I fell trying to get away from Archileta. But how did you find me? How did you know where I was?"

"I didn't, at first, until I got up on the top. Eventually saw your light," Jax said as he gathered up her belongings. He helped her arrange her backpack on her back, tied the laces of her hiking boot around one of the straps and looked around for anything else.

"We won't be able to get out the other entrance," said Dana. "It's completely blocked."

Jax simply nodded his head in acknowledgement and continued to arrange her belongings.

"Okay, here's what we're going to do," he said as he adjusted something on his belt. "I'm going to turn around. I want you to climb on my back, piggyback, and we're going to get out of here."

"Are you sure?" she asked tremulously. "I'm not exactly a lightweight."

"I've done it before," Jax said, "carrying camping equipment. We don't have that far to go. We'll be fine, just wrap your arms around my chest and hang on tight. I promise not to drop you."

CHAPTER 35

Later that night, Dana was settled on the sofa back in her apartment with Jax supporting her injured foot on his lap. She had been to the hospital's emergency room, had her foot x-rayed and placed in an air-cast with a sturdy boot on over that. She had also been given a prescription for the pain. The doctor who had looked at her ankle explained that she had chipped the cuboid bone that connects the ankle to the outer side of the foot. He recommended she stay off her foot for at least two days, then walk on her casted ankle only sparingly, using crutches, until he checked her again in a week.

The doctor had cleaned the cuts and scrapes on Dana's hands and knees and had applied a bandage to the deepest wound on her right hand. After learning of her escapade in the guano-barnacled cave, he had also given her a tetanus shot.

Jax had called his uncle en route to Lander to tell him Dana had been found, that she had an injured foot, and that they were headed to the hospital. But also that she was safe.

Dana explained to Jax, in emotional spurts, how she had come to be in the side of the canyon wall. She told him in detail about her struggle to escape from Archileta on the hillside and once she was inside the cave and about her feelings of fear, anger, and despair when he dynamited the opening shut. She went on to recall her disgust when she discovered she had spent time wandering around under a bat colony, only for the creatures to prove her salvation. They were both able to chuckle, albeit grimly, at her story.

In return, Dana gathered more about how Jax had happened to find her and pluck her to safety from the cave opening and ascend the fifty feet back up the face of the cliff.

After Jax's phone call to Stubby, the sheriff's department had sent deputies up to the trailhead in the canyon. The fact that Leon Archileta had tried to shoot Dana and had barricaded her inside the cave, backed by evidence they had found in the facility where he kept his horses, had persuaded them to launch a full-blown manhunt. They also wanted to question him about the game warden's death. In his storage area, they had found the skins of various wild animals, including a cougar and a black bear as well as the heads of three buck deer. There was also an ice chest with several large frozen trout.

At the parking lot, the deputies had found Archileta's pickup, but without the horse trailer. Even though the shadows were getting long and darkness wasn't far off, they had saddled up their horses. From past experience they had learned it was best to come prepared for any eventuality, and in the rough terrain where they would be searching horses made for easier going than walking.

The two deputies had started up the trail and had quizzed each group of hikers they met, asking about the man they sought. They had also met three young men on a clean-up crew for the forest service who knew who they were looking for once they described him, but they hadn't seen him. One man with another group of four thought he might have seen him up near the falls. The man in question had been climbing back up to the main trail with a full rucksack on his back.

By 9:30 p.m. darkness had forced the deputies to call it quits without spotting Archileta. They returned to the trailhead and discovered his pickup-camper was no longer on the lot. Feeling upset and foolish that Archileta had obviously circled around them and got back to his truck, they loaded up their horses and drove back to town.

As the sheriff's deputies were driving back to Lander, they received a communication from Sheriff Rolston concerning Archileta's pursuit of Dana, that he had dynamited her inside a cave in the canyon wall but that she had been rescued and was safe. An all-points-bulletin had been issued for Archileta, throughout the county.

While they were still at the hospital Jax had called Stubby to ask if he had a couple of guys who could run up to the trailhead and return Dana's Honda to her apartment. Stubby had said he would take care of it and came by the emergency room to pick up Dana's car keys. He had one of the laborers with him and said they would leave the keys under the front seat of the car when they got back to town.

Still wired after her rescue from the side of the cliff by Jax and the trip to the E.R. to treat her injuries, Dana was unable to calm down. She still shivered, picturing Archileta's angry glare when he accosted her and realizing that he was willing to kill her. But for what? Because she had put two and two together and realized he had been stalking her for some time? Why had he been stalking her, anyway?

Flag had sniffed around the cast for a few minutes, but had then quietened down and was now curled up beside Dana on the sofa.

"You really need to go home," she said to Jax. "It's already after midnight."

"I'm thinking it might be a good idea if I just stretch out here on your sofa tonight."

"Why?" she asked, looking at him quizzically.

"Think it might be wise, in case you need help during the night."

"But I can get around pretty good."

"You know what the doc said about being on your foot."

Dana's cell phone trilled. She looked at Jax with an alarmed expression before hesitantly picking the phone up.

"Hello?"

"Miz Cameron, it's Ted Morgan of the police department."

"Yes?"

"Sorry to call you so late. Thought I should let you know that all our evidence points to this Leon Archileta as the person responsible for your recent problems. We still don't have the DNA report on that cigarette butt but this guy has a felony record as long as your arm. He's been arrested in Utah and Montana, as well as Idaho, for poaching and is also apparently still a suspect in a missing person case in Montana." Morgan paused briefly as if there was more to say, but he didn't. "Uh, we located the place where he keeps his horses boarded and found several trophy deer heads and the skins of a black bear and a mountain lion in an old barn on the property, as well as several small animal skins and probably the trout missing from the pond where the Sinks rise. Apparently this guy had a pipeline to an outlet on the west coast for sports shops that display game animals."

Small animals like foxes, Dana was thinking.

"Sheriff Rolston said his deputies thought they had him cornered tonight up in Sinks Canyon, but he evaded the officers. There's an APB out on him for this area of the state."

"Should I be concerned?"

"We'll send a patrol car by your apartment every hour or so in case he should try anything. Hear you had quite a run-in with him this afternoon."

"You could say that," she said. "He chased me into a cave, shot at me, and then dynamited the entrance shut."

"Are you doing okay?"

"I am now." She adjusted the phone so Jax could hear what was being said.

"Just to be on the safe side, I'd recommend you make sure all your windows and doors are locked."

"Thank you, officer, please keep me posted."

"To be sure."

Jax waited as she switched off the phone. "Well, that confirms what I said earlier. I'll be staying here tonight," he said firmly.

Dana breathed a sigh of relief. Even though she was safely back in her apartment, she was happy Jax would be close by.

"For all he knows, I'm still enclosed in that cave."

"Unless he has a police frequency radio and has been monitoring all the action this evening," Jax pointed out. "I feel better that the police will drive by here during the night, just in case he should be foolish enough to try anything."

Dana frowned. "I had the feeling Officer Morgan was going to say something further when he called."

"Yeah, he kind of stumbled over something."

"I'm wondering if they suspect Archileta of killing the game warden but he didn't want to say anything yet."

"That or they've discovered something else about him they're not ready to disclose. I've wondered all along if the guys who found Trig Henderson's body may have seen more than we know, too. You know, the big mystery to me is why a guy like Archileta thinks he can come into this valley and flagrantly poach all the animals he apparently has."

"And eliminate any person who questioned what he did."

"Which came close to happening," he said, touching her hand tenderly.

"Oh my god, Jax, what if he had disposed of our bodies in the Sinks?"

"Don't tell me you're still dwelling on that addle-brained theory my uncle and his pals have talked about. Dana, you know the authorities would be all over that if there was any evidence such a thing had happened."

"I suppose you're right," Dana admitted reluctantly. "But you didn't just spend a whole day trapped in a cave."

"Why don't you take one of the pills they gave you at the hospital. Might make you drowsy."

"Ummm," she said, clasping his hand. "You just want to get me high."

"Hadn't thought about that. Might not be such a bad idea, but I think they would have the opposite effect on you."

But Dana's thoughts continued to swirl about in her brain. "Jax, will they find Leon Archileta?"

"The police said they had an APB out on him and law enforcement is scouring the area looking for him."

"I can't understand how he got around the deputies up in the canyon. You know, I may have seen the lights from the deputies along the trail just about dusk."

"Sounds like they didn't have a tight enough net drawn and he somehow slipped through. I know it had to have been nearly dark by the time they got up there."

"Where do you think he will go?"

"Anybody's guess. He might try to get out of the state and back to Idaho, or he may have something else in mind."

"Guess you'll be looking for a new mason to do the work on your project."

"I'm thinkin' Stubby is already working on that."

Chapter 36

Dana took one of the sedatives she had been given and slept surprisingly well. She awakened Saturday morning to the smell of coffee brewing. It took her but a moment to feel a sharp pain shoot up the side of her right leg when she attempted to stretch. She had forgotten about her injured ankle. Then the events of the previous day flooded back, encircling her again...

Hearing her stirring, Jax appeared in her bedroom doorway, sipping from a cup of the coffee. He had been out earlier and had brought back freshly baked scones from a bakery a few blocks east of Dana's apartment. On his way back, he had seen a police car cruising slowly down the street past her residence.

Dana reached for the crutches he had propped against the wall by her bed the night before and slowly, stiffly, pulled herself upright. She was familiar with crutches, as she'd had to use them before when, as a teenager, she had torn one of the lesser ligaments in her left knee. Now, however, she had to put her weight on the crutches while wearing a thick bandage on her right hand and with a raw wound on her left hand.

She maneuvered to the bathroom and brushed her tangled hair into some semblance of order before tentatively making her way out to the table. After eating a warm roll filled with preserves, she washed another painkiller down with her coffee.

Once she had showered, dressed, and was settled on the sofa with her foot elevated on a small hassock, Jax left to go meet with Stubby. With the TV remote at hand, the computer on the end table by her side, her cell phone in her lap, and the painkiller starting to take effect, she felt reasonably comfortable and happy to obey Jax's orders not to move until he returned. Flag was curled up on the back of the sofa behind Dana's head.

After catching up with the latest news, she flipped through several channels before shutting the TV off in exasperation. She was unused to being home at this time of the day. She had no idea what programs were on, and those she had come across were of no interest to her.

As she set the remote aside, her cell phone began playing her theme song.

It was Arnie.

"Well, good morning, Sunshine, just took a chance I might catch you at home."

"Hi, Arnie."

"Wanted to let you know I've learned more about Jeremy Vanderhoff. It seems he's in jail down around Denver for dealing drugs."

"That's good to know," she replied, dully.

"I thought you'd be relieved to hear that news. You sound a little deflated."

"I am. But I guess I already knew it wasn't Jeremy. I had a serious run-in with this other guy, who's apparently been responsible for all the things that have happened to me." She went on to relate the incidents from the previous day.

Arnie listened quietly as she told about her harrowing experience of being chased into a cave by Archileta. When she told him about the bats and how they had actually led her to safety, he couldn't keep silent any longer.

"Shinola! You mean you were wallowing around in bat guano the whole time?"

"Yeah, nice, huh?"

"And this guy who rescued you off the cliff face... sounds like you've known him for a while."

"I must not have mentioned him. He's Jed Ahrens's nephew."

"Just a slight oversight," he responded, chuckling. "Well, if he's anything like Jed, guess he must be okay."

"You'll like him."

"So, I guess you're laid up for a while with your ankle, then. Maybe you should put your project on hold and just come back to Laramie."

"I haven't quite figured that one out yet. Imagine it'll keep me from any field work for a bit, but I'm virtually finished with that aspect of my project and am hoping to do a great deal on my laptop here at home."

"I hope they hang this mountain man from the highest tree. Tell Jed hello for me when you see him, and take good care of your injury."

They hung up.

Dana leaned against the back of the sofa, thinking about what Arnie had just told her about Jeremy. Her imagination must have been working overtime when she thought she had seen him in downtown Lander. Hopefully, Jeremy would get some help now that he was incarcerated or, as happened with some, he would come out a hardened criminal with little expectation of rehabilitation. Simply because she had cared so much about him at one time, she was pulling for the former.

A pensive smile tugged at the corners of her mouth as she realized she now thought of their relationship as a part of her past. With a sigh of contentment, she felt some of the weight she had been carrying around for so long lifted from her shoulders.

She really should check in with Aberdeen but knew the old lady would want to come right over and mother her once she heard what had happened. That would be trying, as her landlady tended to become even more indecipherable thanks to her Scottish brogue when excited. She vowed to call Aberdeen later in the day after she had rested some.

The pain medication she had taken with breakfast was making her drowsy. After scooting around, trying to find a comfortable position, she rearranged a pillow Jax had used the night before under her head and shoulders. She could smell a faint trace of his after-shave and she smiled as she snuggled into it.

She was recalling the night before when they had returned from the hospital. She had been hurting, felt grimy, guano-covered and stinky, and she had wanted a shower. Clumsily, she had pulled off her soiled clothing and attempted to lift her injured foot over the edge of the tub-cum-shower. Jax, who had been waiting outside the door, had heard her struggles and had entered the bathroom with his eyes diverted, and without comment had lifted her up and into the tub. When she finished, he had stood outside the curtain, holding a large towel that he wrapped around her as she emerged. She smiled as she remembered how sweet and caring he had been.

Pulling a much-used afghan her grandmother had crocheted for her when she was still in high school around her shoulders, she nodded off to the steady drone of a lawnmower coming from a neighbor's yard down the street.

She had been dozing for only a few minutes when her cell phone began ringing. It took her drug-addled mind a moment to orient itself as she dug for the phone under the afghan.

It was a local call. Looking at the screen a second time, she recognized Jed's number.

"Hello?"

"Dana. It's Jed." His voice sounded strained.

Dana sat up straighter, thinking he wanted to talk about her ordeal of yesterday. "Hi, Jed."

"Dana, I wonder if you would be able to come out here."

Had he fallen? Was he sick or injured? Something had happened, she was sure of it.

"Jed, are you alright?"

There was a muffled reply then the line went dead.

Dana threw the afghan aside. What to do? If Jed had fallen again and was injured, she needed to get to him as soon as possible. But the doctor had said to keep off her injured ankle, and how on earth was she going to drive with her left foot? She clicked on Jax's number on her phone. It rang and rang, but there was no answer.

Maybe Aberdeen could help. But that would involve a full-blown explanation about yesterday, her injury, the endless questions she would have and again, trying to interpret Aberdeen's tongue was more than Dana wished to undertake right now.

There was no way around it. She would take it a step at a time and go check on Jed.

Her crutches were propped against the backside of the sofa. She wrestled them around in front of her, dislodging Flag in the process. She lifted her right leg down to floor level and struggled to an upright position.

Dana realized there was no way she could drive her car with the cumbersome boot so she pulled the series of Velcro fasteners apart, opening the apparatus. Her entire foot, ankle and lower half of her leg were enclosed in an air-cast. She laid the boot aside and, with the crutches, pulled herself to a standing position. Whether from the pain medication or from just awakening she wasn't sure, but she was a bit unsteady.

Taking a deep breath, she took a few tentative steps away from the sofa, shuffling along with a slipper on her uninjured foot. She could do this. She just had to remember to put any weight meant for her right foot on the crutches. She picked up her cell phone from the sofa and slipped it into the front pocket of her shorts.

Hang on, Jed, she was thinking, *I'm coming.*

Dana snagged her handbag from the peg by the door and put the strap over her neck in order to free up both hands. At the last moment, she picked up the boot she had just removed from her ankle and wedged it under her right arm. She unlocked the door and slowly made her way through it and the storm door out onto her stoop. She had forgotten she had two steps down to the driveway. After two attempts using the crutches, she sat down on the stoop and scooted down step by step, then stood upright.

She opened the door of her vehicle, turned facing outward and slid into the front seat. She pulled the crutches inside and stuck them between the bucket seats, into the back, and threw the boot into the passenger seat.

Locating her keys under the front seat, she started the Honda and experimented for a couple minutes with how to manage the pedals. She discovered that by drawing her right knee up as high as possible, she could let her right foot rest comfortably while her left foot negotiated the gas and brake pedals. *Just keep focused,* she kept saying to herself as she backed out of the driveway, onto the street.

CHAPTER 37

Only once, when she reached Fourth Street, which had no stop signs and let her speed up, did she forget and move her right leg to touch the accelerator. The sudden movement got her attention as pain shot up the front of her leg. She quickly slowed down and concentrated more on her driving.

What was happening with Jed? She assumed he had fallen, but perhaps he'd just had a brainstorm on something he had recently discovered. He was a very plainspoken individual when it came to his geology and he definitely didn't like speaking on the phone.

Perhaps she should have told him she was supposed to stay off her injured ankle. On the other hand, he hadn't sounded quite right so she felt she had to check on him.

She crossed Main Street and drove north to the edge of town before coming to Jed's street. She knew Jax wouldn't be happy that she had left her apartment but it was too late to worry about that now. Driving her car wasn't so bad. She just had to stay alert and not make any quick movements. Hopefully, she would be back home, settled on the sofa, before Jax stopped by to check on her.

Finally, she came to the dirt lane that led to Jed's property. The trees and shrubs that lined it were a haven for birds, which were busy grubbing food for their demanding offspring, but Dana spared them barely a glance as she parked in her usual spot, near the walkway to Jed's shop. She debated about putting the boot back on, but commonsense won out. Grabbing the boot, she reversed the steps she had taken to get into her car and strapped her right foot and leg into the device. She was soon standing outside her vehicle, wobbling and placing the tips of the crutches carefully to give her the greatest balance on the gravel driveway.

As always, the flowerbeds along the walk were in full bloom. Day lilies in pinks, reds, and yellows were holding forth, but she didn't stop to admire them as she would have done any other day.

Assuming Jed would be in his shop, that was where she headed. She peered in through the screen door and could see Jed slumped to one side in his overstuffed chair before the fireplace. She tapped lightly on the door before opening it and sliding in sideways.

The first sense that something was seriously wrong gripped her when she noticed the overturned table where Jed normally worked. Papers and pieces of equipment were strewn on the floor. Jed's wheelchair lay on its side, and an angry, red welt was forming on the side of Jed's head as he struggled to right himself in the chair near the fireplace.

"Jed?" she said hesitantly, advancing into the room.

She was nearly by his side when a voice with which she was all too familiar spoke from behind her.

"Well, Miz Nosy Parker, good you could make it."

A feeling of horror overwhelmed her. As she turned, Leon Archileta emerged from the shadows behind a storage closet just inside the door. She swallowed hard and tried not to flinch at seeing him there.

"What have you done to him?"

With his usual repulsive sneer, he advanced toward Dana. She noticed that his face looked bruised and raw, presumably from the falls he had taken on the scree the previous day.

"So, you escaped your little cave dwelling, I see, but not without some damage. That's what happens when you stick your nose into somebody else's business."

"Mr. Archileta, I don't know what's going on with you but this nonsense has to stop!"

"Oh, so it's Mr. Archileta, is it?" he said, snorting out a laugh. "I like that!"

Dana shifted closer to Jed.

"Stay where you are," Archileta commanded.

"He's hurt!" Dana protested, her voice raised in anger. "What did you do, slap an old man? I'm going to make sure he's okay."

"He'll live. The question is, *what to do about you?* When I heard on my police scanner you were out of the cave, I figured I needed to find a way to finish this job, and since you're so tight with the Ahrens I knew just how to do that..."

Dana was having trouble keeping her body steady. She had been standing upright for much too long and the painkillers she had taken made her shaky. She needed to sit down.

How, her befuddled brain demanded, was Archileta able to move around town and evade law enforcement? According to Officer Morgan last night, it was only a matter of time before they'd rein him in. But here he was. He had obviously learned of her connection to Jed and got him involved in his on-going plan to wreak chaos in her life.

"I don't know what your problem is," she spat at him.

"My problem is having somebody riding rough-shod over my shit, looking over my shoulder every time I turn around. First, it was that game warden and now it's Miz Hoity-Toity thinkin' she has the same right."

That got her attention. "You killed Trig Henderson! There was no so-called accident, right? What? Did he catch you poaching?" The anger she had experienced the day she found him digging out the fox den returned with a vengeance. "And just what is your *shit* anyway?"

He ignored her outburst and went right on with his rant. "Can't even get back to my property to feed my horses with the sheriff's cars all over the place."

"Perhaps you should go in and talk it out with the sheriff then."

"Oh, you'd like that wouldn't you, little lady! That would solve all your problems. Well, it ain't gonna happen that way."

Jed moaned slightly. Dana glanced at the old man, who was grasping the arm of his chair and attempting to sit up straighter.

"I'm going to check on Jed," she said coldly, glaring at Archileta.

"Make it quick," he growled.

Dana maneuvered around a small table so she was able to get in front of where Jed was sitting. Using the cross bar on her crutches, she awkwardly lowered herself to her knees, with the cumbersome boot putting her at an awkward angle.

Jed seemed disoriented and appeared to be drifting in and out of unconscious. Dana reached out to take his trembling hand, which lay on the knee of his withered left leg.

"Jed?" she whispered, "Are you okay?"

He stirred groggily, saw Dana peering at him, and again struggled to sit up straighter. His bent eyeglasses dangled from one ear and she could only imagine how Archileta had man-handled him.

"D-Dana…" His voice came out in raspy spurts. "I-I'm sorry. He forced me to call you, t-to get you over here."

She removed his damaged eyeglasses and laid them aside, then picked up a half-full water bottle on the table beside him, opened it, and put the bottle to his lips.

"Oh, Jed," she said sadly, "I'm so sorry you had to get involved in this."

"Come on, sister!" yelled Archileta. "Enough of this time-wasting crap. We're gonna take us a little ride."

Dana looked balefully over Jed to where Archileta stood. "He needs a doctor's attention. I can't just leave him like this."

Dana's eyes searched the table and the floor surrounding his chair but saw no phone. It had likely been on his worktable and now lay amidst the jumble on the floor.

Archileta was searching for something in the pockets of the vest he always wore. As he did so Dana slipped her cell phone out of the pocket of her shorts and eased it up along the edge of Jed's chair, sliding it between his right leg and the side of the chair. Then she placed his hand over the phone in hopes he would be aware enough to use it.

Now Archileta was advancing on her, car keys in his hand. He grabbed her by her right upper arm and yanked her to her feet.

Dana stumbled and then screamed as she tried to keep her balance in the clumsy boot as he propelled her toward the back door of the workshop. Had he not been forcing her along, she would have fallen without the crutches that were left lying on the floor near Jed's chair.

CHAPTER 38

Hildy Gullickson was just finishing cleaning the tiled floor of Jed Ahrens's kitchen. She still needed to strip his bed and put clean sheets on it before starting lunch for her cantankerous employer. There was a load of dried clothing that needed to be sorted, folded and put away this morning as well. Several minutes earlier, she had heard a car arrive and assumed it was a customer of Jed's or one of his cronies who had stopped by for a jabber.

Jed was becoming just a tad more dependent upon her for some things he had insisted on doing himself in the past. Maybe it was just her imagination, but he seemed to flip-flop more frequently after deciding to do something a particular way. She supposed she should check on him, and see if he still wanted the lamb chop she was planning on for his lunch.

At the side door leading from the kitchen, she looked out to the driveway. The car she had heard was now parked in the driveway. She recognized the green Honda of the student Jed was consulting with. *Oh good*, she thought, *they were probably deep in a conversation about their rocks and plants.* Hildy had noticed that Jed had become much more interested in his reading and research since she—*now, what was her name?*—had been around. Dana, that was it. She was such a nice young woman, too. Young Mr. Jackson seemed quite taken with her as well.

She would at least have time to get that bed stripped and re-made before preparing his lunch.

***

Just as Hildy smoothed out the final wrinkle on the brown and gold comforter on Jed's newly made bed, she heard the house phone ring. She walked around to the opposite side of the bed to the nightstand on which the phone sat.

"H-Hild…" a voice whispered, raspingly.

"Who is this?"

"It's m-me, you old crow."

"Jed? Is that you?" she shouted, loud enough to be heard outside.

"H-help me."

Now what? She had picked him up more than once when he had slipped getting from his wheelchair into the easy chair out in his workshop. *Must have happened again*, she muttered. He thought she hadn't noticed, but she had seen the recent bruise on his left cheek that he had kept covered with a Band-Aid and which, she surmised, was the result of a fall he had neglected to tell her about.

She hung up the phone and hastened out of his bedroom, down the hall, and out through the kitchen.

Dana's car was still parked in the driveway. Well, wasn't that odd? If Jed had fallen, she surely would have assisted him or summoned help.

Hildy opened the screen door to Jed's workshop. His worktable was turned over and she could see his electric sander on the floor to one side. She looked around the room before spying Jed in his easy chair. He was slumped to one side. There was a pair of crutches lying on the floor near his chair. *Where did they come from?*

"Oh, my god!" she exclaimed, rushing over to the old man.

She set his wheelchair upright and pushed it away before getting down on her knees in front of him, trying to straighten his body. Jed seemed barely aware of her presence. He was clutching an unfamiliar cell phone in his hand.

"Jed, dammit, what has happened to you?"

"Dana…" He was trying to point out the back door of the shop.

This was not good. Hildy grabbed the cell phone from Jed's hand and punched in 9-1-1. Before she could speak, Jed's flopping arms knocked the phone from her hand onto the floor. She retrieved it and could hear the emergency line responder saying, "What is your emergency? What is your emergency?"

Jed frantically snatched at Hildy's arm and mumbled something. The look on his face got her attention and she knelt back down.

"G-gun, in the cab-cabinet…" He motioned toward a cupboard in the corner of the workshop. "Dana… he's got Dana."

"Okay, who is it that has Dana?"

"Outside…" Jed ran out of strength and sagged back into his chair.

Hildy stood up and walked to the cabinet, where she knew Jed kept a varmint-shooting gun. She found two guns inside, a .22 rifle and a shotgun. She grabbed the rifle.

If she understood Jed correctly, someone had Dana outside. What on earth had happened? Jed was certainly disoriented. He also had a nasty weal on his face and his eyeglasses, now resting on the table, had been damaged, suggesting someone had given him a knock to the head.

Hildy wondered if this had anything to do with a vague conversation she had overheard between Jed and Jax a couple of nights before. It had been about some guy that had been stalking Dana. Apparently, Jax had got the police involved. Hildy checked to see that the rifle was loaded and walked to the back door.

An empty blue pickup-camper was parked on the short gravel drive behind Jed's shop. She walked around to the back of the unit and opened the camper door. There was no one in it. So where was this guy? More importantly, where was Dana? She scanned the grass that extended out to the apple orchard to her left before gazing back to the right.

Caught in the late morning dew was a trampled track through the grass where someone had recently walked in the direction of the wind-break. She was just in time to see a bulky figure disappearing into the spruce trees. Was he chasing Dana?

Hildy hesitated to leave Jed alone, but she knew the police and an ambulance would be on the way. And time might be of the essence.

CHAPTER 39

Only minutes earlier, as she shuffled out the rear door, Dana had looked back over her shoulder. Jed hadn't moved and she wasn't sure how well he was tracking what was happening. Had he realized she had placed her cell phone near his hand and would he have the presence of mind to call Jax?

She stumbled on the doorsill as Archileta pulled her outside onto a small concrete pad. To keep from falling she grabbed onto a wooden side rail. Had she not had the boot on, she'd have already gone over.

His pickup with the over-cab camper was parked a few feet away on a gravel pull-in. She shivered as she recalled her recent foray inside that camper.

What was he thinking? Did he plan to load her inside the pickup? Surely he realized law enforcement officials were looking for him and that he likely wouldn't get far.

Beyond Archileta's truck was a large expanse of neatly mowed grass that extended the length of a football field and wrapped around the back of Jed's house. Along the edge of the grass was a dense wall of towering blue spruce trees and, farther to the left, a small apple orchard. Dana had seen the apple grove from Jed's patio on a couple of occasions. In the distance, she could hear water running and recalled Jed saying a nice trout stream ran along one boundary of his property.

Archileta looked around as if uncertain about what he was going to do next. He pulled a cell phone from a pocket, entered several commands and briefly studied something on it.

Dana was aware of a growing weakness in both her legs and leaned heavily on the rail. The pain medication she had taken earlier was making it difficult to stay alert and think clearly. She could feel warmth spreading throughout her body as perspiration beaded across her forehead.

She gripped the support and waited for the shakiness to pass. She was disgusted with the condition she had found Jed in.

She inched slowly back toward the door they had just come through. If she could get inside, perhaps she could grab one of Jed's tools to defend herself. She had seen crowbars, shovels and other equipment hanging on fasteners just inside the back door. If she could just lay her hands on one of them.

But Archileta raised his head from his cell phone, with a decision made. Seeing that she had moved toward the door, he once again latched onto her shoulder. "Don't even think about it, Missy. We're gonna take us a little walk."

"I can't walk without my crutches," she whimpered.

"We'll see about that." He stepped down off the pad and motioned for her to follow. "C'mon, git down here."

"I'm not going anywhere."

"You might want to think twice about that," he said, removing the same short, stubby handgun he had used to shoot at her yesterday from one of the long pockets of his cargo pants. He held it by the grip and swirled it around in a circle, then gave Dana a smirk. "You wanna take your chances with this little gadget?"

Dana could feel what little buoyancy she had drain out of her body. He was wielding a lethal weapon. It seemed there was no end to his ruthlessness. She knew very little about guns other than that they could cause serious damage or death. Having experienced Archileta's mercilessness previously, she knew he would have no qualms about using it on her.

She recalled that Trig Henderson had been shot in the back. He had probably been shot with this very gun. Archileta may also have used it to kill the buck deer. And how many other animals?

She stepped gingerly down with her left foot. He was motioning for her to walk ahead of him. Instead of going to the pickup-camper, he was indicating she should walk toward the spruce trees. Had he changed his mind? Hadn't he said something about going for a ride? For the first few steps, she was able to move quite well but the farther they went across the grass, the slower she went. When she faltered, Archileta threatened her with the gun, so she gritted her teeth and shuffled on.

What was he going to do once they reached the big trees? Would it be the gun, or would he use the knife? Perhaps he hoped to stuff her body under a log. She had to keep from getting to the trees.

How quickly situations change. Just an hour ago, she had been comfortably ensconced on the sofa in her apartment, relieved that she knew the whereabouts of Jeremy and confident that the police were closing in on Archileta. She had felt so relaxed and safe.

Now this.

"I have to rest for a minute," she said, turning to him.

"Fat chance," he replied, slamming the butt of the gun into her right elbow.

Dana yelped in pain and frustration as a stinging sensation covered her whole arm and an angry red welt appeared. He was enjoying this.

She limped forward. Walking on the grass was painful and awkward. Because of her weakened state, she was unable to lift the boot high enough to avoid it scuffing the thick grass, which threw her off balance. The fluffy slipper on her left foot didn't help. Perhaps she should just kick the slipper off. Or not.

Oh god, I hope Jed was able to call Jax or someone to help me!

Clenching her jaw once again, she tried to concentrate on not falling down.

As she glanced at Archileta, she saw he was looking from right to left along the open area and occasionally over his shoulder. "Move it along, sister," he said gruffly. "I haven't got all day."

She bit her lip to keep from retorting.

They were nearing the tree line. The spruce trees had grown into each other and made a thick mat of foliage. Archileta was steering her toward a slight opening between two of the mammoth trees, where a clearing had been made.

With each step she took closer to the trees, the louder a mantra ran though her head—*think, think, think*—she had to find a way to escape from this madman. Would there be rocks or sticks or something she might be able to use to dislodge the gun from his hand? Recognizing she was not exactly agile on account of her injuries and the burdensome boot, she had no idea what to do.

She moved slowly through the opening in the trees, latching on to a strong spruce branch to give her a feeling of stability. The air was pungent with the heady scent of pine.

Once through the opening, the terrain was dry and scattered with large rocks, scrub bushes and short grasses. It sloped down about fifty feet toward a slow-moving stream that meandered along the edge of Jed's property.

Archileta nudged her forward.

"You won't get away with whatever it is you're planning," Dana said.

"I'll be finished with you and out of here before anybody knows what's happened."

"Your truck will be stopped before you get halfway through town."

"Maybe I won't be in my truck," he sneered, threatening her once again with the gun. "There's a little green Honda parked out in the driveway that will suit me just fine."

She looked at him in bewilderment. At the same moment that she turned sideways to look at him, she stumbled over a rock and went down on her knees before she could stop herself. She cried out in pain as her stinging elbow hit the ground. The bandage on her right hand was torn off and the thin beginnings of scabs on her hands and knees were scraped raw once again. Her right leg splayed out uselessly to the side.

Archileta cursed. He pointed the gun at her and moved back a few steps as if looking for a more efficient angle to aim at her.

Dana slowly righted herself and pulled the knee of her injured leg up against her chest as a keening moan escaped from deep inside her.

But now was not the time to stay slumped on the ground. She had to find a way to disable his gun. She looked around for anything she could reach to use as a weapon. There wasn't a stick in sight and the rocks around her were half buried in the ground. Her arms, wrapped around her injured leg, became aware of the stiff boot. It was worth a try.

Archileta had walked a few feet away, apparently checking to see that the gun was fully loaded.

Dana quickly ripped apart the Velcro fasteners on the boot, removed it from her foot and ankle, and struggled up onto her knees. She was afraid he would hear her unfastening it but he was intent on checking his weapon.

She held the boot behind her back with her right hand and, waiting until he was within striking distance and had raised the gun, she swung the foot end of the boot at his outstretched hand with every ounce of strength she could muster. The weapon went flying through the air while the bullet that had been meant for her blasted out over the nearby stream.

The look on Archileta's face was one of shock. He hadn't heard her remove the boot. He was baffled.

Knowing she had won only a minor postponement of the inevitable, Dana tried to regain her feet. But she had spent the last of her energy. Shakiness and pain enveloped her body once again and she found she just couldn't get up off her dirt-encrusted hands and knees.

Cursing, Archileta walked to where his weapon lay. Picking it up, he inspected it and again pointed it at Dana.

"I wouldn't do that if I were you," said a husky voice from just behind Dana.

Archileta raised his head, startled by the interruption.

Dana blinked and turned to look over her shoulder to see who was behind her.

Hildy Gullickson stood on a slight rise just inside the windbreak with a rifle jammed against her shoulder. She was dressed just as Dana had seen her before, with an incongruous frilly yellow apron protecting the front of her clothing.

"Drop it," she said, gesturing toward the weapon Archileta was still pointing at Dana.

Instead, he moved the gun, pointing it at Hildy.

"Well, what do we have here?" he jeered, looking scornfully at her attire.

A rifle shot rang out. The gun flew from Archileta's hand, and he began waggling his right hand back and forth.

"You just shot me!" he shouted as drops of blood dripped to the ground.

"Take one more step and I'll take out your knee."

Archileta blasted a string of insults at Hildy. The index finger of his right hand appeared to be hanging by a thread.

"Are you all right, Dana?" Hildy asked, moving to stand beside her.

"I'm so glad to see you, Hildy," Dana replied, through sniffles of relief.

In the distance they could hear the faint sound of sirens.

Hildy stood stone still, keeping a bead on Archileta, who was holding his right hand with his left and swaying from side to side as if he might collapse at any moment. Dana watched as his aggressive, sneering countenance dissolved into the pathetic, tear-stained grimace of someone who was no longer in control, no longer calling the shots.

CHAPTER 40

At the hospital construction site, Jax had been obliged to spend time with Stubby and a couple of the men working for the plumbing contractor. The plumbers had nearly finished installing the heating and air conditioning equipment Jax had brought back from Denver and were ready to move on to the next phase of the project.

Now, driving west on Main Street, he was headed back to Dana's to see how she was doing. As he stopped at a light on Fourth Street, a Honda similar in color to Dana's went through the intersecting street, going very slow, headed north, a couple of cars ahead of him. The light changed and Jax turned onto South Fourth Street toward Dana's apartment. He realized it was getting on toward noon and decided he should probably pick up something for lunch.

He stopped at a supermarket, hurried inside and steered his cart toward the deli aisle. He grabbed a couple of sandwiches, some salad, a bag of chips and, at the fresh fruits, apples and bananas, then he hurried back to the check-out stations. There were only two checkers on duty. On one line a young woman had her cart piled high; at the other was an older woman with only a few items. Jax rolled his cart into line behind the older woman. She waited until the clerk had scanned each of her items and she checked the total before bringing out her purse and carefully counting out the necessary bills and the exact change.

Meanwhile, Jax was getting impatient. He had unloaded his purchases and now waited for the transaction ahead of him to be completed.

C'mon, lady, he thought anxiously.

He had his debit card ready and ran it through the scanner as the clerk bagged his purchases. He signed the display monitor and was out the door before the older woman reached her vehicle, which happened to be parked next to Jax's truck.

He exchanged greetings with the elderly shopper and climbed into his truck.

Minutes later, Jax turned into the driveway of Dana's apartment. To his surprise, her car wasn't parked where it had been when he left. He slammed his fist against the steering wheel. Was it possible that had been her car he had just seen? When he had left a couple of hours before, she had been settled on the sofa in front of the television and should be drowsing by now.

He gathered the two bags from the supermarket, left his truck, and glanced through the half-open blinds as he passed the front window. The lamp on the side table was on. He inserted the key Dana had given him and opened the front door.

The afghan she had been using was lying on the floor.

"Dana?" he called, thinking maybe she was in the bathroom or had even gone back to bed.

There were no crutches in sight. He set the food bags on the counter, turned the corner to the bedroom and checked the bathroom. She wasn't there. Everything was as he remembered it from the morning. No signs of any disturbance.

Flag jumped off the bed, leisurely stretched first one front leg then the other, and walked toward Jax.

He bent to stroke the cat. "Where's Dana, Flag?"

A satisfied purr was her response.

What had happened? Had Archileta somehow got around the police net and taken her? Or had that car he had seen just minutes earlier on the street actually been hers, with her driving? He tried to recall what the driver looked like, but he hadn't had a clear view of the vehicle. It had just been a passing observation and he didn't recall even noticing the driver, or if there had been a passenger.

He pulled his cell phone from his pants pocket and dialed Dana's number. The phone rang and rang and eventually went to an automated answering service.

Jax left the apartment and walked over to Aberdeen's side door, hoping to find out if she had seen Dana's car leave or had noticed any other vehicle in her driveway. After rapping loudly on her door, he glanced up to the glass at the top of the door. Attached to it was a note to her son, who apparently was expected, saying she had made a quick trip to town but would be back for their lunch date.

Jax turned and stood for a moment, puzzling over what to do.

Assuming the car he had seen earlier was Dana's, where would she have been going? And why had she left her apartment when the emergency room doctor last night had told her explicitly to stay off her injured foot for a couple of days?

It seemed all he could do was come up with questions he had no answers to. If she were going to his uncle's place that *could* be the route she might take. But why? He raised his phone again, and entered Jed's number. It, too, rang without an answer.

Jax returned to his truck, backed out onto the street, and turned onto Fourth Street, headed for his uncle's. He might be wasting precious time running here and there if Archileta had somehow abducted Dana. Another thought passed through his mind. What he probably should be doing was checking with the police…

As Jax turned onto the dirt road that led to Jed's home, through the trees he could see a flashing of red and blue lights. He sped up, spewing gravel from the truck tires as he threaded his way along the two-track road.

An ambulance, a large white SUV, and five city police cruisers were parked in the circular driveway with the roof, bumper, and front bar lights blinking on each of them. Dana's green Honda SUV was parked near the walk back to his uncle's shop. As Jax's truck skidded around the last curve, he slammed on the brakes and was barely stopped before he was out the door and running toward the shop.

Inside, nearly a dozen officers, including the County Sheriff Rex Rolston and Officer Joe Morgan were crammed together to one side. Paramedics were busy working on Jed.

Jax scanned the room. Dana wasn't there.

CHAPTER 41

"Unc!" Jax shouted, pushing his way between the two medics and grabbing his uncle's hand.

"Give us just a moment, sir," one of them said.

They had Jed on a gurney, were checking his pulse, his heart rate, and the abrasions on his face. He was also hooked up to an IV line. His uncle lifted his hand and raised the oxygen mask covering his nose and mouth.

"Jax," he whispered hoarsely.

Ted Morgan walked up behind Jax and touched him on the shoulder. "From what your uncle has been able to tell us, it sounds like Leon Archileta forced him to call Miz. Cameron and get her to come over here."

"What? I thought you guys were watching her apartment so nothing like this would happen? So where is she?"

"We are, we were, there was a change of shifts, and she must have gotten the call when we didn't have anybody covering Canby Street."

"Does Archileta have her right now?"

"That's what we're trying to determine."

The law enforcement personnel, who had only just arrived, stood around sheepishly, discussing their next move. Sheriff Rolston was on his cell phone, attempting to get information from someone, while another officer was down on his knees, studying the chair Jed had been sitting in near the fireplace.

Then a rifle shot went off in the distance.

The policeman by Jed's chair stood abruptly, cell phones were dumped, and they all unholstered their service weapons as they bolted out the back door.

Jax glanced at his uncle and the two medics attending him.

"Go ahead," one of them said, seeing the concern on his face and sensing he needed to follow the officers outside, "we'll take good care of your uncle."

Jax ran out the door and followed in the wake of the policemen, who ran in the direction of the tall windbreak at the back of Jed's property.

When the officers reached the spruce trees and emerged on the other side they found an odd scene awaiting them. Leon Archileta was bent over, holding one of his hands, while Hildy Gullickson was covering him with Jed's rifle and Dana Cameron was sitting on the ground, dazed and struggling to replace the straps on a walking cast.

"Lay your weapon on the ground, ma'am," called Officer Morgan as he pointed his revolver at Hildy, unsure of what was going on.

Hildy jerked her head around to see who was shouting at her, then complied with Morgan's command and laid the rifle by her feet. Several other officers moved to restrain Hildy until they could determine what was happening.

Morgan walked past Hildy and approached Archileta. Then he bent to pick up what remained of his handgun. "You have anything to say for yourself, Archileta? Guess you know you've got some serious charges against you."

Archileta stared at the officer with wide eyes. "That woman shot me just now. What are ya gonna do about that?"

Ted Morgan removed a set of handcuffs from his belt, ignoring Archileta's rant. "Leon Archileta, I'm placing you under arrest for the murder of Trig Henderson, the attempted murder of Dana Cameron, twice," he paused to glance at Dana, "as well as the poaching of wild animals."

"Dana!" Jax burst through the hole in the windbreak and hurried over to where she still sat on the ground.

"Jax," she murmured, stretching out to reach him.

He knelt beside her and enveloped her in his arms. "Are you alright?"

Jax raised his head and looked over her shoulder at Archileta, whom Officer Morgan was patting down, checking for more weapons.

Two of the other officers were examining the remains of Archileta's firearm. One of them held the weapon up while another opened an evidence bag in which it was then placed for later inspection.

Sheriff Rolston motioned Hildy aside and spoke quietly to her. "Was he threatening this young lady?"

She looked at the sheriff as if he had just sprouted tentacles. "See that piece of scrap iron they're looking at? That was a handgun. He was about to shoot her with it."

"Seems you're a pretty good shot, ma'am."

"I know my way around firearms."

Morgan read Leon Archileta his rights. They cuffed him and began walking him up the incline to the spruce trees, paying little heed to his dangling finger. As he passed the two women, Archileta's face was twisted in impotent rage.

Hildy and the sheriff followed the line of policemen as they all moved back toward Jed's shop. "Say, how'd you manage to get through this windbreak without Archileta seeing you?" asked Sheriff Rolston.

"Came in through the apple trees. Some of the branches are pretty low so I was able to get within range without him seeing me."

"Yeah?"

"I could hear things were getting pretty tense, so I crouched down and kept low 'til Dana whacked him with her boot. That's when I made my move."

Sheriff Rolston, a good foot and a half taller than Hildy, nodded solemnly and looked impressed.

Jax wiped some dirt from Dana's cheek and touched his forehead to hers.

"Is Jed okay?"

"I think so. The EMTs were working on him. Dana, when I heard that Archileta had you again, I didn't know what I was going to do."

This time she touched her fingers to his lips, silencing him. "I know." She mouthed "I-I love you, too," trying it on for size before saying it out loud.

Which she did.

Jax lifted her into his arms. She was still clutching the boot in one hand as she buried her head in his neck.

**

After the paramedics had completed a cursory inspection of Archileta's hand, an officer placed him in the back of a cruiser. They drove off, with the sheriff following close behind.

Ted Morgan and Officer O'Brien were examining the cab of Leon Archileta's pickup-camper and preparing it to be towed to the police department to gather evidence. Morgan had his head through the open passenger door and was looking at some papers on the seat when his partner nudged him. Morgan looked up to see Jax walking slowly through the windbreak, carrying Dana in his arms. Morgan smiled, clapped his partner on the back, and slammed the door shut.

Inside the shop, one of the EMTs was talking with Jed, who was propped upright on the gurney.

"Dr. Ahrens, I think it would be wise to let us take you in to get checked out."

"I'm fine. Don't need any further checking out," Jed said adamantly. At that moment Jax came through the door, carrying Dana. "My nephew will tell you, I'm as strong as an ox."

"Yeah, but that guy knocked you around some," one of the medics said as he began putting their equipment back into its metal carrier.

"Good luck with that," said Hildy ironically as she returned the rifle to its cabinet. "Not only is he strong as an ox, he thinks like one, too."

Jax gently lowered Dana onto a stool to one side of Jed's gurney. She reached out and put both of her hands around Jed's free hand. Jax stood behind her, his hands resting on her shoulders.

"If you guys want something to do, take care of this girl's injuries," said Jed, seeing her wounds broken open and bleeding.

"Jed, are you sure you shouldn't go in and let the doc see you?" Dana asked.

"Yep."

One of the EMTs re-bandaged the palm of Dana's right hand, applied antiseptic to her knees, and examined the painful bruise on her right elbow. The other checked Jed's pulse one more time before putting his equipment away.

Hildy stood at the foot of the gurney, hooting with laughter over something one of the officers had said. The police were still praising her for slipping through the apple trees along the spruce windbreak and approaching Archileta without being seen.

"Hildy, what are you doing standing around, woman?" Jed growled. "I haven't had anything to eat since breakfast."

Hildy placed her hands on her hips and glared at him. "Yeah, yeah, yeah, you old carcass. You're lucky you're still around to eat anything!"

After the rescue crew and the police had gone and Hildy had returned to the house to prepare lunch, peace descended on the Ahrens property once again.

Epilogue

Later that afternoon, Dana and Jax were back at her apartment. He was preparing, reluctantly, to go to the construction site after a call from Stubby involving a question that had come up requiring a decision that "was above his pay-grade to make."

"Um, Dana… Unc and I were talking before we left his place," he said, fidgeting as he perched on the edge of a chair next to the sofa where she reclined.

Dana looked up from mail she was opening. "Is everything okay with him?"

"Everything's fine. He… well, he was wondering about my intentions."

"What, some job he needs done around his place?"

"About you and me."

Dana dropped the envelope she was holding. "He's a darling, but that was rather forward of him… wasn't it?"

"You know Unc, he says what's on his mind."

"And you said?" she teased.

"I told him we hadn't actually talked about our future. I have this job here, which is still a good year away from completion. He knows you will finish your degree next spring and that you will likely be relocating, but also that I want to be with you..."

Jax moved self-consciously from the chair to the sofa to sit beside Dana.

"Ahrens… is this your round-about way of suggesting something?"

"It is."

"And that would be?" she asked, smiling as they reached for each other.

"I want us to be together, always."

"Me, too."

"Are you sure?"

"Never been surer of anything in my life."

About Patricia Jones

Patricia Jones is a native of Wyoming where she resides with her husband. She is the author of two previous novels: *Sloe Eyed Sentinels* and *The Post*. She has lived and worked in Illinois, Minnesota, and Wyoming, and is a lover of nature and enjoys flower gardening, particularly hybrid iris.

Other Books by Sastrugi Press

2024 Total Eclipse State Series by Aaron Linsdau
Sastrugi Press has published state-specific guides for the 2024 total eclipse crossing over the United States. Check the Sastrugi Press website for the available state eclipse books:
www.sastrugipress.com/eclipse

50 Wildlife Hotspots by Moose Henderson
Find out where to find animals and photograph them in Grand Teton National Park from a professional wildlife photographer. This unique guide shares the secret locations with the best chance at spotting wildlife.

A Small Pile of Feathers by Gerry Spence
Gerry Spence reveals his spiritual, loving, and sometimes humorous sides, depicted in his devotion to family and preserving the wild places he writes of as though they were inscribed on his own bones and in his own blood.

Along the Sylvan Trail by Julianne Couch
Along the Sylvan Trail dips into the lives of linked characters as they confront futures that aren't clearly dictated by conventional planning. The conflicts of the small town change and pressure residents of Sylvan Grove to look beyond their world to the outside.

Antarctic Tears by Aaron Linsdau
What would make someone give up a high-paying career to ski alone across Antarctica to the South Pole? This inspirational true story will make readers both cheer and cry. Fighting skin-freezing temperatures, infections, and emotional breakdown, Aaron Linsdau exposes the harsh realities of being on an expedition.

Cloudshade by Lori Howe, Ph.D.
The poems of *Cloudshade* breathe with the vivid, fragrant essence of life in every season on America's high plains. Extraordinarily relatable, the poems of *Cloudshade* swing wide a door to life in the West, both for lovers of poetry and for those who don't normally read poems.

Is It True? by Eugene Gagliano

This delightful collection of children's humorous poetry encourages parents to interact in an enjoyable way with their children, to help them understand common expressions used in our daily language.

Lost at Windy Corner by Aaron Linsdau

Windy Corner on Denali has claimed lives, fingers, and toes. What would make someone brave lethal weather, crevasses, and slick ice to attempt to summit North America's highest mountain?

Prevailing Westerlies by Ed Lavino

With clarity and intensity, Ed Lavino's photographs express a longing for the natural world and hope for its future through his black and white photography.

Sleeping Dogs Don't Lie by Michael McCoy

A young Native American boy is taken from his home after tragedy strikes, grows up in middle America, and through his first real adult summer searches for Wyoming artifacts, and attempts single-handedly to solve the murder of his treasured coworker.

So I Said by Gerry Spence

The collected sayings of Gerry Spence provokes readers into thinking about their own vision of the world. His insights provide a grander vision of how the nearly invisible world of the justice system in *So I Said*.

Voices at Twilight by Lori Howe, Ph.D.

Voices at Twilight is a guide takes readers on a visual tour of twelve past and present Wyoming ghost towns. Contained within are travel directions, GPS coordinates, and tips for intrepid readers.

Visit Sastrugi Press on the web at www.sastrugipress.com to purchase the above titles in bulk. They are available from your local bookstore or online retailers in print, e-book, or audiobook form.

Thank you for choosing Sastrugi Press.
www.sastrugipress.com
"Turn the Page Loose"

www.ingramcontent.com/pod-product-compliance
Lightning Source LLC
Chambersburg PA
CBHW032037240626
47154CB00003B/957